THE DOOMSDAY CARRIER

Jean Blackwell works at Fadledean, a Ministry of Defence research station. Involved in a new project, her work with a chimpanzee named Charlie involves research into biological warfare. But security there is severely compromised when, alone on duty, Jean falls down in a faint. And despite Fadledean's strict safety regime, Charlie is able to make his escape from the station. The chimpanzee, having been injected with plague bacilli, will become highly infectious after a three-week incubation period. Now, the hunt is on for Charlie . . .

Books by Victor Canning
Published by The House of Ulverscroft:

BIRDS OF A FEATHER
THE BOY ON PLATFORM ONE
FALL FROM GRACE
VANISHING POINT

The Arthurian Trilogy:
THE CRIMSON CHALICE
THE CIRCLE OF THE GODS
THE IMMORTAL WOUND

VICTOR CANNING

THE DOOMSDAY CARRIER

Complete and Unabridged

ULVERSCROFT
Leicester

First published in Great Britain in 1976

This Large Print Edition
published 2012

The moral right of the author has been asserted

British Library CIP Data

Canning, Victor.
  The doomsday carrier.
  1. Suspense fiction.
  2. Large type books.
  I. Title
  823.9′12–dc23

  ISBN 978–1–4448–1320–3

Published by
F. A. Thorpe (Publishing)
Anstey, Leicestershire

Set by Words & Graphics Ltd.
Anstey, Leicestershire
Printed and bound in Great Britain by
T. J. International Ltd., Padstow, Cornwall

This book is printed on acid-free paper

For Adria with love

1

As Jean Blackwell turned away from closing the window of her sitting room some loose petals fell from the yellow roses in the bowl on the table at her side. She picked them up to drop them in the waste-paper basket. George had given her the roses some days before and on the hand that held the petals was the engagement ring he had placed there four months ago, a platinum ring with a large topaz set in a circlet of small diamonds.

Standing there, idly crumpling the yellow scallop shells of petals, a tall, good-looking, dark-haired woman in her early thirties, she smiled to herself at the thought of George; dear George, the giver of unexpected gifts, simple and expensive . . . a painting she had admired at an exhibition smuggled into her flat to be found hanging in just the place she would have chosen, a large smooth pebble with a hole in the middle, beachcombed, to use as a paper-weight for her desk, a china mouse with daisies for eyes and using its tail as a bow to play a violin to add to her collection of odd animals. When he had given her the ring he had said, 'And remember

— when we are married there's no bloody larking about any more with all this micro-whatever-it-is caper. I want a wife and I want kids. Just a plain, old-fashioned setup.'

There had been no argument. It was what she wanted more perhaps than George could ever know; George a knight in shining armour to rescue her from her work and a too often troubled conscience. She dropped the petals into the basket and felt the slow, familiar tremble of her body that the touch of his hands could bring, and with it came the impulse to give George a surprise gift.

She went to her desk and began to write him a letter. The night before she had told him that she would be tied up all this day. They were beginning a new project at the Research Station and she would have to sleep there because she had been drawn first on the night duty roster. A rearrangement of the timings had given her an unexpected few hours' freedom this afternoon and she had driven back to town to do some shopping and to tidy her flat.

She wrote swiftly and impulsively, writing what she knew he would want to hear, picturing him coming in late from his business trip and finding it on his pillow . . . Dear George, who wanted no bloody

larking about, wanted a wife and kids
. . . wanted her.

George lived in a block of flats on the
northern side of the town. Jean parked her
car in the forecourt, smiled at the porter as
she went through the hall and took the lift to
the top floor which held two flats. Turning the
corner of the corridor which led to his flat she
stopped, as she often did, to look out of the
window. The world outside lay under the heat
of a fierce June afternoon. Far below her,
rising clear above the huddle of houses and
streets, the great spire of the cathedral thrust
like a rapier into the sky, grey against a smoky
blue with a moving, ragged garland of
pigeons circling it. Beyond it, clear of the
town, a loop of the river showed through tall
poplars like a silver horseshoe, and distantly
the land rose into the great folds and curves
of the downs.

She opened the door with her key of the
flat and went in, her feet sinking deep into the
lush carpet. Lush and good, she thought.
George had had his early struggles but now
that his business was successful and fast
growing only the best was good enough.

She hesitated at the door to the lounge.
Should she leave the letter there so that when
he came in late and sank into an armchair
with a nightcap he would see it? No, he might

3

miss it. She went along to the main bedroom and took the letter from her bag. She would turn his bed down and lay the letter on his pyjamas.

The door was a few inches ajar. She pushed it half open and it swung noiselessly on its oiled hinges. George was an engineer and everything he owned was scrupulously maintained in first-class order. The inner smoke-grey silk curtains were half drawn and a great bar of sunlight fell across the room. She stood in the doorway and was invaded by an ice-cold numbness, all feeling robbed from her.

A woman's clothes were sloughed in a heap at the side of the bed . . . a summer dress, scarlet poppies on a yellow background, the stitching broken away for two or three inches along part of the hem, a pair of shoes, one lying on its side, the polished fawn sole only faintly scuffed. Her eyes marked the details but the coldness in her barred all emotion.

George lay on the bed, sleeping. His mouth was slightly open, his dark hair tousled and sweat-damp, and he wore nothing except a pair of short grey silk socks. His breathing was heavy, breaking into a snore now and then. One of his hands lay lax over the naked woman's navel. She slept without sound, fair hair in disorder over the crumpled pillow.

4

Jean watched them for a moment or two and then, as thought and reason, bereft of all emotion, came back to her, she let the letter drop from her hand to the floor and turned away.

Leaving her flat key on the heavy silver tray on the hall table, she closed the door silently behind her and went down to her car and drove off, taking the road to the Research Station. Some time or other she knew that real feeling would come to ravage her, that the icy coldness which she inhabited would thaw and free a new Jean Blackwell. For the time being she had no interest in that person.

As she pulled up at the main gate of the Research Station, the guard gave her a routine smile and flicked his eyes at her identity card with its Ministry of Defence embossed stamp franked across her photograph. He nodded her through and the red-and-white barrier pole rose, sweeping a slow quadrant against the cloudless summer sky. She drove to the car park, past the low, precisely set buildings and the freshly hoed, neat beds of flaming geraniums, and found a vacant place in the shadow of the water tower. She sat for a while, untroubled by the heat, her body — like her mind — insulated against all normal feeling.

From the tower a stretch of rough,

summer-browned grass ran to the high-wired perimeter fence. Beyond it the downs fell away to the far valley of the River Avon. Although the city of Salisbury was hidden from view, the top part of the cathedral spire just showed against the brazen sky. The rough grass at the foot of the perimeter fence was marked here and there with the scarlet of poppy blooms. George was wearing his socks in bed. He very often did. And the hem of the dress needed stitching. They would make love again when they woke. She knew George. The giver of surprises.

She got out of the car and walked to the laboratory and project building. *No bloody larking about with all this micro-whatever-it-is caper.* She unlocked the heavy entrance door and watched it swing back to self-lock before she went into the cloakroom to wash her hands and tidy her face. Once you came through the entrance door then Armstrong's law ruled.

When she went into the administrative office Boyson was sitting sideways at his desk with his feet propped up on the wastepaper basket. He was reading an old copy of *Nature*. The window was partly open at the top and the blue drift of his cigarette smoke was coiling through it in slow trails.

He looked up, a man in his late thirties,

long-faced, mild surprise showing on it briefly at the sight of her. A lock of lank fair hair fell over one eye. His white laboratory coat rode high and untidily about his shoulders. Boyson always looked as though he had been loosely and hurriedly assembled.

'Hullo, Jean.' He glanced at the wall clock. 'You're a bit early, aren't you?'

'A little. How's the patient?' Her voice was normal, betraying nothing of the cold emotion still frozen deeply within her. And that, she thought, was helpful. When you came in here you left the warm, normal world behind you. Forgot it. It was easier that way.

'Charlie's all right. You're not due to take over for half an hour yet. I was just going to do my last round.'

'Don't bother. I'll do it for you.'

'Sure?'

'Yes.'

'Well, thanks. That's a bonus. I promised to take the kids swimming as soon as I got back. I can't wait to get in the water, either.' He sighed. 'Flaming June . . . The weather never does anything by halves in this country.' He nodded at the desk. 'The check list is there. Armstrong is coming in around six. No need, but you know him. Just can't keep away once the green light goes on.' Standing up and slipping off his white coat, eyeing her, he said

7

gently. 'You all right?'

Jean nodded. 'Yes.'

Boyson smiled. 'I know the feeling. The first day of a new project always brings up the old problems. Moral indigestion. But it passes quickly. Thank God.'

As he went by her he paused briefly and laid the back of his hand against her cheek. It was a rare touch of physical comfort. Nobody liked the first day.

Alone, Jean went to the desk and picked up the check list for Charlie. It was headed Monday, 21st June, and the page was ruled in blue lines marking off the half-hours. The first entry had been made at ten-thirty that morning and there were entries for every half hour since. The last five had been made and signed by Boyson. Jean read them through absorbing them clearly but mechanically.

She heard Boyson whistling softly as he went down the corridor and then the long sigh of the outer door closing; Boyson the happily married man with a boy of three and a girl of five, both with their mother's dark hair, a tight little family. She and George had gone swimming with them the previous weekend. *I want a wife and I want kids. Just a plain old-fashioned set-up.* She saw without emotion the woman's body, sun-tanned, the breasts large-nippled and flattened by their own weight as she lay on her back.

Going back to the cloakroom she took her white coat, rubber gloves and a new mouth mask from her locker and then, check list and the key of Charlie's quarters in hand, she went down the corridor.

Charlie's quarters were at the far end of the building. They were entered through two spring-loaded, self-locking doors operated by the same key. The first door was of wood with a small circular observation window of security glass at head height. Ten feet beyond it was an iron-barred door with the bars set a few inches apart. The space between the two doors was empty except for a wooden cupboard against the left-hand wall. In this cupboard were kept brooms, brushes and pails and other odds and ends used for cleaning the quarters.

Jean looked through the circular window, checking that the space between the two doors was empty. She unlocked the door and went in, standing and waiting until the door swung back to self-lock.

Going up to the open bars of the next door she looked into the quarters. There was no sign of Charlie. She unlocked it and entered. The door swung back and locked itself. She was in the main section of the quarters, a large solarium with a glass roof. Three of the four blinds were unrolled behind their protecting iron framework. Above the door the air-conditioner hissed gently, and at the side of the door the wall thermometer behind its iron grill read 75 degrees Fahrenheit.

Jean entered the temperature on her check board, and then crossed the solarium to Charlie's sleeping cubicle. The door was open and clamped back against the wall with a strong padlock. The bed — a low wide crib — was against the far wall and Charlie lay on it sleeping. There was no other furniture in the room. The ceiling light was protected by a strong grill. The guarded thermometer in the wall showed 78 degrees Fahrenheit. Jean entered this on her list. It was two degrees above Armstrong's stipulated temperature. When she left the quarters she would have to adjust the thermostat control in the corridor. The regulator on the air conditioner had given trouble before. The station electrician would have to be telephoned to come and look at it. Pleasant as Armstrong could be — he was a stickler for details. From this day on not the slightest risk could be taken with Charlie. Thinking this and looking down at Charlie, Jean knew that the thought came from a stranger . . . the ice-cold Jean Blackwell, carrying out her duties automatically and efficiently.

Charlie was lying with his head buried in his forearms. He could be sleeping or, as he often did when not in the mood for company, feigning sleep.

At the door, as she was going out, she turned her head quickly and looked back. Charlie's right forearm had slid a little from his face and one open brown eye watched her. Almost immediately the eye closed and the forearm re-covered it. Going out into the solarium there was no familiar smile on her face at this familiar ritual . . . nor even the sudden, sharp but quickly suppressed stir of conscience because of the way they were using Charlie.

Charlie lay on his straw-filled bed, listening to the sound of Jean Blackwell moving in the solarium. Charlie was a seven-year-old chimpanzee. He had been born in a forest on the eastern shores of Lake Tanganyika. At some time in his young wild life his left ear had been bitten or torn in a fight, leaving a large nick in it. When he was four years old, barely weaned and still with his milk teeth, he had been illegally trapped on the fringes of the Gombe National Park and taken from Tanzania. Over the years he had moved from public to private zoos and finally to the Fadledean Research Station, high up on the Wiltshire Downs in the South of England where, because he was the closest living relative to man in the animal world, he was a creature of particular importance and value to the Ministry of Defence at this moment. Man and Charlie's kind had probably shared a common ancestor in the past, but since the things Man will do to Man are without limit, Charlie and his kind in other scientific laboratories merited no special concessions even though they shared the same number and form of chromosomes, the same blood protein and the same circuitry of the brain. That Charlie's kind had thirteen ribs instead of Man's twelve was not significant. Plenty of men had thirteen and behaved far worse than chimpanzees. The main point was that Charlie was important to Man. He had been since ten-thirty that morning when Armstrong, the Scientific Co-ordinator of the Fadledean Research Station, had injected him in the upper right forearm.

Charlie rolled over on his straw and lying on his back raised his left arm and slowly beat with his hand against the boarded wall of his room. Most animals in captivity develop stress mannerisms. This was Charlie's. When he was upset or unsure of things about him he would thud or drum against a wall, sometimes with a fast tattoo. Normally, because they treated him well and he liked them, he would be eager for company when any of the laboratory people came in. He liked to play games with them and to be scratched or quietly groomed. But today, in order to give him his injection, he had been treated with a short-lived anaesthetic to immobilize him. He still felt the after-effects of it and there was no desire in him for company . . . not even the company of Jean Blackwell, who, of them all, was the one to whom he gave the most friendly and trusting responses. As he thudded at the wall, he pursed his broad upper and pendulous lower lips together into a pout and almost inaudibly made gentle hooing sounds.

Outside in the solarium Jean crossed to the low-set drinking fountain. She kept her finger on the porcelain press button until the water ran from lukewarm to cold, its coolness reaching through her rubber glove. Suddenly aware of a faint prickle of heat on her forehead she cupped some water in her hand and dabbed it on her brow. She heard Charlie's drumming almost as though it were a faint thudding inside her own head.

Going back to the open-barred first security door she looked sideways and saw Charlie lying on his bed, one hand slowly pounding the wall. There had been a time when this kind of work had seldom troubled her. But in the last years the seldom had become often. Boyson had guessed that. Maybe Armstrong had, too. The wall thermometer now read 76 degrees. The moment she got out she would telephone the electrician, and then Armstrong. *Any irregularity whatsoever and I must be called.*

As she reached into her pocket for the door key she felt a sudden fierce prickle of sweat at the base of her throat and between her breasts. She thought of Boyson and his family swimming. It would be good to be stripped and in the water. The last time she had swum with George and they had sunbathed afterwards he had put out a hand and let it rest, cool and lax, on her navel . . . George the giver of gifts, the knight in shining armour who would have rescued her from all this. She put the key in the lock.

Pulling the door open, she felt the beaded sweat on her throat break and run between her breasts, and suddenly her head began to swim so that she was forced to lean back against the half-open door to steady herself. Then, as she fought the swimming in her head and a fast growing weakness in her legs, she knew with a swift panic what was going to happen . . . remembering the times, distant now, when she had come round to stare stupidly up into the faces of other girls, her

14

mother and father or complete strangers.

A violent wave of nausea rose in her. The door key in her hand, she fainted, collapsing to the floor. The door swung back and was held partly open by her legs which lay across the threshold.

Charlie heard the thud of her body on the floor. He stopped drumming and lay listening. All the movements and sounds made in his quarters were familiar to him, the click of keys in locks, the soft sighing of self-closing doors and the sound of footsteps — always quickly recognized — in the vestibule between the doors. There was no further sound of doors opening or shutting. He picked up a straw and chewed at it.

After a moment or two he went out into the solarium and ambled on all fours over to the water basin. He pressed the porcelain button and sucked at the water as it ran. Turning away he saw Jean's body lying beside the partly open door. He went across to her and squeezed through the open door space above her legs. Squatting on his heels he looked into her face. Her eyes were closed. He put out a long, hard-skinned finger and touched her face. When she made no move he gave two or three anxious sounding panting hoots and then turned and left her.

Going up to the large cupboard he rose on

15

his hind legs and rattled at the handle. Now and then the people who looked after him, he knew from experience and watching, kept a few titbits in there for him . . . a banana, or onions of which he was fond. Unable to open the door, he gave the panel a frustrated smack.

Grumbling to himself he went past the cupboard and sat down in the recess made by the angle of its side with the main wall. He sat with arms locked across his chest and rocked himself gently, watching Jean's head which he could just see.

Five minutes later Jean came round. She slowly sat up, the barred door closing quietly behind her as she drew her legs forward. Her head was swimming and her stomach began to heave with a swift attack of nausea. Dimly, hardly knowing what she was doing, but realizing that in a few moments she would be violently sick and wanted to reach the cloakroom, she climbed to her feet. One hand across her eyes and forehead to steady the throbbing in her head, she stumbled across to the main door, the key still in her right hand. She leant against it, fumbled the key in the lock and turned it with only one desire in her . . . to get to the cloakroom quickly and be sick. She pushed the door wide and went through swaying as she walked, one hand out to steady herself against the wall.

As the door started to swing slowly back, Charlie rose and slipped through it. He ambled down the corridor on all fours, his body swinging with a gentle roll, following Jean. She turned into the cloakroom a few yards ahead of him and the door closed.

Charlie sat on his bottom in front of the door, raised his head and gave a few rapid grunts. Then he turned and, seeing the door of the administration office opposite open, he went in, his grunts ceasing. He went to a chair below the window and looked out and blew a series of *hoos* through his pouting lips. Then, seeing that the top half of the window was partly open, he climbed on to the sill, pulled himself up and squeezed through the opening and dropped to the ground outside.

Without any hurry he ambled along, the back of his hands just touched the ground, the sun burning the rich dark brown fur of his pelt, across a lawn and into a small shrubbery of flowering viburnums. On the other side of the shrubbery he came out on to the path that ran all the way around the inside of the perimeter fence. Talking to himself in low, excited grunts and little pouting sounds of pleasure, he climbed the tall stout-meshed wire fence easily, balanced himself on the barbed-wire stranded overhang — designed to keep people out not in — and jumped the sixteen feet to the ground easily.

Without any idea where he was going and, in fact, with no desire to go anywhere in particular, content solely with this new freedom, he went slowly across the downland and was soon out of sight of the perimeter fence and Research Station buildings. Above him the larks were singing and the warm air was full of the scent of thyme and marjoram.

As he walked, he caught two copper-coloured grasshoppers and ate them.

Five minutes later he came to a spinney of tall beech trees. He climbed thirty feet up one of the inside trees, settled himself into a fork and, lying back with his legs crossed, reached out and gathered a handful of the silky green leaves. Chewing the leaves into a moist wad in his mouth he looked around him. High summer lay over all the land and the sky was pearl grey with heat haze. Through a gap in the trees Charlie watched the movement of distant cars on a main road. Beyond the road a narrow river threw loops of silver between meadows studded with the resting, cud-chewing shapes of black-and-white cows. A large caterpillar crawled up the smooth bark of the tree trunk. Charlie picked it off and put it in his mouth to flavour the leaves.

As he chewed contentedly he scratched

absently at the slight irritation that came from the small shaven patch at the top of his right arm where he had been injected. Then he began to drum against the tree trunk with one hand faster than he had ever done in his quarters and opening his mouth wide, displaying all his teeth, the wad lodged in the pouch of his cheek, he called loudly *waa-waa-waa*.

★   ★   ★

Charles Armstrong the Scientific Co-ordinator of the Fadledean Research Station, fiddled with the half-empty glass of whisky on the desk before him as he listened to the Director of Micro-Biological Research on the telephone. Armstrong was an amiable man who believed in taking no chances and no extreme initiatives. Outside of his official sphere he led a happy life with his wife and his two children and allowed them to exploit and manipulate him so long as they did not interfere with his chief pastimes of golf and shooting. One of his recurring dreams was of himself winning the British Open Championship as an amateur. His handicap was sixteen and never likely to be lower. As a micro-biologist of international reputation his eminence in this sphere also gave him dreams — from most of which he woke in a cold sweat — but he had learnt to live with them. He was fifty, plump, almost bald and his cheeks were crested with little tufts of grey-white hair.

As his Director spoke to him he made notes from time to time on the pad beside the whisky. Now and then he managed a small sip of whisky which he knew at this moment he damned well needed. Because of what the Director called 'the sensitive areas concerned', practically all action was being taken out of his hands, certainly concerning anything that had to be done outside the perimeter of the Station and absolutely regarding any communication with the civil or police authorities. Armstrong congratulated himself that — after the Station guards had reported that there was no sign of Charlie in the camp — he had stayed his hand in the act of reaching for the telephone to call the police. Thank God for that . . . No mention of Charlie's escape must as yet go beyond the Station. The outside world was for others to worry about.

The Director ran on, detailing the immediate steps which he had taken, steps he was confident would see Charlie back in the laboratory very soon. That night, maybe. He sounded very sure of himself and made one of his weak jokes at which Armstrong dutifully laughed faintly — knowing that whatever happened there would always be a stout umbrella above the Director to shelter him from the storm. But against himself, even if Charlie came ambling back with a cheerful grin on his face in the next hour, Armstrong knew there would always be a black mark simply because he had not been able to foresee the one chance in a million which had freed Charlie. That damned Jean.

The Director finished, 'So just sit tight and look after your own little plot. If you get a call from the military then cooperate to the limit. As far as the police and the public are, if ever, concerned . . . well, all that will be handled from the holy of holies. However, I'm sure that once Charlie is spotted a bunch of bananas will bring him to heel.'

Armstrong put the receiver down, picked up the whisky glass and drained it. Well, he just bloody well hoped the Director was right because if not the balloon would go up.

He flicked his intercom and asked his secretary to send in Miss Blackwell.

When Jean came in he nodded her to a chair and then pretended to occupy himself with his notes for a while to give himself time to decide how to handle her. He liked her and, indeed, there had been the odd times when, satisfying a timid sensuality, he had

21

imagined her naked and himself making love to her. At the moment as she sat waiting for him she prompted no such fantasy. She was the one who had poised a sword above his head. If there was real trouble he knew that it would come right back to him. From the corner of his eye he saw her fiddling nervously with the ring on her engagement finger. Security had checked the man and had found nothing against him . . . George Somebody-or-the-Other, the proprietor of a prosperous engineering firm . . . well heeled, well liked, sociable . . . hardly her type, he would have thought. Security would have done better to have checked her past medical record . . . a chance in a bloody million.

He pushed his notes away, looked up and in his official no-nonsense laboratory voice said, 'I've just been speaking to the Director. Staff not on duty are being recalled at once. All project staff will sleep here until further notice. Except for essential family messages — which must be cleared through me and telephoned in my presence — there will be no communication with anyone outside the Station. Does that pose any immediate problems for you?'

'No, it doesn't.'

'Good. Nothing is being said to the police or the public at the moment. The whole thing is in the hands of the military area command. There will be a discreet and wide troop cordon centred on this Station and also a helicopter search while the light lasts. That's one reason why you have to be on hand. Charlie comes to you more readily than to anyone else.'

'Yes, I know.' She spoke briefly, knowing that was all he wanted, guessing his mood and knowing that she was entirely to blame for it. But Charlie had a mind of his own. No matter what bond she had built with him over the past months, Charlie had never been free from his quarters, or other quarters for years. Sudden freedom changed people, and it might change Charlie.

Armstrong stood up and moved uneasily to the window. His back to her, he said, 'The Director naturally, wants a report on the whole business. I want you to write your own report — in the fullest detail — on what happened. And I want to send it off tomorrow morning.' He swung round suddenly and shook his head at her. 'Christ, Jean — you could really have put the cat among the pigeons!'

'I'm sorry . . . But this isn't the African jungle. There's no possibility that Charlie could stay free long — '

Armstrong smacked a hand on his bald

head and said, 'Don't talk about possibilities. There was no possibility that Charlie could escape. We went over everything . . . and then the million-to-one chance happens!'

He went across the room, picked up his whisky glass, and opened a cupboard door. As he filled his glass he said in a suddenly changed tone of voice, 'You like a drink?'

'No, thank you.'

'You're all right now?'

'Yes, thank you.'

She knew he was making a peace overture. He was a decent man. Knowing what Charlie's escape already had and — with bad luck — might still further involve him in, knowing how much his professional reputation meant to him, she realized that it was a gesture that would never have come from one in fifty of his superiors in the Ministry.

He turned, eyed her for a moment, glass in hand and then shrugged his shoulders. He said, 'I was going to blast hell out of you. Almost looked forward to it.' He grinned ruefully and sat down at his desk. 'No point though. It's happened. Let's assume it will all be sewn up without trouble. Meantime, I'd like to know about this fainting business.'

She said uneasily, 'Well . . . when I was much younger, a schoolgirl, and two or three times in my early twenties, if I got over-excited or very much upset I would faint — right out of the blue. But it hasn't happened to me for years and years. I thought I'd outgrown it.'

'Did you mention this at your medical when you came here?'

'No. It had gone completely from my mind. I wasn't asked the question specifically.'

Armstrong sighed. The question would be asked in future. For a moment he had a vivid picture of the things that might happen if someone had a sudden fainting fit during some of the tricky moments of working here. He said, 'Were you under any exceptional stress or emotion today?'

For a while there was no answer. Watching her, sitting there, cool in her blue dress, the sunlight through the window raising high points on her dark hair, he wondered if the stress might have come from a swift attack of conscience or self-repugnance. Everyone had them at times . . . people who couldn't handle them soon left. Others learned to live with them. The need for national survival and self-defence in these times had bred a new morality. He saw the lift of her shoulders as she breathed deeply.

Then flatly she said, 'You altered the schedule this morning and Charlie was injected at ten-thirty instead of two-thirty. The duty periods were rearranged, which gave me an unexpected few hours free this afternoon. I went down to Salisbury to do some shopping and to tidy my flat. Then, although I'd already told George that I wouldn't be seeing him, I thought I'd give him a surprise . . . '

Armstrong listened as she went on baldly telling the story, wondering why on earth this damned George could not have been content with the prize he already had. If he had been George . . .

Jean finished. 'I was perfectly calm about it all. Just frozen up inside. Then as I opened the barred door in Charlie's quarters to leave — it hit me.'

Armstrong said quietly, 'I'm sorry. I didn't know I was going to drag this kind of thing from you.'

'You're entitled to know. Do you want me to put it in my report?'

After a moment's consideration, Armstrong said gently, liking her, feeling sorry for her, and knowing that when all this was over she would have to go. 'Yes, Jean — you must put it all in.'

Jean stood up, grateful for his kindness and wanting to repay it somehow. She said, 'I'll go and start it now. But surely as far as Charlie is concerned there's no need to worry? He can't possibly stay free for three weeks in this country, can he? It's not possible.'

Suddenly, forgetting her personal problem and his sympathy for her, Armstrong said brutally, 'We didn't think it was possible for Charlie to escape — but he bloody well has! So anything is possible. I don't have to tell you that if Charlie does stay free long enough what kind of walking time bomb he will become!'

2

Captain Hector Stevens, Royal Corps of Signals, temporarily attached to the Army School of Aviation in Wiltshire for an advanced flying course in helicopters, with a Sergeant Observer by his side, swung his machine gently into a wide turn and levelled out at three hundred feet along the third leg of the sector which had been allotted to him. As he flew he whistled gently through his teeth and listened to the network chatter coming through his earphones, his eyes watching the ground passing below.

He had two more sectors to fly before dark — and they would take all that time — in a search for a chimpanzee, codename Charlie, male, which had escaped — so rumour already had it — from the Research Station at Fadledean. If so, it was a damned good place to escape from he would have thought, for man or beast. Not that he would ever have said so in the Mess. He knew when to keep his mouth shut. If the animal were seen, report location and keep under observation. A rum place, Fadledean, and some rum goings on if you believed everything that rumheads said. Personally he believed nothing unless it was in one of the manuals or came from the mouth of a superior officer. Keep your mouth shut, your private thoughts to yourself and your ambition daily burnished — that way lay promotion. So, he told himself, the fact that he was in a rush operation to search for a chimpanzee with God-knows-how-many helicopters in the air and ground patrols, R/T trucks and all the rest spread out for miles around might make this chimpanzee no ordinary chimpanzee; there was not the slightest speculation in him about the special nature of the animal. Which was sensible, he knew, because after the animal had been captured none of the other pilots and observers in the air now, or the troops below, would be made any the wiser about the reason for the animal's importance. Why plague yourself with questions which would never have any answers? Idle.

The small chalk-stream he was following curved through a meadow mottled with kingcups and yellow patches of flowering iris, long streaks of green weed marbling its flow. Here and there a line of willows or alders overhung the bright water. A man on the bank fishing looked up and waved to them as they passed over. Not a friendly wave,

Captains Stevens guessed. Get that something-something thing out of here. Bloody racket.

He grinned to himself and took the machine down a hundred feet as they approached a ragged wood of poplars and ash trees through which the river ran. He quartered over it slowly and at the far end dropped down to close above tree level, the rotors setting the topmost branches waving and tossing. If VIP Charlie-boy was anywhere up in them, he thought, he would be a stout number not to be flushed by the noise and the wind storm which was setting twigs and leaves scattering into the air. He took the machine twice over the wood fast and then went up a hundred feet and hung, watching verges. A pair of magpies — two for joy — and a rocketing cock pheasant went away, but nothing else moved.

Stevens went to normal search level and cruised slowly down the stream. Beyond Salisbury the setting sun hung low like a red ball, shimmering in its own heat haze, the great pointed shaft of the cathedral spire a raised black stiletto against its glare. Somewhere down there was the girl he had been taking out to dinner tonight. Tough titty, old man . . . still, plenty of other girls, plenty of other nights. Get your priorities right, old boy . . . more to be got from being the first to spot old Charlie than there was to be had in the back seat of a car . . .

As the sound of the helicopter died away, Charlie — who, after months in his quarters at Fadledean, was well used to the sight and sound of low-flying army helicopters — ambled out of the wood and crossed the stream by a wooden footbridge. He made a quick snatch at a dragon-fly that neared him, missed it, and went on chattering softly to himself. A narrow path led up the valley side along the edge of a field of tall wheat. Charlie pulled off some of the unripe heads and began to chew them into a moist wad. He moved along easily on all fours, hidden from sight by the growing wheat, hands touching the ground, lightly taking his weight.

At the top of the field the path turned sharply to the right and ran along the side of a garden which fronted a low thatched cottage. The garden gate was open and carried the sign — SPURBROOK. Charlie went through the gate, stood erect — when he did so he was just over three feet tall — and spat out his wad.

The front door was shut. At its side a stout wisteria trunk ran up to the top windows and branched left and right along the face of the cottage. The right-hand window had its middle section partly open, set on a bar catch.

Charlie pouted his lips and blew a series of soft hoos of contentment. He was enjoying his freedom. Then he shuffled slowly up to the front door, grasped the wisteria trunk and climbed up through the foliage to the open window and slipped inside.

★ ★ ★

It was almost dark when Captain Brauning, Royal Navy retired, in his seventies, hard as oak, able to walk and drink plenty of men half his age off their feet, the man who had been fishing the chalk-stream, returned to Spurbrook Cottage.

Leaving his rod on the rack in the hall, he went through to the kitchen to put the one small trout he had caught in the refrigerator. The fishing was useless, the weather too hot, the trout insolently indifferent to all artificial flies, there had been no evening rise and the midges had given him hell. It would take two large whiskies, he told himself, to put him back in good humour. No, maybe three. Plenty of time for that because his wife was out playing bridge and wouldn't be back until late.

He washed his hands under the kitchen tap and went into the large sitting room where, he knew, the table would be set with a cold supper left for him by his wife, but the supper could wait. The whisky decanter was on the sideboard.

He switched on the lights to be met by a scene of disorder. Magazines and newspapers, many of them torn to pieces, were strewn about the floor. Two armchairs had been overturned and the cloth had been pulled half-way off the table. On the carpet alongside it lay plates and dishes and cutlery, some of the china broken. A half-eaten loaf of bread was still on the table, the lid was off the cheese dish and there was no sign of the large slab of ripe Gorgonzola which he knew had been under it. Nor was there any sign of the cold sliced ham which his wife had left, napkin covered, on his plate. Near the fireplace a small glass pickle jar lay on its side in a pool of vinegar, but there was no sign of the pickled onions which it had once held.

Captain Brauning, not a man easily shocked by words or deeds, took a deep breath to ease his indignation and then began to swear. He swore long and with a rising anger, an anger only slightly mollified when a quick glance showed him that the sideboard was untouched and that the whisky decanter stood undisturbed, the room light striking bright gleams from its cut-glass sides. Anger somewhat eased, action followed. He turned and began to go quickly through the rest of the house.

Nothing else had been disturbed except in one of the bedrooms. The half window was off its bar and wide open. A small single bed had been pulled away from the wall, its covers on the floor and one of the pillows torn open and the feather-filling scattered around the place as though a fox had been enjoying himself hammering at a couple of frantic geese. In one corner of the room was a toilet alcove. The cold tap had been turned on and the water was still running away through the waste pipe. A large tube of toothpaste, its bottom bitten off, lay below the basin, near it was a decorated drum-shaped toilet powder container empty, the powder thick across the polished boards like a heavy hoar frost. One large footmark was imprinted on the powder.

Captain Brauning, advising himself to ease the pressure that was rising in him, relieved himself with a scabrous flow of lower-deck language as he turned the cold tap off and then clattered down the stairs to report the vandalism to the police.

The duty officer, when he answered, seemed possessed of a stupidity deliberately designed to complicate a simple matter and keep Captain Brauning as long as possible from his whisky decanter. He was given no chance to reply to Captain Brauning's parting shots — 'And I might add that the bugger who did this has damned bad table manners, doesn't like whisky, and bloody well goes about bare-footed!' He slammed the receiver down and headed for the sitting-room and the first of his glasses of comfort.

Half-a-mile away, in an open corrugated iron roofed barn, Charlie lay on top of a tall stack of hay bales in a comfortable nest he had hollowed out for himself. He was sleeping, holding in one hand the chewed length of one of Captain Brauning's club ties, softly whimpering to himself now and again as Gorgonzola cheese and pickled onions fought intermittently in his stomach, and clasping the other hand over the place where he had been injected that morning.

★　★　★

Sitting on the teak table in the window of his office, John Rimster looked out over St James's Park and the sunbright London morning. London's and the country's mornings had been sunbright too long now. People — even those who normally talked nostalgically of the glorious summers of the past — were getting fed up with blue skies. Through the screen of hanging willows at the lakeside he watched a shelduck bully a mallard into water-frothing flight. Two girls walked up the far pavement towards Wellington Barracks, a Cadillac with a CD plate passed, momentarily truncating them, but the details it fleetingly obscured were in his mind and so were the details of the car as it disappeared. Over the years you learned to suck in everything, digest it with ease and throw it up like an owl's pellet when needed. Two blackheaded gulls began to fight and scream over a floating bread crust.

He lit a cigarette and went back to his desk and began to tap one finger absently on the locked despatch box which he had opened at eight o'clock that morning and closed ten minutes ago at nine. Nice stuff. It made you proud to be a member of the human race. He was used to such stuff. It no longer — since when, God help him? — gave him indigestion; and the human race . . . well, when he gave them up he would have to give himself up. If only they could be indecent efficiently. He smiled, this last was a favourite phrase of Grandison's. But beyond everything he hoped that he was not going to be mixed up in it. It was far from his line of country. But it damned well looked like it. He bit the edge of his lower lip, frowning.

He sat there frowning, thinking about Charlie and the Fadledean set-up. He was a man not far into his forties with close-cut, iron-grey hair. The craggy hardness of his build was in his face too, except when he smiled, furrowing and scarping it. His eyes were a dry slate grey and, although he was meticulously shaven, there was the faintest bloom of obstinate stubble at the sides of his chin. Everything about him was neat, trim and hard. His clothes were good, a hound's-tooth check suit, a light blue shirt and a darker tie. He was neat and precise in everything he did. And he had done some extraordinary things, most of which he had learned to forget quickly.

Grandison came in at quarter past nine precisely. He was a great pirate of a man — a wooden leg and a black eye-patch all that were missing. In the place of a patch he wore a monocle, its red silk cord looping over the lapel of his grey linen suit. His bulk was enormous, but never clumsy. He was black-haired, black-bearded and his broad red face was time-creased and experience-scarred from fifty years of hard, violent, devious and joyful living. There was now a warm, friendly smile on his face, but that meant nothing. When he wanted to he could make Privy Counsellors and Cabinet Ministers sweat under the armpits. He had the ear and the confidence of all those who mattered and had dined once a fortnight with all the Prime Ministers under whom he had served in a highly confidential capacity which had never been precisely defined. The section he commanded, an unlisted and unpublicized offshoot of the Ministry of Defence, had an ambiguous mandate, and its members were all smoothly endowed with a variety of skills and — when necessary — an inhumanity which set them apart from most other people. Their training had been long and dedicated and the percentage of would-be members over the years who had been rejected was high.

Grandison went to the window without greeting Rimster and looking out said, 'Well?'

Rimster said, 'Doesn't seem to be up my alley. Opposition — one male chimpanzee. I know he's special, but . . . '

Grandison turned. 'Three weeks? Mr Charlie no-can-do?' He grinned.

'He could — by a miracle.'

'They happen. That's why he's free . . . the time, the place, and the loved one altogether. Incidentally, I met her once. She's a nice-looking girl. You'll enjoy holding her hand, even if it's only for a few days.'

Rimster knew it was his moment to probe.

Grandison was silent for a moment and then with a shrug of his shoulders said quietly, 'You know better than that, Johnnie.

You've known the answer for some time. Do you want me to put it in words? The moment comes for us all — sooner or later. If you don't want to do this, you know the alternative. Appeal to you?'

'Not yet.'

'Good. Then get down there. If Charlie stays out long the public are going to know he's out. What they are never going to know is the truth about him. All the press stuff will be done this end. I just want you sitting there keeping an eye on things.' He smiled. 'A nice rustic interlude for a change — and pleasant company. Enjoy yourself and keep an eye on things for me.'

Rimster touched the knot of his tie and smiled back. 'Beagles smoking eighty cigarettes a day. The anti-vivisection-and-experiments-on-animals lobby. The Englishman and his dog. That can be handled. But if he stays out over the limit, the balloon goes up plain for everyone to see.'

'That won't happen. But assuming it did . . . well, that's where we pull out and others take over. How good are you on micro-organisms?'

'Not too hot. But I get the drift. No doubt the charming, heart-broken Miss Blackwell will enlighten me further. What's the brief?

'Watching. Full access to places and

persons. And you stick by her side. People under stress often rediscover their consciences.'

'You're telling me.'

Grandison chuckled and came to the desk. 'I'm not worried about you. You never had one. Now get down there. Here's your brief and all the trimmings.' He dropped a sealed envelope on to the desk, and then took out a cigar and began to prepare it for lighting. When it was going — no one interrupted him when he was lighting a cigar — he said, 'Good security comes from having the right kind of outrageous imagination. Scientists don't have that. He's out — by a miracle. He could stay out by the same dispensation.'

Rimster shrugged his shoulders. 'Possible, but not probable. He'll be spotted. The higher an ape climbs the more he shows his bare backside.'

'Sure, my boy. Unlike clever man — he invented trousers on the way up. Now read that brief and off you get.' He nodded at the envelope and then picked up the locked despatch case and left the office.

Rimster lit a cigarette and began to read his brief. When he had finished it — it was three pages long — he went to his safe and locked it up, but every fact, date, name and figure in it would go down to Wiltshire with him.

* * *

Charlie woke at sunrise on his first full day of freedom. His digestion had settled overnight. He dropped down from the hay bales and ambled out into the sunlight which was throwing long shadows across the small bowl of land in which the barn stood. He squatted down and began to comb loose hay from his pelt. Over his head, swallows flew in and out to their nests in the roof of the barn, and above the centre of the hollow a kestrel hung on quivering wings, scanning the ground below. On the far side of the hollow, a few sheep grazed in the shadow of a small fir plantation.

Charlie began to move towards the sheep, stopping now and again to raise himself to full height and watch them. They saw him as he neared them and began to move away, slowly at first and then breaking into a lumbering gallop. He chased them for a hundred yards, screaming *waa-waas* and then broke off and turned towards the plantation.

When he was a few yards from it, a rabbit, lying in a patch of nettles, bolted from almost under his feet and headed, its white scut flicking, for the fir plantation. Charlie raced after it and the rabbit in its panic ran straight into the close-meshed wire fence that

41

surrounded the firs. Charlie caught it and squeezed the life from it.

He sat down in the shadow of the firs and ate part of the rabbit. It was a long time since Charlie had eaten raw meat and he stopped now and again to roll and lick his lips and to make gentle hooing noises. Since his hearing was acute, he heard the coming of the helicopter long before he saw it, its noise gradually drowning the buzzing of the bees and flies which worked the downland flowers in the grass of the bowl and the high, monotonous flighting song of the larks above.

The machine came diagonally across the bowl, its awkward shadow flaying the ground behind it, and passed over the far end of the wood. The pilot and the observer missed seeing Charlie because his dark coat merged completely into the black shadow of the firs.

When it had passed, Charlie threw what was left of the rabbit carcass to the ground and began to follow the line of the fence. He stopped once, picked up a dead branch and stood beating it quickly on the top strand of wire, grinning and barking with excitement.

Half an hour later, Charlie was seen for the first time by a human being since his escape. A motor-cyclist came fast round the corner of a narrow lane cut deep through the downland chalk and found Charlie in the middle of the road. The man braked and swerved violently. The machine skidded past Charlie and smashed into the road bank. The rider was thrown through the air and crashed into the hard white bank of the lane. His crash helmet saved him from death, but not from concussion. He was two days in hospital before his memory returned.

Ten minutes later, Charlie crossed the main Salisbury to Winchester road on all fours, leaving the downlands behind him and moving towards the lusher country of the valley of the River Avon. A lorry driver saw him from a distance, as did a commercial traveller approaching the lorry. Both took him for a large sheep-dog.

★ ★ ★

It was three o'clock before Rimster got to Fadledean. He had stopped at the Army Aviation Centre near Andover, where a communications centre for Operation Charlie had been set up and he stayed for lunch. During this time the radio telephone link in his car had been adjusted to the allotted army frequency and all the equipment checked over. He sat now talking to Armstrong in his office.

He made Armstrong uneasy. He had met

the type before, but not often. Rimster's slow, easy smile and almost casual manner he guessed meant nothing. Underneath, the man was prepared to be whatever the job and his superiors demanded of him.

Armstrong said, 'Do you want to be shown round . . . see the lab.? Scene of the crime?' His own jocularity almost stuck in his throat.

'No, thank you. That's not my business. I've just come to baby-sit. The man from head office. But don't worry, I shan't be staying here. You know Redthorn House?'

'That's the Army Command place, isn't it? VIP guest house?'

'That's it. That's where I'll be — and let's hope not for very long. That's where Miss Blackwell will be, too.'

'Why her?'

'Because the bananas are there. She's the one Charlie responds to best. This is no place to sit around and wait — not for a non-scientist like me, anyway. I might pick something up.'

Armstrong smiled, but not at the mild joke. He was relieved to know that he was to be left alone. Unwisely, out of his relief, he said, 'I give Charlie two or three days at the most because — '

Rimster shook his head, interrupting.

44

'That's what you give. I hope you're right. But Charlie might take more, the limit and perhaps far beyond. What happens then?'

'Then the public must be warned.'

'Nice situation for a government. But I imagine they would find some way of facing it. At the moment though the main concern is that the public know nothing — until they have to.'

Armstrong scratched his bald head and shrugged his shoulders. 'Well, nothing will leak from here. Only a handful of people know the full truth and they've all been vetted and know how to keep their mouths shut.'

'I'm sure. But it's none of my business if it does. I'm just here to pass news back and to keep Miss Blackwell under my wing. Liaison man. Redthorn House is very comfortable, they tell me. After London in this heat it's nice to look forward to a few days in the country. I'd like to see Miss Blackwell now in here — and alone.' It was said with no change in the pleasant easy voice, but momentarily the smile was gone from Rimster's face.

'Do you want me to tell her anything before she comes in?'

'Why not? I'm a liaison officer — civilian — from the Ministry. She's the banana girl.

We'll be working together, amicably as far as I'm concerned.'

With Armstrong gone, Rimster leaned back and lit a cigarette. He'd been a little jaunty with the man, for he could sense that behind all the bluffness there was nervousness . . . maybe less concern for Charlie than the beginning of a shrewd calculation about his own future. He needn't have worried. That was nothing to do with him. All he had to do was to hold the girl's hand and see Charlie safely back. Of his own future he decided not to think. Grandison never made his mind up in order to change it. There was no place for sentiment in official life.

Looking out of the window and seeing part of the distant perimeter fence, he thought — Good old Charlie, over the fence and away into the good old summertime. That's what everyone wanted. Over the fence and away. Nearly everyone, anyway.

Jean came in and they made their introductions. She wasn't what he'd pictured in his mind's eye. But he had no complaints with the change.

He said, 'You're moving quarters — to Redthorn House. We may, though I hope not, be there some time. I'll run you down to Salisbury to your flat and you can pick up what you want there. Charlie-chasing clothes.'

The weak edge of a nervous smile touched her lips, following his own broader smile. Nice smile it would be when given full life to break up the solemn, good-looking face. When she laughed she'd be a different woman. There was no temptation in him to speculate beyond that. 'I assume there's a telephone in your flat?'

'Yes, there is.'

'Good. Let's go.'

She sat mostly silently by him as they drove. She was nervous of him and, without any obvious reason, felt a little frightened. Perhaps she had picked that up from Armstrong's manner when talking about him. He looked hard, precise ... no, neat, unruffled, and dead sure of himself.

Now and again he made some passing comment.

Seeing her looking at the radio-telephone equipment in front of her, he said, 'From now on, twenty-four hours a day, we'll be in touch with the operations centre, wherever we go. But don't worry, I'll see you get your sleep.'

As they crested the ridge by Old Sarum, the city below came full into view. She said, 'My flat is on the far side of the town, beyond the cathedral.'

'You just call the directions as we go.' He nodded towards the cathedral. 'One of my

47

favourites. Early English and the highest spire in England — four hundred and four feet. Most of it built in record time by an old boy called Elias de Derham. Impress you?'

He glanced sideways at her and she saw the fine-crowfooting around his dry, slaty eyes tighten as he lowered an eyebrow.

Feeling far out of touch with him, she said, 'Yes.'

'Don't let it. My father was a clergyman. Three boys. We had all the cathedrals of England and a few more at heart. We were traipsed round most of them, too.'

When he parked the car outside the flat he reached over and picked up the telephone. He asked her the number of her telephone and called the operations centre and, giving it to them, said that he would be available on it until further notice. Although she made no move to suggest it, he came up with her and she left him in the sitting-room while she went to pack the things she might need.

★ ★ ★

It was mid-afternoon, the heat oppressive and not enough movement in the air to stir a leaf. Charlie lay along one of the broad mid-boughs of a chestnut tree, his back partly propped

48

against the main trunk, his right hand clasping a thinner branch above him. He was eating the remains of a spring cabbage which he had pulled from a row in a smallholding a quarter of a mile away. The man working in the smallholding had been sitting under the shade of a hedge, resting and drinking cold tea from a bottle. Charlie, at the bottom of the holding, had been screened from him by two tall rows of runner beans. Before taking the cabbage, Charlie had squatted between two rows of netted strawberries and, picking them through the meshes, had eaten his fill.

Now and again, as the flies and honey bees which were working the spikes of the chestnut blooms buzzed around his head, he waved them away with a cabbage leaf. As he lay there, eating and flicking away the flies, Charlie watched a small boy who, a hundred yards away, was sitting on the bank of a narrow carrier stream fishing for roach. Charlie was well acquainted with children, for he had spent a period in a children's zoo on the Continent before coming to England.

Over-bothered with the flies about him and no longer hungry and feeling the need for a drink, Charlie leaned forward, seized a smaller branch and dropped to the ground. Leisurely he shuffled his way through a low growth of scrub willows towards the stream.

He crossed the stream path and sat down a couple of yards from the boy who, watching his float move down the swim he was fishing, had his head turned from him. The boy already had acquired the complete absorption which overtakes fishermen as they watch their moving floats.

Charlie, moved with a desire for company, ambled forward and, suddenly making a series of gentle, panting hoos, reached out and touched the boy on the shoulder.

The boy jerked round at the unexpected touch, found Charlie's face within inches of his own and, scared out of his wits, let out a loud cry of fear and alarm. Dropping his rod, he jumped to his feet and ran as fast as he could along the path. Two hundred yards away he had left his bicycle propped on the other side of a stile which gave access to a small road.

When the boy reached the stile, he stopped, panting, and turned round and looked back along the path. Charlie was sitting on the bank, holding the long roach rod and beating the water with it. Concern for the rod over-rode some of his shock and quick fright.

The boy's name was Andrew Garvey. He was thirteen, stoutly built, and had sandy-coloured hair and a flattish square face, slightly freckled, and for his years he was self-confident over the average, and far from lacking in courage. He knew a chimpanzee when he saw one, and he knew that he was seeing one now. He began to walk slowly back along the path.

As he did so, Charlie dropped the rod and picked up the small tattered fishing bag which lay in the grass. Standing upright Charlie held the bag aloft in both hands and suddenly began to bang it on his head as he went into a silent and mild burst of display. The hairs of the fur on his head and body rose and bristled and he danced and ran around thumping himself and the ground and the bushes with the haversack. As abruptly as it had begun, the display ceased. Charlie went back to the bank and, sitting down by the rod, put one corner of the haversack into his mouth and began to suck gently at it like a baby while his free right hand thumped a slow tattoo on the ground.

Andrew Garvey, his heart beating faster than he would ever tell anyone, approached him slowly.

Charlie had been long aware of him and as the boy neared him he dropped the haversack, turned his head towards Andrew, pursed his lips, pouting them forwards and began to issue a series of soft and friendly *hoo-hoo* whimpers.

When Jean came back into the sitting room, changed and carrying a suitcase, Rimster rose and took it from her. He put it down on a chair by the door and said, 'Would there be any beer or something cool to drink in your fridge?'

Surprised, Jean said, 'Yes, yes, I think so . . . well, lager anyway.'

'Good. No — don't you bother. I'll get it. I'm used to finding my way around.' He smiled. 'I wanted to have a talk with you and I thought this was the best place. Lager for you, too?'

She nodded, feeling awkward and aware that for all his easiness there was something beneath it which was deliberately designed not for her benefit but his. Before she had gone into the office to meet him Armstrong had said, 'He's one of the top grey men. They don't pay social visits. They're wound up and set going and then nothing stops them.' It meant nothing to her and she had the feeling that Armstrong was hardly aware of what he was saying to her, that he was talking to himself.

Rimster came back, a glass in each hand. He handed her a lager. 'Couldn't find the tray.'

He sat down in an armchair opposite her,

took out his cigarette case and offered it to her.

'No, I don't smoke.'

He lit a cigarette for himself, sipped at his lager and then said, 'Relax.'

Stung a little she said, 'Is that an order?'

Rimster laughed quietly. 'Oh Lord, is that what I'm doing to you? I must be slipping. Look, I'm not an inquisitor. I'm not after you because it was through you that Charlie went out on the loose. I've read your report on how it happened and I know all the details about you and your career and so on which are on the official files. So we can forget all that. I'm only interested in Charlie and his recapture. I know something about human beings but not much about chimps, and nothing about Charlie. So, while I smoke and enjoy my lager I'd like you to fill me in. And after that I'd like you to translate into simple terms the reason why, if Charlie stays out over the limit, he's such a cause for concern.'

'But surely you know that?'

'I've read the micro-biological notes about the project without my head spinning too much, but sometimes if miracles keep happening I may have to explain it all to, say, a Chief Constable or an Army general. Underneath the glitter they're just ordinary men, some of them even a little stupid. So — when you've finished with Charlie and his habits, needs and reactions and so forth, I'd like the cause for concern in simple language. All right?'

'I'll try.'

'Good.'

'I think I'd better start with Charlie, and not his kind in general. You see he was comparatively quite young when he was captured and his life up till then can mean very little to him now. He's used to human beings and he depends on them. They're his source of food and shelter. That doesn't mean he likes all of them. He likes some and dislikes or doesn't like so much some others. Although basically he's quite friendly, he's not entirely reliable in his actions because of the unnatural stresses which captivity has caused in him. He has nervous mannerisms which he uses to ease some of these frustrations. Sometimes he just beats a hand or fist against a wall for a long time. Other times he will go into a display mood, either playful or angry. You can't tell right away . . . '

Rimster sat there listening to her and he saw, as he had often seen before in others, the naturalness return when she spoke of a subject she knew, and he marked the moments now and again when the tone of her voice or the stress on some words faintly gave away something of her personal feelings. The more she said the easier it was to read her and to guess at her feelings. She didn't like what she had been doing for years now although — wisely — he guessed she had never said so openly to anyone else. And she didn't like animals being kept in cages and even more so she disapproved of experiments on animals or the use of them for laboratory research purposes . . . Oh, yes, it was all there. It was there in all of them, because they were human, just as it was there with him in a different profession — if what he did merited that world. You could deny God, but that didn't explain the word. You could use a thousand arguments to justify what you were doing but nobody believed them. Most people not involved turned aside, not wanting to know, and quickly forgot all about arguments, justifications and the greater good of the greatest number. The world was a jungle; the wise thing to do was to move away from its dangerous areas — if you could. He couldn't and Jean Blackwell hadn't been able to. Tough.

When she came to the end of her account of Charlie, Jean took a sip of her lager and then went on, 'When I said I didn't smoke — I meant not very often.'

Rimster gave her a cigarette and lit it for her.

She gave him a little nod of thanks and the ghost of a smile. Talking about Charlie had been easy. Talking about what had been done to Charlie was like going into a confessional and knowing you could never come out with any dispensation or in a true state of grace.

She said, 'Yesterday at ten-thirty Charlie was injected with a new and highly complex form of plague bacilli. Basically it's a combination of the three forms of plague — bubonic, pneumonic and septicaemic. The special thing about this form is that except for a few minor effects like slight vomiting and shivering spasms which will quickly pass, he will at the end of twenty-one days be in normal health and, while immune himself from plague, will be a carrier. If he's loose then, not under strict laboratory control, he can spread the disease. If he coughs the minute droplets could infect anyone within three feet range of him. That's the pneumonic side. If he's bitten by a flea — at the moment of his escape he was free of all body vermin, but he won't be for long — then the flea takes his infected blood into its own and any person who is bitten by that flea will contract the disease. If the flea gets on a rat, that rat becomes a carrier and its faeces and urine deadly. That's the septicaemic side . . . ' She paused, drew hard on her cigarette and went on, 'Pretty bloody, isn't it? Charlie's own urine and faeces will be similarly infective. The virus is very resistant to external conditions and will survive in the ground or water for a very long time — like the anthrax bacillus, which can survive in an infective state for a hundred years or more. Overall too, this form of plague is very difficult to diagnose . . . That's a pretty generalized picture. I'm sure I don't have to tell you the thinking behind all this. You probably know more about that than I do.'

Rimster said, 'All this after twenty-one days? Do you mean *exactly* twenty-one from the time of injection?'

'No — there could be anything up to a two-day spread on either side. No more though, and very rarely that.'

Rimster got up and walked to the window. Through gaps in trees and houses some of the greensward of the cathedral close could be seen. There was nothing she could tell him about the thinking behind it. Almost every government had its own chemical and biological warfare establishment.

Without turning, he said, 'You'd have gone on using Charlie? Putting, say, another chimpanzee in with him and waiting for it to be infected and die?'

'Yes. He was going to be transferred to

57

another lab. — specially built, but not at Fadledean — next week.'

'And if it worked? Then eventually it would have been used on a human — some brave volunteer?'

'Yes. Does that surprise you?'

Ignoring the emphasis on the *you*, he said, 'No. But how did you get into all this?'

'It creeps up. I was a bright girl, scholarships, university and medical school. Micro-biology always fascinated me. Government research establishments often farm out minor projects and research work to university scientific departments. I did quite a few. My work must have impressed someone and I was offered a post eventually at Fadledean.' She shrugged her shoulders and made a wry face. 'You begin to paddle in the water and then you find one day you're right out of your depth. You must know that.'

He turned. He knew all right. But he had long, long ago learned to live contentedly with it. Just for a moment he saw a handful of men, plague carriers, moving openly and peacefully into some country, some troublesome or strategic emergent state . . . oh, in a hundred different places, and leaving behind them, unsuspected, a growing epidemic that would disrupt economies, social services, weakening law and order. The brave new

58

world . . . which he served.

He moved towards her and picked up her empty lager glass.

'Yes, I know. But there's always a moment when you know you could escape — I didn't take my moment. What about you?'

Jean said coldly, 'I was to have been married in four months' time. For love and for escape. I should have done it on my own years ago. But I kept putting it off. But now — as soon as Charlie's back — they'll sack me. I'll sign the Official Secrets document and be free. Well, as free as I can be.'

For a moment or two she thought he was going to make some answer. The slate-grey eyes watched her and the corners of his lips showed two tight, stubble-touched clefts. Then with a little shrug of his shoulders he picked up his own glass and went into the kitchen. She heard the tap running as he rinsed them. A tidy, neat, hard man, wound up long ago and set going, and still going, and — she wondered — with no real sympathy for anyone.

He came back, picked up her case and they went down to the car. He called the network to give them his change of place, and asked for the latest on Charlie.

The latest on Charlie was that there was nothing to report.

3

The Garvey family lived in a cottage in the hamlet of Petersfinger, which was outside Salisbury and just off the Southampton road and a little to the east of the river Avon. Andrew's father was a carpenter, working mostly on building sites, an amiable, easy-going man; his mother was amiable, too, but less easy-going. He had one sister, Judy, who was sixteen and looking forward to the freedom of leaving school and working in any job which was not too demanding but well paid.

At supper-time, as Andrew Garvey finished his sausages and baked beans and began to wipe the plate clean with a piece of bread, he said casually, 'Guess what?'

'You'll have the pattern off the bottom of that plate in a minute, that's what,' said his mother.

Andrew grinned. 'Guess what happened to me this afternoon — after school when I went fishing.'

'You sure you went fishing after school, not skipped it all afternoon?' His father cocked an eye at him dubiously.

'Course I did. But guess what happened.'

Without looking up from the magazine she was reading as she ate, Judy said, 'Some old lady fell in, you rescued her and she gave you a five-pound note. Can I borrow a quid?'

'Oh, shut up, you!'

'Enough of that.' His mother took his plate from him.

'But guess what happened. You never will.'

His father grinned. 'Don't suppose we will. It's always something with you what never happens to anyone else.'

'Like seein' flying saucers or nearly catching a fish as big as a shark. Always nearly.' Judy reached out a hand for the sauce bottle and smothered the last of her sausages.

'Well, this weren't no flyin' saucer and it weren't nearly anything. It really happened.'

His father finished eating and sat back. 'Okay, lad — let's have it.' He winked at his wife. 'Andrew Garvey will now tell us one of his celebrated — '

'This is no make-up thing! This really happened! Not like some of the others. That was just for fun.'

'What's this for then? Money? We got to cough up when you pass round the hat afterwards?' asked Judy.

'Let him be,' said Mrs Garvey. She ran her hand affectionately across his sandy hair.

'One of these days you're going to wake up and find you're living in a real world. It's all this TV, and those comics and books you read.'

'Batman and Asterix. And Dr Who,' said Judy.

'They're not bad stories, his, though,' said his father. 'I liked that one he told about seeing Princess Anne and Prince Philip mending a puncture on — '

'This is real, I tell you! I was just sitting there fishing away when something taps me on the shoulder — '

'Not the Queen Mother or good old Snoopy?'

Andrew made a threatening gesture at his sister and almost shouted, 'All right! Don't believe me then. But I turns round and there's this chimpanzee thing — '

'Riding a bicycle?' His father leaned back and laughed at his own witticism and went on, 'One thing I got to say for you, son, is you're always good value. So what did you do? Now — keep quiet, everyone. Andrew Garvey speaks.'

Andrew sighed. 'Well, you can believe it or not, it really happened. There was this chimp, staring right at me. Cor, I tell you it made me jump. I just ups and away, fast as I could go. But when I got to the stile I looked back and, you'll never guess' — he debated with himself and succumbed to temptation — 'there was this old chimp sitting with my rod and quietly going on fishing. He looked all right and harmless, so — '

'You went back and gave him a few tips about the best baits.' Judy giggled.

'I went back all right,' said Andrew firmly. 'And what's more I sat down with him and just as I did that, what do you think?' He had their attention now and loved it, and the temptation to improve reality by art was again too great. 'He caught a fish. A nice grayling, it was. About three-quarters of a pound.'

'How can you catch a grayling on a roach rod?' asked his sister innocently.

'Oh, very funny!' Andrew made a mock gesture to hit her.

'Enough of that, Andrew,' said his mother.

His father shook his head. 'It's this heat. Goes to your head and makes you see things. All afternoon I've been seeing a bloody great pint of beer with a frothy head on it — and now I'm off to get it.' He stood up and winked at Andrew. 'What did you do with old chimpy? Give him a lift back to Salisbury on your crossbar so that he could get a haircut and shave before going back to the zoo?'

Andrew gave up. But a few minutes later, left alone in the room with his mother, and helping her to clear the table, he said to her quietly, 'It really happened, you know, mum. After a bit he just started to lark around and then went off into the bushes. He was quite nice really. He liked it when I scratched him. Sort of made blowy kind of noises at me.'

Busy with her work, Mrs Garvey said, 'I'm sure it happened. But all in your mind, son. But that's not a bad thing' — she pushed a strand of hair back from her eyes, her face flushed from the heat of the small room — 'so long as you don't make too much of a habit of it.'

Andrew said nothing. Sure, lots of things happened in his head and he told about them as though they were real. But then, in a way they were real, like stories in books were real as you read them because if they weren't then they weren't any cop as stories. But this . . . well it was real — except for catching the grayling, of course.

*   *   *

After leaving Andrew Garvey, Charlie had wandered idly up through a long pasture to a clump of poplars which dominated the rise. He had climbed one of the outside ones and some way up had made himself a rough nest by bending the smaller leafy branches over on

64

one of the outspreading limbs. While the light slowly went from the summer sky, he lay contentedly, dozing sometimes, and at others watching the view which the tree commanded over the railway and then the road which lay between him and the intricate lacing of streams and carriers that marbled and veined the broad water meadows flanking the river Avon. Twice a jay perched nearby and screamed at him. At sunset a returning colony of rooks, which roosted in some elms on the far side of the clump, spotted him and flew around his tree, calling and croaking at him for a while.

As the dusk thickened, two helicopters flew up the river valley below him, their navigation lights showing, and away to his right he could see the loom of town lights washing up from Salisbury and the still, solitary aircraft warning light that burned at the tip of the cathedral spire.

Now, as the night began to cool a little, Charlie suddenly started to shiver. He huddled himself into a tight ball, drawing up his legs and clasping his arms around himself.

His shivering increased, coming in spasms at irregular intervals. Occasionally he slept, only to be wakened by a bout of shivering.

Not long after midnight, disturbed and unwell, he left his nest and dropped from branch to branch to the ground.

He went down the hillside, over the railway and then through the large garden of a house — where a dog in a stable scented him and began to bark — to the roadway. A car came sweeping up the road, its headlights chalking the bordering foliage of trees and shrubs and for a moment spangling Charlie's pelt with moving high points. Two or three more cars came along the road. A little frightened of them, Charlie chattered to himself and then, as the road for a while lay deserted and dark, he came down from the hedge and crossed it. He climbed through the hedge on the other side of the road and dropped down a steep grass bank to a meadow which flanked the run of the river Avon.

Shivering now and again and feeling unwell, Charlie moved down the river southwards, away from Salisbury, following a fisherman's path. To his left, cattle grazed in the warm night and he could hear the sound of their slow breath and the rasp of torn grass as they fed. Once or twice a soft-winged barn owl came drifting along the fringe of river reeds searching for water-voles. A heron got up a few yards ahead of him, screamed in fright, and flapped awkwardly into erratic flight, long legs trailing. Charlie, alarmed by the sudden appearance of the bird, called *waa-waa* angrily.

An hour later the thin crescent of the moon, almost at the end of its last quarter, rose clear of the fine drift of mist which now coiled high above the river and the water meadows, and Charlie came to a point where the river divided into two arms around a long island matted with rank rush and low alder growths. The branch of the river on Charlie's side was narrow and shallow and he waded into it and stopped in midstream to drink avidly against the thirst which was rising in him. On the far side he found a path trodden through the high growths and followed it to the end of the island. Here the river arms joining spread out into wide shallows of faster-running water that swept around two smaller tree-studded islands, which lay off the end of the first island.

Charlie, shivering still, splashed across to the larger of the two islands and screamed as he disturbed a handful of feeding mallard ducks which got up from the weed beds with an outburst of alarm calls, their threshing wings and webbed feet creaming the water.

As the birds disappeared, Charlie was suddenly sick, crouching to the ground, his body shaking and heaving. The spasms passed quickly and he moved away from the smell of his own vomit. He trampled his way across a patch of wild musk into the trees, and began to climb up the trunk of an ancient ash tree. Ivy spread a thick mantle over its trunk and many of its lower branches, slowly killing it. Its top branches were already bare, grey limbs. He found a wide branch crotch close to the main trunk in a tangle of ivy creepers just below the first of the dead branches. He bent and trampled the thick ivy spread and young ash branches over and made himself a bed. He lay down, curled into a ball, his arms clasped tightly round himself, and shivered now and again.

★   ★   ★

Redthorn House was a small, red-bricked eighteenth-century manor house standing in its own grounds of six acres, most of it walled, on the bank of the river Avon, some miles above Salisbury and not far from Amesbury. The terraced front of the house faced the river and the gardens, parterres and walks ran down to it. It was staffed by the army for visiting VIPs — home and foreign generals, admirals and airforce commanders, government heads and politicians who came from time to time on visits to the army installations on and around Salisbury Plain. It was comfortably, though not quite luxuriously, furnished, the service was discreet, intelligent and efficient, the food of a high order and the wine cellar notable. Its security was unobtrusive but highly efficient.

Jean and Rimster had bedrooms on the top floor — rank or prestige was subtly marked by the rooms you were given, the higher the room the lower the ranking.

Rimster lay in bed after midnight, the room unlit, the window curtains pulled back to show the thin wash of moonlight on the field slopes across the river valley. On his bedside table was a telephone with a direct line to his London office, also to the operations centre at the Army School of Aviation.

So far there had been no sighting reported of Charlie. This would be his second night of freedom. He was into his third day, the twenty-third of June. By all the odds, he felt there was no possible chance of Charlie staying free until the end of his earliest incubatory term, the tenth of July — unless a miracle happened, as Jean had put it when they had been talking over their coffee after dinner. However, he had no belief in miracles. Time and chance now . . . they were birds of a different feather. Charlie was not, however, particularly likely to shun the presence of human beings. Time and chance would have to dance a fine fandango to keep him on the loose. But — if they did — it could turn into a dance of death. Melodramatic? Possibly. Not a chance. Night thoughts were always grey. Christ, what people did. Men like Armstrong and Boyson ... family men driving up to Fadledean each morning and putting on their sterilized blinkers to shut out the world. The girl, too. And John Rimster, Esquire ...

A bat went erratically across the window space. Time had been when his ears could catch their notes. But not now. He was a man; not a boy lying in bed of a summer night in the top bedroom of an old rectory, his elder brothers marked in age for the Army and then the Navy, and himself for the Church, the old Rimster family pattern. What had happened that the angels had missed him and the Devil had got him? Anyway (and he had to confess, regretfully) it was all coming to a close now. He had reached his limit of full usefulness. That's why he was here. Burnt out, but still useful. No more missions that set the adrenalin being pumped out ...

He turned over, away from the moonlight-pale window and was asleep in ten minutes.

Not far away, Jean, wrapped in a dressing gown, sat by her open window, smoking one of her rare cigarettes. The room light was out. High over the limes that fringed the bottom of the garden the thin slip of moon threw its broken reflection on the moving waters of the river. Somewhere out there, too, the moon's light probably touched Charlie. Instinct and memories of his early years had probably sent him up a tree, maybe to make himself a clumsy nest. If their estimate of the clinical developments from his injection was right he should about now be entering on a first phase of shivering and vomiting. If he survived that period then there was no doubt that at the end of his time he would be a self-immune carrier . . . they had already established the sequences with rats, a dog and a marmoset, a silvery Amazonian marmoset with pink face and ears and a black tail contrasting with its whitish body fur called Igor, engaging and affectionate . . . all of them long killed and incinerated. Charlie was the first of the primates and after him would come some human volunteer . . .

She heard herself saying, *You begin to paddle in the water and then you find one day you're right out of your depth.* Those dry-looking, slate-coloured eyes on her showing no emotion. What emotion would her father have shown had he known? Retired now from doctoring, living in the Channel Islands, a round of golf each day and a greenhouse full of orchids and a long life behind him full of service to humanity. Shrug

71

his shoulders and say, 'We make our own lives. God gives us a bundle of choices and then turns away to leave us on our own' — Familiar phrase. She smiled in the darkness of the room. Well, when this was all over and she was free of Fadledean, maybe she would follow his profession, make it an act of contrition. Obtruding, unbidden, she suddenly wondered what George would have said. Security had long prevented her from telling anyone outside what she did. One answered vaguely and after a time one's friends asked no questions.

Idly in her mind she put George alongside Rimster ... George, unreliable in his appetites, but bursting with vigour and enthusiasm and chasing his dreams of the future with buoyant and ever-flowing optimism, George making love to her as no one else had ever done ... and the other, neat, hard, slate and granite and even his touches of kindness and humour calculated precisely for his own purposes. She fancied, even while she shunned the picture, herself in bed with him, and her skin prickled with a chill of disgust.

At three o'clock that night, Charlie, half in sleep, vomited, voiding the spew over his legs, hardly aware of what was happening and then dropped back into a fitful, shiver-touched sleep. A pipistrelle bat flew around him momentarily and then dipped to the riverside and went upstream hawking for moths over the flags and mace reeds. A moorhen in midstream rooted among the current-drawn lengths of water crowfoot and bitter-cress, and a hen salmon, four months in from the sea, threw herself into the air with a great curving leap and smashed down on her side, spray spouting into the moonlight like the sudden blooming of a silver flower.

Andrew Garvey, lying in his bed sleeping, suddenly twitched and mumbled something aloud in his dreams.

And not far away, just outside Salisbury, the motorcyclist who had crashed woke, dazed and confused in hospital and wondered where he was.

* * *

George Freemantle's alarm woke him at five o'clock. He got out of bed and shaved, bathed and dressed quickly. Somewhere overhead he heard the distant sound of a helicopter passing.

He walked quickly to his car parked in the forecourt, a large, fleshily built, strong-bodied man, moving briskly, full of confidence in himself and his own power. George Free-mantle, successful and his own boss, all the way up from primary school, keeping an eye on the main chance, using his brains and his guile and seldom letting his good nature be ruffled, astonishing his jobbing-gardener father and timid mother, both now comfortably pensioned off by him.

He drove across the city and let himself into Jean's flat with his own key. They both had keys to each other's flats. Trust, he thought, as he opened the door quietly and stood listening. But sometimes trust could undo you, and it was no good then trying to explain the difference between someone you loved, really loved and wanted, and a woman you took after a few lunchtime gins and a bottle of wine because she was there and was willing. But he meant to try. Jean was what he wanted. He'd been here twice before, night and day, and no sign of her, and no damned good phoning that bloody Fadledean place where all you got was *I'm sorry, but Miss Blackwell isn't available* or *Miss Blackwell isn't here. Can I take a message?* Oh, sure, tell her I love her and won't do it again or, if I do, I'll take damned care she never knows. The flesh is weak, but I want a wife and kids and all the trimmings otherwise what am I burning my ass off for making a success of things in a country which takes most of what you earn to give away to a set of idle scroungers who think honest work is some kind of disease?

Moving into the sitting-room he saw that she had been back. There was a lipstick-marked cigarette end in a tray by an armchair and another, unmarked, in the tray on a table at the end of the settee. They hadn't been there yesterday lunchtime.

He went through to the bedroom and opened the door quietly. The bed was still made up, untouched, but a blue linen dress and a pair of tights lay across the end of it. Methodically he went through her wardrobe, the chest of drawers and the low cupboard under the window where she kept her shoes. The expensive lightweight suitcase he had given her was gone from under the bed. He knew exactly what she had taken because he knew her wardrobe and outfits. Wherever she had gone it was for more than a night.

He went through to the kitchen, found a bottle of milk in the refrigerator and drank it. Two empty lager cans stood on the draining board. Who was the man, he wondered? Armstrong or Boyson or one of the other boffins with acid-stained fingers?

Outside in his car he debated for a moment driving up to Fadledean, and then rejected it. No pass, no entry. Sorry, sorry, sorry. Big deal, they were all busy putting together another Frankenstein or inventing some pill that would keep a man alive for ever or kill him if he as much as looked at it. For God's sake, in four months' time he was to have put her across his saddle and ridden off with her. That's what she wanted, though she'd never put it in so many words — to be rescued. He could read her like a book. St George. Well, no one could tell him that there weren't saints who'd had a bit on the side now and then. But love was the thing — and marriage.

He drove off to his factory, grinning to himself. The boys would jump at his early arrival. They'd jump higher later when lack of breakfast began to touch up his temper.

Going down the river valley along the Ringwood road to his factory at the village of Downton, he saw three helicopters, widely spaced and flying low, come up the broad reaches of the river meadows. Buzzing around like a lot of bloody wasps, burning up fuel at God-knows-how-much-a-gallon for which he paid out of his income tax.

$\star$ $\star$ $\star$

Charlie, from his ivy bower, saw the helicopters go over. When they had gone he went on rubbing at the vomit-matted fur on his legs with handfuls of ivy leaves. Charlie hated to be unclean or unkempt. Although he lacked the company of his own kind to take part in mutual grooming, he rubbed away at his legs, removing most of the mess and then turned to finger-combing the pelt of his arms and chest. On his travels he had picked up a sheep tick in the long grass and two or three fleas from his first night in the open barn. He picked off the bloated body of the tick, leaving its head still buried in his skin, and caught two fleas which he nipped to death between his front teeth and spat away. Now and again his body shook with an uncontrollable spasm of shivering. When it did so he whimpered and drew his large lips back over his teeth in a wide grin of resentment. He was not hungry but a strong thirst rose slowly in him.

After a while he dropped, hand to hand, through the tree branches and waddled half upright to the water. Wading into the shallows on the fringe of the island, he crouched over and drank. When he had satisfied his thirst he climbed back up the tree and, rejecting his broken and vomit-smelling bed, swung round the bulky trunk and made himself another a little lower down. It took him some time before he was satisfied with it. When he eventually settled down he found that he could look through a gap in the island's tree foliage straight down the river.

Two or three hundred yards away, a stone bridge carried a private estate road over the Avon to Longford Castle. Two swans with a brood of cygnets foraged slowly upstream. A Land-Rover crossed the bridge and a little later a tradesman's van. The shadows of the trees and shrubs in the castle grounds slowly grew shorter and the coolness of the morning was shredded away by the power of the rising sun. Distantly, Charlie could hear the hum of the traffic on the Ringwood road, and nearer, the sound of a motor mower working in the castle gardens.

Charlie lay still in his bed, not wanting to move, the intervals between his shivering fits gradually lengthening. Once or twice he fell asleep, and once he woke and lay unmoving as a tree-creeper worked its mouse-like way up and around a dead branch above his head and then flew off as Charlie shook his head to ward off the flies which were beginning to buzz around him.

★　★　★

Back at Redthorn House, Rimster came into the lounge from the administrative wing where he had been called to the telephone to talk to Grandison.

Jean was sitting by the open french windows reading a morning paper.

He said, 'That was my master speaking from London. If there's no sign of Charlie by tonight the powers-that-be have decided to issue a press and radio release. And the police will be informed.'

'What will they say?'

He shrugged his shoulders. 'I wasn't given the exact wording, but I'll get a copy when it comes. Certainly it won't be anything like the whole truth. Not within a hundred miles of it. In the meantime, there's no point in our sitting about. I'll get the people here to put us up some lunch and we'll take a drive around. Can't offer to buy you a lunch anywhere — we've got to stay by the car in case anything comes through. Who knows, we might might strike lucky and sight Charlie ourselves.'

'What happens then?'

'Well, we'll have a bunch of bananas and while you charm him I'll call up the operations centre. They've got a truck all fitted up to take him. You think he might give trouble?'

'He could. If things are going as planned with him he should be . . . well, not very happy at the moment.'

'Too bad. In that case we'll have to get the

truck party to shoot him.'

'What?'

'Don't be alarmed. Not with a four-o-four nitro express bullet. Just a knock-out nembutal dart.'

When she was gone to get ready he lit a cigarette and stood looking out of the window. The car was outside and he had ordered the picnic lunch before coming in to her. Grandison, unusual for him, had been nearing bad temper on the telephone which meant that it was one of those rare occasions when his advice had not been taken.

Although he hadn't told Jean so, he knew how the report for the press and police was to be worded. A chimpanzee, named Charlie, being transferred from a private collection on the east coast to a new owner in the south of England, had escaped from its travelling cage on the truck when the vehicle had been involved in a minor accident on the Winchester-Salisbury road. If Charlie were soon caught the story would hold. But if he stayed out too long some bright boy from one of the national papers might begin to poke around. June was the silly season for newspapers ... good fill-ups were always welcome and Charlie would be a change from the Loch Ness monster. Everybody loved a good animal story, and chimps were lovable.

And the press boys were no fools. They would — if Charlie stayed out — soon be poking into his background. Private collections on the east coast and wild-life parks in Dorset wouldn't hold up for long. Whoever had overruled Grandison had to be carrying a lot of weight — and, maybe, not much imagination.

By five o'clock that afternoon there had been no sign of Charlie or reports about him. The police were informed and the story went out as a small news item on the local television and radio channels. At ten o'clock that night, Rimster had a call from the operation centre. A motor-cyclist recovering from an accident in hospital who had heard the news over the radio had reported that he was certain that the chimpanzee had been the cause of his accident on a small side road near Salisbury.

The Garvey family had heard neither radio nor television because Mr Garvey had taken them all for an evening drive in his car to visit Mrs Garvey's mother on the outskirts of Southampton.

Rimster, taking his coffee alone after dinner while Jean walked in the garden, guessed that more sightings would soon follow (even though some of them would be the product of old ladies' imaginations and false, mischievous calls). He felt that Charlie's days were numbered well below twenty-one. It was a pity from a professional point of view, because he would like to have seen how Grandison and the big boys would have handled the ticking time bomb of public relations if Charlie had managed to run them close up to the limit.

★ ★ ★

Charlie himself stayed all day on the island and most of the time in his tree. He had no desire for food, his shivering fits gradually became less frequent. He had vomited only once during the day when in the afternoon he had dropped down to drink some more water from the river. Most of the time he had rested in his bed, watching the country and castle grounds and sometimes dropping off into fitful bouts of sleep. But by the time the moon was riding well over the horizon, blurred by the rising river mist, he was feeling better and restless.

At two o'clock in the morning he came down from the tree and waded across the shallow run to the left bank of the river and began to move downstream. A herd of young bullocks saw him and, with the curiosity of their kind, began to follow him and now and then cavorted and circled round him. Charlie, frightened by the thudding of their hooves and their movement around him, ran from them and escaped over the iron railing on to the private road by the river bridge.

An hour later, as he moved across a sedgy patch of ground a hundred yards away from the river, he disturbed a late-sitting semi-wild muscovy duck from her nest in the reeds at the side of a small ditch. There were seven eggs in the nest and Charlie ate six of them before he moved on. A little later, feeling stronger, even now and then making con-tented hoo-hooing noises to himself, he crossed from the left bank to the right bank of the river by a narrow iron bridge. Below the bridge a long run of red-brick farm buildings and a concrete-built milking parlour stood back from the Avon, well above flood level. One of the buildings had an open front. A farm tractor stood inside under a half-loft which was piled with a few bales of old straw.

Charlie climbed on to the tractor, reached up and swung himself up to the loft. He pulled straw from the bales, gathered more loose straw from the floor and made himself a bed. As he lay down and curled himself up, a shivering fit, far less intense than any of the others he had had, began to move through him.

He lay there, his teeth chattering gently, and slowly, as the fit passed, he drifted off to sleep. After a while the few rats who lived in the loft came out from their hiding places and began to move around. From the nearby river came the sound of an occasional fish rising and now and again the calling of a pair of tawny owls as they hunted the river fields. A rat, emboldened by Charlie's stillness, and smelling the eggs he had eaten, came to his right hand and nibbled at the dried yolk remains which matted the hairs above his wrist. Charlie felt it in his sleep, flicked his hand and the rat scurried away.

Charlie slept until the first light of his fourth day of freedom woke him, aided by the chattering and quarrelling of sparrows on the roof of the building.

4

Early the next morning the Garvey family were all having breakfast together and listening, as they always did, to the radio.

Andrew was only half-listening to it, the heavy aftermath of sleep still with him, as it always was when the morning promised only the prospect of going to school. At the week-ends it was different. He would be up before anyone else and as bright as a button.

Mrs Garvey was shuttling between the kitchen and the living room with food. When they were all away she would settle down and have a quiet breakfast by herself.

Judy ate in much the same kind of half-daze as her brother, but wishing that her father would hurry up and finish with the newspaper. She wanted to read her horoscope for the day. Sometimes, of course, it was really daft, but then again it was sometimes just spot on . . . *Today is one for caution in business affairs, but brings unexpected romantic possibilities.* That was the day, three weeks ago, when she had had her purse stolen from the cloakroom and had met Teddy, her current boy friend. Teddy's charms were quickly beginning to wear thin. It was time something new popped over the horizon.

Mr Garvey, eyes on the sports page, read, ate and listened to the radio and, although it was no good for his trade, wished that they might have just one day of really belting rain to freshen up things in his allotment patch where lettuces and spinach were bolting into seed heads unless you stood by to catch the right moment to cut them.

In the kitchen, Mrs Garvey dropped a plate and broke it. Father, son and daughter looked up and into the sudden spell of their alert attention came the voice of the radio announcer.

'... the animal escaped from its truck as the result of a minor accident on the Winchester-Salisbury road. Charlie is a seven-year-old chimpanzee and, while not dangerous, anyone seeing it should keep away from it and report the sighting at once to the police. Charlie is believed to be somewhere in the Salisbury area. Here is the telephone number to call if — '

The rest was lost as Andrew banged both his fists on the table and shouted, 'There you are! I did see him! A chimpanzee. Charlie the chimpanzee — he came fishing with me!'

Judy grinning said, 'He told you his name was Charlie, did he?'

Mr Garvey rose., 'Come along, lad. The call box at the end of the road.'

Andrew was out of the room before his father, his sister calling after him, 'Don't forget to tell them how he caught that grayling.'

But Andrew was away with his father, laughing, following, and there was only one thought in Andrew's mind. The police would want to know everything, take ages that would, maybe he'd be driven off in a patrol car to show them where it was and all that . . . and with any luck he wouldn't see school today. Good old Charlie.

At that moment, Charlie, who had awoken early feeling hungry and much more himself, had long left his loft and was moving idly back up the river towards Longford Castle. But instead of crossing the iron bridge he had kept to the right bank, following a narrow fishing path.

He stopped once to drink from the river and then pulled a few leaves from an overhanging willow branch and chewed them into a wad. Half a mile above the bridge the river swung round in a great curve, widening into a long, deep pool which was the haunt of large pike and an occasional salmon. Sand martins flew low over the water, pattering it with small rings as their breasts flicked it, rings that matched those made by the trout which were rising to an early morning hatch of fly. Reed warblers fluted among the rushes and sedges bordering the river, and distantly a solitary cuckoo called brokenly.

From the top end of the pool came the sound of heavy splashing. Made curious by this noise, Charlie walked half-way round the curve of the pool and saw over the high, fringing reeds the bald head and naked shoulders of an elderly man swimming slowly but clumsily against the gentle current.

Clarence Bedew, a retired civil servant, a bachelor who lived in a small cottage just off the Ringwood road, three-quarters of a mile away across the fields to the west, was taking, as he always did when the weather was fine and the season right, his early morning swim. He was a puffy, noisy and not very strong swimmer, but he was enjoying himself and relishing the calm and peace of the early morning. He was a good-natured man, but also hasty-tempered. At the moment, sure of his solitude, he was quoting poetry aloud to himself . . . *What was he doing, the great god Pan, Down in the reeds by the river?* His feet touched gravel and he stood up and massaged his bald head and then his shoulders. *Splashing and paddling with hoofs of a goat . . . .* He did a little dance, relishing

88

the buoyancy that took his body. *And breaking the golden lilies afloat with the dragon-fly on the river* . . .

Charlie moved up the bank towards Mr Bedew but stopped when he came across the man's clothes piled on the grass by a break in the mace reeds and bullrushes. He sat down, the reeds hiding him from sight, and began to turn over the clothes and hunger for a while gave way to his instinct for play. There was something about cloth which always excited him. He liked to chew and suck it and he liked to throw it about.

Chattering and pouting his lips with pleasure, he draped a shirt over his shoulders, stretched a sock between his hands and then threw it into the water. A few seconds later he sent an immaculately polished brown shoe after it. He turned over Mr Bedew's trousers and, reaching into a pocket, found a key-ring and a penknife. He dropped the keys to the grass, scratched himself behind his right ear with the penknife and then put it in his mouth and sucked at it while he picked up the man's jacket. Although his sense of smell was not as keen as his sight or hearing he picked up at once two smells familiar to him, one was tobacco and the other was chocolate. Rooting in the pockets he pulled a tobacco pouch from one and a half-eaten bar of chocolate, loosely wrapped, from the other. In his time, Charlie had had a keeper who, discovering his passion for tobacco, had occasionally given him a cigarette to chew. Charlie, tearing the loose paper from the chocolate, put the half-bar into his mouth and added to it a generous helping of loose pipe tobacco.

Shaking his head as flies buzzed around his ears, his dark, lustrous eyes shining with pleasure, Charlie rolled the wad around his mouth and now and again gave a soft pant-hoot of contentment. He picked up Mr Bedew's well-worn panama hat and flicked it into the river. It landed crown up and floated away, gently spinning on the current.

A few seconds later, Mr Bedew, who always finished his bathe with a little swim under water, surfaced in the gap in the run of reeds and stood up, waist deep, water rolling from his body. Short-sighted, and the water in his eyes not helping him, he saw Charlie as a very blurred shape. In fact what he saw, as sudden rage rose in him, was some darkly dressed gypsy boy sitting there with his . . . his! . . . clothes scattered all around and calmly wearing his shirt around his neck like a scarf.

No coward, Mr Bedew charged forward through the water and roared, 'What the bloody hell do you think you're doing? You damned rascal!' Grabbing his walking stick from the grass, he swung it angrily at the gypsy lad and cracked him across the shoulder.

Charlie, startled and hurt by the stinging cane blow, gave a loud scream of pain. He rolled over backwards, twisted to all fours, and galloped away up the river path as fast as he could go, Mr Bedew's shirt falling from his shoulders as he went.

For a little while, Mr Bedew went after him but when he reached his shirt he realized he could never catch the small, dark figure. He picked up his shirt and went back to the rest of his clothes. When he found his glasses in the top pocket of his jacket and put them on and saw what had happened, his mounting anger drove all the pleasure of the glorious June morning from him and banished all poetry from his mind.

Charlie kept going until a turn in the river put him out of sight of Mr Bedew and, as the smart of the cane blow died, he slackened his pace to an amble. Turning away from the river, he climbed over a field gate and made his way towards a clump of tall birch trees which overhung a narrow side road which led to the main Salisbury-Ringwood road a quarter of a mile away. Keeping on the field side of the birches, Charlie followed the line of the hedge towards the main road.

A hundred yards off the main road a

canvas-topped lorry was parked on the grass verge of the side road. The driver, who had been travelling since before daybreak from the West Country with a load of vegetables and fruit, was in his cab taking a short nap after finishing his breakfast. Before him he had the long run to the London markets.

Coming abreast of the lorry on the other side of the hedge the warm morning breeze wafted towards Charlie the faint smell of early strawberries, gooseberries and vegetables. He stood upright and saw the lorry. He climbed through the hedge and went to the back of the lorry. Two canvas flaps covered the rear end of the vehicle above the raised tailboard. The sides of the flaps were held together loosely by cording through eyelets in the canvas.

The smell of food moving him strongly, Charlie climbed up on to the tailboard and pushed hard at the canvas. It bulged inwards, leaving a narrow gap through which Charlie squeezed himself downwards and under the canvas into the lorry. Light came through the loose cording of the canvas join. Charlie sat down on a netted sack, ripped part of the mesh with a tug of his strong fingers, and pulled out a handful of young carrots.

With a low grunt of pleasure he began to eat.

Rimster came through the open french windows of the lounge and down the brick-paved path between the terrace rose beds. He wore an open-necked green shirt with a paisley foulard at his throat and immaculately creased light cord trousers. He looked clean, hard-chiselled and impossible to ruffle. It was the first time Jean had seen him this morning. He had breakfasted before her. She guessed that he had been in the administrative wing.

In the short time they had been together she had realized that he considered it no part of his duties to keep her company — not that she wanted his company or anyone else's for that matter. Sometimes he ate with her and sometimes not. When they drove around together he was pleasant enough but clearly had no wish to move beyond some clearly marked line of social conduct. At first she had been untouched and indifferent at his polite remoteness, but now she found it beginning to irritate her and to provoke in her speculation as to how he was with people who could make a claim to his friendship . . . or, maybe, his love. Perhaps there were no such people.

He came up to her and held out a letter,

saying, 'Good morning.' His eyes flickered momentarily skyward. 'Glass is still high. Flaming June. This came for you.'

'Good morning. Thank you.' Jean took the letter and glanced at the handwriting. It was somehow familiar but she could not place it.

She opened her handbag and was putting the letter in when he said, 'Would you open it, please. I'd like to know who wrote it.'

'Why?' Her sudden annoyance came over clearly.

'Because only a few people are supposed to know you are here. And don't look so offended. I could have opened it myself and you would never have known it had been tampered with. Sorry, but I must know.'

She shrugged her shoulders and opened the letter. Inside was another letter, the envelope folded in two, and a sheet of notepaper with a few lines from Boyson which read: *George came round insisting that he had to get in touch with you. I'm not allowed to say where you are — damned if I know why — but I said I would see you got the enclosed. Harold.*

She handed the note to Rimster and after he had read it asked flatly, 'Do you want me to open this and show you, too?' She held up George's letter.

'George is Freemantle, your fiancé?'

'Was.'

'No, I don't want to read it. But if you make any answer then I shall have to see that. I've told you that any letters you send out must be censored.'

Jean shrugged her shoulders. 'Don't worry. I shan't be replying to it. And I understand perfectly that I'm considered unreliable. An unstable, unreliable female who might let the cat out of the bag.'

'That's your description. But you are a security risk. You could say something quite innocently and someone with a little help on the side might put two and two together, plus a little guesswork, and then Charlie's potential danger to the public might be uncovered. It's a very long shot — but that's my job. To see that nobody gets a chance of sniping.' He handed back Boyson's note to her and then, with a note of easy friendliness, went on, 'There's no reason to get a dagger out for me. You of all people should understand what the lobby is like against the kind of work you've been doing. If the public ever knew the truth about Charlie — even though we picked him up today, or long before he becomes a real danger — then the balloon would go up. That your kind of work is done is accepted and people push it to the back of their minds. But let them find out that it's done carelessly, without proper precautions — and the lid would blow off. Think of it their way — the whole of the South of England, and that's only for a start, put at deadly risk because a woman faints with the emotional stress of finding her fiancé in bed with another woman. The press and the public wouldn't spare anyone. Heads would roll right up to the inner Cabinet level. Charlie could spread plague, but the public would spread mayhem through the government, the Ministry of Defence and institutions like Fadledean.' He grinned suddenly. 'No fairy story. The gods for their own good reasons might be working for Charlie. But let's hope not. As for now, I'll have the car round in a few minutes. The police have reported that a boy spotted Charlie the day before yesterday near the river south of Salisbury.'

As he walked away she had a sense of having been chastened, could acknowledge to some extent that it had been deserved, and, not for the first time, she was aware that working at Fadledean forced one to shut one's mind to the fears and claims of the outside world.

She opened George's letter. It was typically George. Bouncy, not over-contrite, the whole thing had been of no real importance. For the

96

first time since he had known her he had been caught off balance . . . a few gins too many at lunch and this old girl friend turning up and bingo. But not again, not anything like that would happen. He loved her and wanted only her. After all — if it had been the other way round . . . Forgiveness, understanding, nothing could touch the real core of the bond between them. And where the hell was she and what was she playing at because he just had to see her?

His pleas and justifications left her untouched, except that she wondered if it had been the other way round what in truth his reactions would have been?

★   ★   ★

Horace Pringle, forty, married with three children, was the proprietor of a small shop in Ringwood where he sold cameras, films, photographic equipment and had a small trade in picture-framing. In addition he was fairly constantly in demand to attend weddings, christenings and other events to take photographs. He was a short, plumpish, dark-haired man of Welsh extraction who had a nice sense of humour, was devoted to his family and loved to drink beer, sometimes immoderately; though he had no high opinion of the stuff which the multiple brewers turned out these days and often said so emphatically. In his early days he had worked for a while as a press photographer in Fleet Street. Younger and single then, they were days he looked back to nostalgically. Weddings bored him stiff, though no one would have guessed it from the jocular, cajoling manner which he employed in order to get the best photographs he could for his clients . . . *Now, could we just have the bride by herself? That's it, love. Just a bit farther forward and the bouquet a little higher . . . That's it. There's lovely you look.* He was on his way to a wedding now at Stockbridge on the Winchester road the other side of Salisbury.

As he approached Salisbury he came up to the tail of a string of vehicles following a big container lorry. He could see that there would be no chance of overtaking any of them yet, so he settled in at the end of the queue without impatience. He had plenty of time to make the wedding.

Immediately in front of him was a lorry with a canvas top. With an observant eye that fussed over untidy details of a dress or a veil which might mar a picture, he noticed that the cording which laced up the canvas flaps at the back had drawn loose at the bottom so that now and again the canvas flapped like a slack idle sail. The thought made him think of boats and he began to whistle gently *A Life on the Ocean Wave.*

As he came down the slope to the river bridge over the Avon on the outskirts of Salisbury and followed the lorry through the roundabout he thought for a moment that he saw something move behind the loosely corded gap. Without giving it much thought he followed the lorry and the traffic on to the ring road round the town which would take him on to the Winchester road. Half-way along the road repairs were being made and there was a set of temporary traffic lights. The line of traffic halted as the light went red against it. Horace drew up close behind the lorry.

As he did so he saw a pair of hands tug at the edges of the canvas flaps pulling them free from their cording into a triangular opening. A head pushed through the gap and Horace found himself looking straight at the face of Charlie.

For a moment or two he just stared, unbelieving. Then as Charlie drew back his big lips, showing his teeth in a wide grimace, Horace came to life, the Horace of the old Fleet Street days, the Horace who, even now, sometimes picked up the odd shot which the agencies would take. A few quid extra was always a few quid extra. And, since he kept up with the news and had heard about Charlie, his left hand reached out automatically for his camera which rested on the seat at his side. He leaned out of his window and took six quick shots of Charlie, varying the angles and getting part of the traffic queue and the nearby houses in them before Charlie's head withdrew and the traffic began to move as the lights changed.

Horace followed the van, thinking . . . well, boy, there's a bit of luck for you, now. He followed the lorry up to the next roundabout, hoping that the vehicle would take the Winchester road. Who knows? He might get a few more shots. The more the merrier. He might be lucky and some editor would want a fill-in or a minor lead story. When he got to Stockbridge he'd phone old Jones at the agency and have a word.

At the roundabout the traffic slowed and stopped, waiting to filter around, and here Charlie appeared again, pushing through the canvas gap and partly lifting it so that his head and half his body were visible. He stared solemnly back at Horace and chewed contentedly at a carrot in one hand, while he held a fine lettuce in the other.

Whether anyone else had seen the animal, Horace didn't know and didn't care. He leant out of his window and took some more shots. Charlie, seeing him, raised an arm, waved the lettuce, and then solemnly rubbed his head with it, his dark eyes sparkling, his lips pouting forward as he hoo-hooed with contentment. Horace heard someone shout from away to his right but, before he could turn to see from whom the call came, the lorry moved into the roundabout.

Horace, aware of a horn blowing impatiently behind, quickly followed and was delighted to see that the lorry was taking the Winchester road. He saw too that Charlie had disappeared from sight. And that was the last that Horace saw of Charlie who had withdrawn to eat his fill of strawberries and gooseberries.

Some miles outside Salisbury the main road split, the right-hand fork going to Winchester, while the other went left-handed towards Andover and Basingstoke to pick up the main London road. Hanging on behind the lorry, Horace had hoped that it would keep on the Winchester road. When he saw by its indicator that it was going to swing off to Andover he was tempted to follow, but the wedding waiting ahead kept him on his own road. Charlie was only a chance few quid ... but a wedding was a wedding and his bread and butter.

He drove on to Stockbridge. In the long main street, and having time in hand, he went to a call box and telephoned his old Fleet Street friend Jonesey, as Welsh as himself, and who would place the story for him if he could.

When he explained about Charlie to Jonesey and of the local search going on for him his friend said, 'I don't know. Sounds more like local stuff. But no harm in giving it a try up here first. Might work. Charlie the wanted chimp riding through the town right under everyone's nose — making a monkey out of the police. What time you free of that wedding?'

'Some time after one o'clock.'

'Tell you what to do. Take the film into Winchester after the wedding and put it on a London train. Phone me and I'll have it picked up. Somebody might go for it. What about telling the police down there?'

'Why should I? Let 'em read all about it tomorrow morning — I hope.'

'Okay, your business. Do what I can. Give my regards to your missus.'

Meanwhile on the Andover road, a little while after Horace had parted company with Charlie, a motorcyclist overtook the lorry, pulled in ahead of it and flagged it down, persisting until the driver stopped.

The motor-cyclist trotted back to the driver and said, 'You know you got a monkey thing in the back of your truck?'

'What you talking about?'

'About a chimp thing. Like them on telly what advertises tea or something.'

'Pull the other one.'

'I tell you you have. Come and look.'

The driver got down and walked around to the back of the lorry with the motor-cyclist.

As they did so, Charlie, who had eaten his fill, dropped to the ground from the tailboard and ambled on to the grass verge. When he saw the two men approaching he moved away from them.

'What did I tell you,' said the motor-cyclist.

Ignoring him, the driver shouted at Charlie, 'Hey you! What you doing up in my truck?'

Charlie moved farther away, sat down and called *waa-waa* loudly.

The motor-cyclist said, 'Eh, are they dangerous?'

The driver said, 'I don't care what they are — they ain't supposed to ride in my truck, not with — ' He broke off and went to the canvas flap and pulled it aside. One look was enough for him. He turned quickly and, moving towards Charlie, shouted angrily. 'Hey, you little bugger, what the hell you been up to!'

Charlie, who knew anger in the human voice when he heard it, seeing the man coming for him, turned and swung up into the road hedge, forced his way through a tangle of briars and small thorns and dropped to the field on the other side. Without looking back and whimpering softly to himself through thinly pouted lips, Charlie loped away quickly on all fours.

The two men watched him through the hedge tangle and the driver said almost accusingly to the other, 'Where'd he come from then? And how'd he get in my truck?'

'How do I know? I only spotted him as I come up with you. What you got in the truck then?'

'Not as much as I bloody well did have. Fair old mess he's made of my carrots and strawberries.'

'Think we ought to tell the police?'

'You ever been to report anything to the police?'

'No.'

'Well don't then — unless you want to be kept sitting on your arse for hours while some old sergeant writes it all down as though it's the first time he's ever had a pen in his hand. That's not for me. I got to get to London.'

'But where'd he come from?'

'How do I know — or care? Way this

104

country is these days you never know what's going to happen. Last week I give a lift to a bloke who turned out a real nutter. Said for a fiver he'd tell me the exact date the world was going to end, dead straight he did. Now this week a bloody monkey crawls out of me fruit. Anyway, thanks for stopping me. Some people'd drive by without a word if the back of the truck was on fire.'

★ ★ ★

The police constable on the desk at Salisbury who was doing his spell of duty on the line which had been reserved for Charlie calls said, 'Very well, madam, we'll look into it. Thank you for calling.'

He put the receiver down and sighed. Amongst the genuine calls on this kind of lark there were all the cranky ones. Lonely people mostly who just wanted to talk to someone . . . he could take those easily enough. But the practical jokers were the ones who got his goat. This old girl had said that from the window of her cottage on the narrow road which ran not far from the Avon she had that morning through field glasses seen a naked man chasing a chimpanzee along the river bank. When asked why she was looking through field glasses she said she always did, every morning, because being crippled with arthritis it was the only way she could do any bird-watching. Also her cat had disappeared. Did the constable think the chimpanzee might have caught and eaten it? If it had been left to him he would never have passed the message on. You could tell jokers and the eccentrics just by the way they talked. Still, the orders were everything, but everything, must be passed to CID.

He was reaching for the internal telephone to the detective branch when the bell went on the outside telephone again.

'Salisbury police station, here.'

A man's voice said, 'That the number for Charlie the chimp?'

'That's right, sir.'

'Good.' The man laughed. 'Well, you'll never believe this. Real rich it was. I'd have called you sooner only I was late for work and then I had to wait for the tea break to get to the phone. Course, none of the blokes here would believe me. Thought I was pulling their legs, like I do sometimes. Well, you got to liven things up a bit, standing all day over a lathe, ain't you?'

The constable sighed gently. He knew the type. Put up to it for a gag by his mates, no doubt. He said, 'Have you seen this animal, sir?'

'I'll say.' The voice was rich with barely held laughter. 'There he was in the back of a lorry on the ring road . . . you know, up by the roundabout where the Winchester road goes off. Standing up in the lorry, bold as brass, laughin' all over his face, and guess what?'

'Look, sir. May I just have the facts. But first of all would you give me your name and address for reference, please?' A joker, he was sure, and if he got a name and address they would be false.

'It don't matter who I am. I can't help you any more nor this. There was this Charlie chimp at the back of the lorry and he had a bunch of carrots in one hand and a lettuce in the other and a great big smile over his face. Laugh . . . I tell you it was the funniest thing I seen in years. Nearly fell off me bike I did. Went off up the Winchester road did the lorry. If I hadn't been late for work I'd have tagged along a bit just for the fun, but my place was the other way. Well, there it is. Don't suppose it's much help to you, but I done my duty like by phoning.'

The man rang off before the constable could say more. Not that there was much he wanted to say. Eccentrics and practical jokers. The world was full of them. However, he dutifully passed both messages to the CID.

Within the next hour he had two more calls; from a woman who said she was sure that Charlie was in her attic because there was an awful rumpus going on there and she was afraid to go in (when the patrol car got there it was to find nothing in the attic but piles of old newspapers and broken furniture and the good lady heavily fuddled with gin-drinking), and the other from a man who said in an affected voice, 'This is the chairman of the Society for the Protection of Higher Primates. A chimpanzee has as much right to live free and unfettered in this country as any of the stinking riff-raff of coloured immigrants we've let in. And, what is more, I personally prefer chimpanzees — many of whom I've numbered among my best friends — to some of the apes in blue uniform who go about interfering with the normal lives of hard-drinking citizens like myself.'

The constable decided not to pass this message on. The world was full of humorists, the sad, the lonely, the mad and the bad. The sooner Charlie was put behind bars the better . . . Nice, though, if you'd lived behind bars most of your time like Charlie, to be out and free for a while in the lovely summertime.

★　★　★

By dusk that evening, Charlie was some miles north of the spot where he had left the lorry. The country he had covered was a mixture of downland and wide stretches of arable and pasture land with only a few minor roads or lanes cutting across it. Well-fed, he was not worried about eating, and he had drunk twice, once from a cattle trough and the other time from a small dew pond. During the fiercer heat of the afternoon he had slept for some hours on some sacks in an old cart shed, lying in the shade. Now and again he had heard the sound of helicopters going over, and once, waking from his sleep, he had watched a patrol of six soldiers spread out into line along the edges of a distant plantation of young larches and then move in and beat their way through it. Far beyond the plantation he could see the rise of a main road over a gentle hill-slope and the flashing of the sun on the windscreens of the cars which sped along it.

As the air cooled and the shadows lengthened, he left the hut and ambled away northwards.

He moved down now into a wide bowl of rough land, dotted with gorse and thorn growths, and idly made his way along its gentle slope, grunting and talking to himself. A hare got up from a clump of grass ahead of him and he squatted on his rump and watched it go bounding and zigzagging down into the bottom of the bowl to disappear into the thick scrub. Away to his left a kestrel hung in the air, wings quivering, and then dropped to the ground to take a vole. Charlie pulled a long grass stalk and began to chew it, shaking his head as a persistent fly buzzed around his ears. On the far side of the bowl the land rose to a prominent knoll which was crowned by a tall, thick growth of beech trees. The knoll was in fact the site of an old hill fortress dating back to the Iron Age, a fortress which was being excavated by archaeologists during the summer season. From where he sat, Charlie could see the movement of people around its outer grass ramparts and with some of them were dogs which they were exercising, for Danebury Hill was a well-known spot for tourists and local people to visit.

Charlie, who had no real fear of human beings, might well have been moved to get up and make his way to the hill. But the sight of the dogs probably stayed him. In the past he had twice been bitten by dogs and he always gave them a wide berth. He sat where he was, relishing the growing coolness of the evening, which was dying to a moonless night.

A helicopter came over from behind and

passed almost directly over him, flying at five hundred feet. Neither pilot nor observer saw him, for they had finished searching their allotted area some way south and were heading back now for the landing ground at the Army Aviation Centre field on the other side of Danebury Hill, their thoughts on a bath, a change to cool clothes and long drinks in the mess.

When the helicopter had disappeared, Charlie got up and moved leisurely down into the bottom of the bowl. A large grass snake slid across the sheep track ahead of him. Charlie stood upright, jumped up and down, and gave a small scream half in fright and half in defiance. He left the path and wandered through the low thorn bushes. He picked up a length of dead branch and carried it crossways in his mouth for a while. A jay flew across the thorns and gorse and screamed as it veered away from the sight of Charlie. Charlie sat down, took the stick from his mouth and began to beat the ground with it. He went on drumming away, giving long-drawn hoo pants and grunts as he thumped the ground.

Overhead, in the gathering dusk, another helicopter went by, its lights flashing.

Its pilot was Captain Stevens who by now was getting bored with the daily search patterns he had to fly. In the mess the feeling was growing that Charlie was nowhere in the area. Or, if he were, he was lying dead somewhere. Some farmer or gamekeeper finding him in corn or covert could easily have blasted him with a shotgun. There were plenty of men who would shoot first and think afterwards . . . would even, when the thinking began, take the trouble to bury him and stay silent. Anyway, why all the fuss about him? At the briefing conference after lunch that day when the new search patterns had been set and allocated there had been present — though not a word did they say — a hard, precise-looking type that mess rumour said was from Whitehall and a woman from Fadledean, or so the rumour went. A lot of quiet rumours were beginning to float in the air. Dark-haired, good-looking woman, but a bit of an ice-maiden, he guessed, though you couldn't always bet on that. Sometimes they exploded like a volcano at the right touch. Still not his kind. Blonde and busty and a shade overweight, that was for him, like Ruthie who would be waiting for him tonight . . . a sleeping-out pass until six tomorrow morning, dinner, drinks and then a large armful of home comforts for the troops. God, that guy with the ice-maiden looked as though he would twist his grandmother's neck if anyone made the price right. The dark

112

ring of beeches at the top of Danebury loomed up on the skyline.

Captain Stevens went up two hundred feet and passed over them. Away to the right at the bottom of the hill near the road a few cars were still standing in the car park. Lovers and their lasses roaming in the gloaming . . . he grinned . . . great place Danebury, many a child had been conceived in the long grass shadowed by the tall trees. Beyond the hill the lights of the airfield showed, patterning the ground, and he began to lose height as he started a slow swing that would bring him in to land.

An hour later, Charlie ambled through the growing darkness up the western flank of the hill, away from the car park and the road, and crossed the deep vallum which ran around the tree-thick summit. He picked his way past the excavated corn and storage pits of another age cut in the chalk to the far side. He climbed one of the outlying trees. After a little search he found himself a bedding place and began to bend over leafy branches and twigs to make himself a couch, twisting and turning and softly grunting to himself until he had made it to his satisfaction. Looking down on the lights which showed from the airfield and its buildings, well-fed, all vomiting and shivering attacks forgotten, he settled himself to pass his fourth night of freedom.

Seventy miles away to the east the Fleet Street presses of the national dailies were already rolling and spinning — and spinning with them were pictures of Charlie at the tail of the lorry, grimacing contentedly, a carrot in one hand and a lettuce in the other.

5

The next morning, just before daybreak, the weather which had been set fine over the whole of southern England for weeks changed. Great banks of heavy-headed clouds rolled up from the west to blot out the paling stars.

As Charlie slept, a great fork of lightning fractured the sky over distant Salisbury, to be followed within seconds by a heavy, explosive roll of thunder.

Charlie uncurled himself and sat up on his nest. Lightning flashed beyond the airfield and another roll of thunder pounded the air. Then a massive artillery of flash and thunder peal began to swing a great barrage of summer storm over the country and with it came the rain. At first it fell in heavy erratic drops that beat a tattoo on the leaves of the beech trees, and then grew into a heavy, steady downpour which added its noise to the rolling thunder.

Charlie reached up a long arm, grasped a branch above him and stood upright on his bed. He raised his head to the sky so that the lashing rain beat fiercely into his face and began to give a series of excited pant-hoots which grew louder and louder as though some ecstasy were rising in him, delighting him with its power and novelty. In his young days of jungle freedom he had known such storms and with his mother and other mothers and young had sat safely in trees or on some high point and watched the adult males, fired by the coming of the rains, welcome the deluge with their wild, charging displays and dances.

Maybe he remembered something of them now, or maybe he moved instinctively to a primate instinct awakened in him because in all the time of his captivity he had never been unsheltered and exposed to the slashing, pounding assault of stinging rain against his face and body as the sky was filled with the boisterous rhythms of thunder and the arcing blaze and jabbing darts of lightning. Whatever the reason, he was slowly possessed by the emotions and responses which the storm drew from him.

Lightly holding the branch above him with one hand he stood upright and began to sway and roll rhythmically from one foot to the other. With his great chin and squat nose raised to the sky to take the rain's onslaught he started to call waa-waa-waa against the surge and violence of the roaring thunder.

The tempo of his dance rose as the rain ran in streams down his dark pelt and now and again, without stopping his swaying, he would shake his body like a dog and send the water spinning from him.

Then, as though there had grown some ecstasy in him demanding more than this treading dance which was breaking up his bed, he suddenly jumped downwards, swinging from branch to branch and calling loudly. He dropped from a branch, fifteen feet to the ground and began to run through the trees, calling, grunting and hooting and striking out with his hands at the bushes and low growths in his path. On the outskirts of the hilltop he leaped into a young ash tree, wrenched off a branch, and then jumped clear to the ground. He dashed down the flank of the hill, swinging and brandishing the branch at the sheets of rain which cascaded about him, rain that exploded on the summer-hard earth in a layer of spumy froth and ran in spouting, growing torrents down the slope while the storm-dark sky above was turned blue and livid by the flaring lightning.

An hour later the storm had moved away to the east, marked now by a distant mutter of thunder, and the rain had steadied to a quiet, persistent downfall which was to last until mid-morning.

117

Half an hour later as the bell in a church clock tower began to strike six, Charlie climbed over a field gate which fronted the main London to Exeter road. The excitement of the storm had gone from him. His fur was slicked with rain and splattered with mud and he was hungry. A few yards down the road was a lay-by and parked in it was a small, shabby green van.

Charlie walked upright to the van and, stopping at its nearside door, looked through the half-open window. Sitting in the driving seat was a young man in his late twenties. He was drinking tea from a mug which he had filled from a thermos flask and eating a bacon-and-cheese sandwich. He had a craggy, weather-tanned amiable face and longish brown hair which turned up in a row of duck-tails at the back of his neck. He wore a shabby white cardigan and light blue and very much stained linen trousers.

This was Duncan Sparrow, single, well-educated, not so well-balanced, an opportunist, and a not very successful smallholder. He ran the holding single-handed and to supplement his small earnings he had a contract to drive to Andover early each morning to collect the day's supply of newspapers and magazines from a wholesale newspaper firm to deliver to shops in six of the outlying villages within a radius of ten miles of his smallholding. Great oaks from little acorns grow was his motto. Though he would have been the first to admit that few of his acorns ever showed signs of sprouting. He came from an old but long-impoverished family, did not mind doing any kind of job, or taking almost any kind of opportunity which might bring in a little extra cash. On the whole, people liked him, but did not entirely trust him — an assessment of which he was well aware without taking any offence. He was in goodly company, for there were millions like him.

When he turned his head and saw Charlie looking in, he stared at him, momentarily surprised, and then he grinned and said in his pleasant cultivated voice, 'You look a bit done in, old chap. Here.'

He leaned over and held out his half-eaten sandwich. Charlie took it without hesitation and began to eat. As he did so, Duncan Sparrow watched him. Two or three cars, their tyres searing loudly in the rain, went by. Duncan had spent a year on a game farm in Rhodesia and was well used to animals, although chimpanzees were a little beyond his field. Still, he thought . . . you didn't get far unless you could adapt to new circumstances and such-like.

He took the last breakfast sandwich from

what he called his fodder-tin and got out of the van, moving slowly and paying little attention to Charlie. That Charlie should turn up out of the blue was a surprise, but Charlie himself was no surprise. He had heard the broadcasts about him and, while he had been waiting for his consignment of paper bundles, he had read about him in the free copy of the *Daily Mail* which was one of the perks of his job.

He opened the small double doors at the back of the van.

It was empty now except for some sacks and a litter of old newspapers, some crushed egg cartons and an untidiness of bits of straw and hens' feathers. Across the van behind the two front seats, separating them from the van's interior, was fastened a loose spread of broad-meshed cord netting.

As he opened the doors, Charlie came to the back of the van, his large chin and lips moving as he masticated the half-sandwich. Seeing the other sandwich which Duncan Sparrow held up, Charlie reached for it, hooing gently through the wad in his mouth.

Duncan tossed the sandwich into the back of the van and then stood back, saying easily, 'If you want it, old lad, you've got to jump in and get it. No tricks, I swear. Just pure kindness of heart. You stay loafing about this road and some bastard'll run you down.'

Without any hesitation, Charlie climbed into the back of the van, retrieved the sandwich and, sitting down on a sack, began to eat it.

'There's a sensible chap. And don't worry, you can trust old Dunky. He'll see you right.'

He closed and locked the doors and a few moments later was driving down the road on the way to his small-holding.

Charlie, to whom the offer of food meant friendship, sat swaying gently in the back eating his sandwich.

When they turned off the main road, Duncan glanced briefly back at him, grinned, and over his shoulder said affably, 'Some storm what? Tropical, you could say. Must have reminded you of home.'

Then, turning away, he began to whistle gently to himself. Just what he was going to do with Charlie he didn't know. But then, there was no point in rushing things. Somewhere there had to be something in it for him. Just had to. After all, the gods had dealt the cards, and they had the look of a good hand, so it was up to him to play them right. It was just a question of figuring the angles like, say, the press or the police and his own profit.

Behind him, Charlie shuffled up to the netting and made soft and friendly pant-hoots.

Outside, the steady rain had freshened the foliage and flowers in the park and the wildfowl on the lake after their first flurries of excitement at its coming were now preening and grooming their plumage. The pavement across the road had bloomed with the coloured umbrellas of the office girls hurrying to work.

Rubbing his beard in thought, Grandison watched the passing flow of traffic and people. People hurrying to work . . . coming into London by train and bus, glad of the freshness the rain was bringing, sitting reading their papers as they travelled, and as a relief from the usual morning recital of the world's woes they had been given Charlie. And why not? No editor worth his salt would have spiked the story. Charlie was fun, Charlie was the element of rebellion against a too-regimented life. Just one look at him standing at the rear of the truck immediately captured their sympathy and delight. Charlie, cocking a snook at authority, against regulations and the bars visible or invisible that fenced them all in, was a hero. No editor would drop the story until everything had been squeezed out of it.

He went back to his desk and sat on the

corner. The four nationals which had run the story were spread over the highly polished red morocco leather top. Two had Charlie on the front page . . . a head-and-shoulders blow-up, showing a toothy grin and the hands flourishing carrot and lettuce, and then two more shots of the truck, Charlie in the back, and a glimpse of traffic and buildings. One of them had a policeman on the pavement in the background which he was prepared to bet had been faked in. It made no difference. It was all good fun — at the moment. Except that the worrying note was there in the *Daily Mail*. Somebody had worked hard and fast on the telephone and with local representatives. *Extensive inquiries to all wild-life parks, and public and private zoos have so far revealed that none has lost a chimpanzee. Where does Charlie come from? The only word from the Salisbury police is that 'at the moment the owner is not available for comment'. Why not?* The police had been landed with a hot potato. With bad luck or bad direction it might become too hot to handle.

Thinking of the two telephone calls he had already made he shook his head. If you wanted to cover up the truth you shouldn't depart entirely from it in any public statement. That way it always left you with a line of escape and recourse to the easy phrase of 'in the interests of the public' and all the other pabular forms to feed to the people without having to come down openly on newspaper editors. For them a nod was as good as a wink and often saved the use of a D notice. One thing that must not happen was that the story should get out of hand and rouse an awkward outcry from the fringe elements and cranks in the country. Frowning to himself, he thought, damn Charlie . . . ambling around down there with troops, helicopters and police looking for him, enjoying himself no doubt while the long length of fuse smouldered gently forward.

He picked up the telephone and called Rimster at Redthorn House. When Rimster came on, Grandison said, 'You've read the morning papers?'

'Yes, sir.'

'What have you done?'

'The police have got the name of the photographer. He phoned in early this morning. I don't see there's anything we can do about him.'

'Neither do I. Tell them to drop him. What about this truck?'

'The number plate shows on one of the photographs. The police are tracing it now. My guess is that he may never have known he had Charlie in the back. He probably dropped off after he had eaten all he wanted. But we'd like to know where, of course. We may get some lead from him. What's happening about the press?'

'Nothing — yet. They got the story by a fluke. If it's killed dead right away people will wonder why. The moment Charlie's picked up it will die a natural death — even if we have to say eventually that he was being taken to Fadledean. They should have said Fadledean right away as I wanted. People know animals are used there and they would have looked the other way — except for the odd cranks and the press wouldn't have given them a look in.' For a moment his own sense of frustration at being overriden from above broke through. 'What I can't understand is why the animal hasn't been picked up yet.'

'Everything that can be done is being done. Time and chance — and maybe the gods — have just been against us.'

'Maybe. And now we'll find some of the public are against us. The man on the run is a romantic figure. Make it Charlie with that happy grin of his and a carrot in his hand and he's not just romantic — he's the stuff of all folk heroes. People will be on his side — not ours.' He sighed. 'Still, if he doesn't soon come to hand, we may have to do some hard thinking about a change of policy.'

125

'The truth?'

'If it should come to it — which God forbid — yes. That's why they should have stuck nearer to the truth from the beginning — and would have done if I'd had my way.'

Going back to the dining-room to finish his breakfast the note of anger in Grandison's voice was still with Rimster. He usually got his own way, usually fought for it because he knew — and had so often proved — that he was right. But that didn't matter tuppence with the people he served if for reasons of political or personal prestige, deviously lodged in their minds, they felt that this was the wrong moment for being asked to handle openly a difficult situation. Truth for politicians was a hybrid growth which flourished best in a half light.

Going to their table he saw that Jean Blackwell was now down and beginning her breakfast, a newspaper at the side of her plate. He gave her a good morning and sat down and poured himself a cup of coffee.

Nodding at her newspaper, he said, 'What do you think of all that?'

Jean smiled. 'Charlie seems to have been enjoying himself — and making a fool of the police and a few others, including us.'

Unexpectedly her attitude irritated him. 'I'm glad you can look on the light side of it.'

'Well, it's there, isn't it? I'm only too aware of the other side — and my part in it. What are the authorities going to do about it?'

'Nothing — for the moment. I've just been speaking to my office. Charlie's just a normal chimpanzee on the loose. If Whitehall tried to sit on the newspapers right away then Fleet Street would more than prick its ears up. There are one or two editors these days who don't answer the rein easily. Anyway, by all the odds, he should be picked up in the next few days.'

'I certainly hope so.'

'I fervently hope so,' he said curtly.

Bending over her plate, going on with her meal, Jean half-smiled to herself. Underneath all the control there was a man of some emotion. What was it that moved him? Professional pride? Or a kind of arrogance which held no place for failure. She was beginning to catch the movement of ghosts somewhere in his background. He didn't like her particularly and, more pertinent, she felt he didn't like this job. She hadn't helped him with the first, and there wasn't much she could do about the second until Charlie was found and she could pick up her bunch of bananas. It could even be that he really felt that Charlie could go the limit, stay free for more than twenty-one days and that he was genuinely concerned for the consequences. But she felt that it was nearer the truth that he was more concerned with the thought of a personal failure. Yet beyond that she was beginning to sense something else in him, something as yet too vague for definition. Maybe his hard façade covered some interior shabbiness or disappointment which he hated and which, for her, if true made him more human.

She looked up and said, 'If you want to smoke with your coffee, please do. It won't worry me. I might even join you later. And . . . well, I change my 'certainly' to your 'fervently'.'

'Thank you.' He smiled. 'I could kill that photographer for not immediately calling the police. We'd have had Charlie in the bag within the hour.'

'If he'd known the truth of what was involved he would have called the police. But we don't live in that kind of world. Truth is a security risk. It's also — when you have to keep it to yourself for the rest of your life — an emotional risk. If or when I get married my husband would never know that I've had a part in planning mass and horrible murder. It's a nice thought, isn't it? And my shame is that it's only recently come to me. So, if at times I'm a bit edgy or distant, you'll know that that's the reason. I'm learning to live with a woman who used to be a distinguished micro-biologist who — through her own fault — was seduced into planning murder.' She smiled ruefully, reached for the coffee pot and went on, 'I think if you'll offer me one I'll have a cigarette and talk about something else.'

As he lit her cigarette, he was thinking that there were many ways of being seduced into murder apart from the remote impersonal kind she meant where the faces of the victims were blanks and the names often meaningless. Little by little you were drawn into the shadowy byways until the day came when you looked down and saw for the first time the face of a dead man, your first kill. Slowly after that, like an anodyne, came professional pride in your skills. You lived at the peak for years, proud, arrogant, deadly efficient . . . and then one day Grandison changed it all, signalling the end by sending you on a job anyone could do . . . a pleasant little jolly in the good old summertime chasing Charlie — a break from the usual run of business; a permanent break.

* * *

Westacott Bottom was the name of Duncan Sparrow's cottage and small farm holding. It lay some miles northwest of Andover in a hollow at the bottom of the high ground which rose to the wooded slopes of the ancient forest of Chute. The nearest village, a handful of houses, a general store, a public house and a small chapel, was two miles away.

The holding was approached by a narrow, private lane a quarter of a mile long, a lane badly maintained, its pot-holes filling with water in the winter. The cottage was a simple two-down and three-up building, roofed with reed thatch which was green and worn in places and needed renewal. Behind the cottage was a big yard hedged by a small enclosed barn, a run of hen houses and an open cart shed. Beyond the yard, Duncan owned ten acres of poor land, some of it pasture where he kept a few pigs and the rest given over to market gardening.

Out of this he made a living of sorts and just managed to keep up his mortgage payments. He liked living there because he liked living alone and being his own master. From time to time he had a woman living with him, but none stayed long. He was content with the way he lived and not at all concerned about his future. Shortage of cash held no great worry for him, but he was always glad to make a little money on the side and did not mind sailing close to the wind in doing it.

An hour after picking up Charlie he drove into the yard, opened one of the double doors of the barn and then put the van inside.

Leaving Charlie shut in the van, he busied himself in setting up quarters for him, whistling to himself as he cleared an old stall and spread hay over the floor. He filled a bucket with water from the yard tap and put it by the stall and then fetched an armful of vegetables and a dozen eggs and put them in a shallow box alongside the bucket. The barn was soundly built, without windows and the roof was hung with large, heavy slates all in fair condition. As he worked, he congratulated himself that at the moment he had no female company. Women's tongues were the devil.

Closing the barn door, he picked up a handful of young peas and went to the back of the van. He unlocked it and Charlie, wet still, his coat messy with bits of straw and hens' feathers, came at once to him and reached out for the peas. Duncan turned and went to the stall and Charlie jumped down from the van and followed him, reaching out to get the peas. Duncan dropped them into the box in the stall and Charlie at once went to the vegetables and eggs and squatted on the ground.

While Charlie was eating, Duncan opened the barn door and drove the van out into the yard. It was the one period when Charlie could have escaped from him. Well, Duncan thought — if you don't take risks you don't make profits, only a pittance. When he went back and closed the door Charlie was still sitting in the straw eating. When Duncan appeared, he looked up and gave him a teeth-baring grin and a few contented grunts.

Duncan went back to the cottage, made himself some coffee and, as it was in the nature of a special morning, he opened a new bottle to lace it strongly with brandy. Flopping into the dilapidated cane armchair in the kitchen, he settled down to consider the possible money angles, well aware that opportunities like this were rare and therefore needed unhurried consideration.

By the time he had emptied the coffee pot and taken a fair amount of the brandy he had decided his line of action. He would keep quiet about Charlie until the next day and then try first — like a good citizen — the police. If that didn't work he would try the press. No hurry — the longer Charlie was at large, surely, the more valuable one way and another he became?

* * *

That evening at eight o'clock the sergeant on duty at what had become known as the Charliephone had a call.

A man's voice, educated and affable, said, 'This the number for the escaped chimpanzee?'

'Yes sir, it is.'

'Good. Well, of course, I might be making a Charlie of myself — sorry, I didn't mean to be funny. No offence meant. But I just thought — '

'Do you mind, sir,' interrupted the Sergeant, who had already had his quota of jokesters' calls, 'if, before you report whatever it is you have to report, you give me your name and address?'

'Not at all, constable. Ulpert's the name. Joseph Ulpert — you want me to spell that, constable?'

'No, thank you, sir. Joseph Ulpert. And the address?'

'Bourne End Cottage, Thruxton. That's just off — '

'Yes, sir. We know where it is. Now about Charlie, please?'

'Ah, yes. Well you see, it's like this. I work in London and go up by train from Andover every day — 'cept weekends, of course. I get the early train which means I leave here about

133

half-past five. Damned early I know, but I'm a bachelor and don't sleep well, and I like to know I'm going to get a seat, and — what's more — I'm in my office — export electronics equipment — and get some work done in peace — '

'Could we come to Charlie, sir?'

'Sure, that's what I'm coming to. I just thought you people liked all the details. I mean, I might be some damned joker ringing up just for a lark. The world's full of them as I expect you know in a job like yours.'

'Do we not, sir.' There was warmth in the sergeant's voice now. 'All right, sir. You just go ahead and tell it in your own way.'

'Well, I was driving in this morning. Hell of a morning, too. Belting with rain. Just the other side of Weyhill there's a bit of a pull-in at the side of the road. As I went by I saw a small, rather battered old green van parked there. Ford, I think. I've seen it before plenty of mornings. Well, there was this young fellow standing out in the rain at the back and he had the van doors open and just to one side of him as I passed I saw this chimpanzee. It looked as though the chimp job was going to get in the van. Pretty odd thing to see, eh? I thought I was dreaming at first, but I know I wasn't. When I got back tonight I thought I'd just phone up and check with you. Do the good citizen act just in case the bloke hadn't turned Charlie boy over to you or reported him. That's what anyone would do isn't it?'

With some feeling the sergeant said, 'It's what a good citizen would do, someone like yourself, sir. But this fellow didn't. You say you've seen this van before and the man?'

'Plenty of times. He's usually sitting in the van having his breakfast or something. Also — '

'Excuse me interrupting, sir. Are you at home all this evening?'

'Nowhere else. Just going to do myself some steak and chips.'

'In that case, sir, we'd like to send someone out to talk to you right away.'

'Yes, that's all right. By the way the chap's name is Wrench. A. Wrench. He's a baker and confectioner. It's written on the side of the van.'

'Thank you very much, sir. We'll have someone out to you right away.'

Half an hour later another call from a pay-box came on the Charliephone, and a man's voice inquired, 'About this Charlie the chimp. It's a very valuable animal, is it?'

'That's right, sir. Could I have your name and address please?'

'Sure, if you want to. It's Lucas . . . Alfred Lucas, Number Seven, Avonbrook Villas,

Amesbury. But I haven't got anything to tell you. I was just wondering if there was a reward being offered to anyone who found this animal?'

'No sir — there isn't any reward being offered.'

'Pity . . . just thought if there was I'd take a couple of days off from my job and have a look around. I've worked in Africa, you know. Big game reserve. Still . . . if there's nothing on offer I'll just forget it. Thank you.'

The sergeant logged the message and then checked the street directory for Amesbury. He found that there was no listing for any Avonbrook Villas. Cranks and optimists with an eye to the main chance. Walk down any street, he thought, and what did you see? Mostly solid, sensible citizens going about their business, as steady and solid as plum puddings . . . or so you would think. Anyway, what was all this fuss about the chimpanzee? Whatever it was, nobody in the force around here knew because the truth would have leaked by now. Higher up they might know, but if they did they weren't saying anything.

Before going to bed that night, Duncan Sparrow, alias Alfred Lucas, went across the yard to the barn to see that Charlie was all right. He took with him a couple of oranges. He unlocked the main doors, slipped inside and turned the light on.

Charlie was curled up in the straw of his stall with one arm across his face. He made no move as Duncan leaned over the low stall door and tossed the oranges across to him.

'Just in case you get peckish in the night, old boy.'

Charlie lay where he was until the lights went out and he heard the door close and the lock turn. Then, in the darkness, he began to drum with one fist against the side of the stall. Lying in the straw here was in many ways like being back in his sleeping quarters at Fadledean.

He drummed for some while and then reached out with a foot and groped in the straw until he found one of the oranges.

In his cottage, Duncan had made up his mind. Since there was no reward for Charlie — after all, it was only right to try and do the decent thing by the chimpanzee's owner in the first place — he was left with the press. If the papers were still running the Charlie story in the morning he would ring one of them. Some fresh photographs of Charlie and an exclusive story about him should be worth something . . . maybe far more than any reward.

★   ★   ★

Just before midnight, Rimster received a call from the operations centre telling him about the sighting of Charlie by Joseph Ulpert. The man had been interviewed and was quite genuine and certain about seeing Charlie and the man with the green van. There was no record in the Andover-Amesbury areas of any baker called A. Wrench but inquiries were proceeding farther afield. It was quite possible that the van was a secondhand one bought at some car mart, whose previous owner had been A. Wrench. Anyway, he would be called immediately there was any news.

Going up to his room he stopped and knocked on the door of Jean's bedroom.

She opened the door to him wearing a dressing gown over her nightdress. Over her shoulder he saw the rumpled bed, a book lying face down on it.

He said, 'I'm sorry to disturb you, but we've had some news about Charlie.'

'He's been caught?'

'Not quite that.'

'Oh, I see . . . ' She hesitated for a moment or two and then stepped back and said, 'Come in and tell me.'

'Thank you.'

She sat on the side of the bed and he stood by the door. Her hair was loose and in the single light of the bedside lamp she looked softer and relaxed.

As he explained things to her, part of his mind considered her as a woman, as a woman he could like and would like to have. There was always that side of the mind working and, anyway, this was a boring kind of assignment. Perhaps, too, it might not be very difficult. Dear George had betrayed her . . . she might think that she was due for a turn. Without arrogance, an imaginative exercise, he saw them making love together and he knew, since she was an intelligent woman and no stranger to love-making, that the steadiness of her eyes on him and the calmness of her face probably masked something like his own thoughts. They had driven miles together, eaten their alfresco lunches together and never once that he could remember had he ever touched her. Maybe that was all it needed. She was easier with him now . . . but what would be the point? A few hours' pleasure and make believe, but behind all that nothing would change.

He said, 'So you see, if things started moving unexpectedly I might have to call you out in the night. The truck for Charlie is at the operations centre and they won't make a move until we arrive with your bunch of bananas.'

When he had gone, Jean got back into bed and lit a cigarette. She was smoking more now than she had ever done in her life. Please, she thought, let Charlie be picked up soon so that she could put Fadledean and George behind her, and get on with some other kind of life . . . so that she could be free, too, of the company of Rimster and of the cold discomfort his looks and his manner sometimes set up in her; a hard, self-contained man, sure of himself and with God-only-knew what memories of his professional life securely stored and sterilized within him. Whatever was done and would go on being done at Fadledean had, at least, some scientific brief and reasonableness behind it. But this man, some sense told her, was a machine programmed to conscienceless actions, any emotion and apparent warmth part of the smooth functions of his profession. What was it Armstrong had said? One of Grandison's grey men. Come on, Charlie, hurry up and be caught. She wanted to be away.

6

At first light, Duncan took Charlie fresh food and water and then drove off to Andover to pick up his newspapers for delivery.

While he was waiting for them to be loaded he looked at two or three of the dailies and saw that all of them were still running the Charlie story, though it had been pushed well into the paper and not much space used on it. There was an interview with a small boy called Andrew Garvey who claimed that the chimpanzee had come and sat with him while he was fishing, and another with the lorry driver who had unwittingly given Charlie a lift. One of the dailies still wanted to know why the name of the owner of the animal had not been made public or any details of the road accident which had freed Charlie. Duncan guessed that without fresh news the story would soon be dropped. Well, that was where he came in.

On the outskirts of Andover he stopped by a public call-box and telephoned the Press Association in Fleet Street which had fed the original story to the newspapers.

Although he had expected some suspicion

about his good faith and a lot of havering and argument about a price he was met by immediate attention and a very nice sum was quoted to him with the promise of a bonus if the story went well. A photographer and a pressman would be at his cottage before midday. In the meantime all he had to do was to keep his mouth shut and look after Charlie.

He drove on and made his rounds, whistling to himself softly and debating whether he should spend the money on luxuries or some minor improvements to the smallholding and cottage. In the end he decided to postpone any immediate decision. As he came back along the Andover road he passed the lay-by where he usually stopped for breakfast. Instead of drawing in he went by it because he had decided to have breakfast at home where he could keep an eye on Charlie.

It was a lovely morning. Summer was back. The larks were singing high in the sky and the grass and trees looked fresh and trim after the heavy rain. God's in his heaven, all's well with the world, he thought. Maybe he would get old Grindle in from the village to keep an eye on the place and he would take off for a week or two . . . Brighton, Bournemouth, somewhere by the briny, where the fresh breezes lifted the skirts of the girls in their summer dresses and money in your pocket paid the entrance charge

142

to a little corner of paradise . . .

As he turned off the main road a police car came up fast behind, passed him and drew in ahead, signalling him to stop. A police constable got out and came to him.

The constable said, 'Mr Sparrow?'

'That's right. What's the matter? I wasn't doing more than forty — '

'Nothing's the matter, sir. Not about speeding, anyway. But I must ask you to drive on to your place and when you get there just sit in the van. We'll be right behind you.'

'I think I have a right to know what all this is about.'

'So you have, sir. And we'll let you know as soon as you get to Westacott Bottom. Just do as we say, sir, if you don't mind.'

Duncan Sparrow did not mind. He knew that he was in no position to mind. Nobody had to wave a red flag for him to know that the firing had started. Somehow the police had got wind of Charlie. Damn. Well, that was that. There went Brighton and Bournemouth and all the delights of a man temporarily monied and looking for a not-too-nice girl to spend some of his cash on. As for himself . . . well, they couldn't touch him. He'd only done what anyone else could have done. Poor old Charlie, drenched to the skin. Took him home, dried him down, fed and bedded him. Damn it, we were all God's creatures and any other decent sort would have done the same. Why hadn't he reported his good deed? Well, he wasn't on the telephone at the cottage and he was a busy man. Going to do it this morning in the village when he'd finished his round. Yes, that was all right. Couldn't touch him. Still, hard luck, Dunky, old boy . . . no cuddling in some sunny cove with an unbashful maiden.

Whistling thinly through his teeth he drove into the yard and the police car pulled up alongside him.

The constable came back to him and gave him a pleasant smile, saying, 'Had time to think it over?'

'Charlie?'

'That's the size of it.'

'Someone saw me give the poor little blighter a lift?'

'Yes. Reported it last night like a good citizen. Green Ford van. A. Wrench, baker and confectioner.' He nodded to the battered side of the van.

'I've been meaning to paint it out for months, ever since I bought it in Oxford.'

'Wouldn't have made any difference. One of our blokes coming on duty first thing this morning read the log and knew you at once. Regular habits like breakfasting in a lay-by, regular routes on a paper round delivery to shops. Regular face, regular van. People remember — especially our kind.'

'Makes me sound like a regular fellow. So what now?'

'Just sit. Where's the chimp — in the barn?'

'Yes. Nice chap, too. Why shouldn't he be allowed to have a little freedom? I get the feeling from the papers that there's a bit of a mystery about him.'

'No mystery. You live alone here?'

'Mostly, and at the moment.'

'Nice place, could be.'

'You can have it for fifteen thousand, lock, stock and barrel.'

'I'll think it over.' The constable went back to the police car.

The driver said, 'They're on their way. Ten minutes.' He tipped his head back towards the van. 'What's he like?'

'A little ray of artificial sunlight. Old school tie. No money and work-shy. Look at this place. It's a damned disgrace. You could take a crop of hay off the cottage thatch.'

Ten minutes later, Rimster, with Jean at his side, drove into the yard. Behind them came a truck with boarded sides and roof and an iron-grilled back with a small doorway in its centre, and two other vehicles, one an army

R/T truck and the other an army command car, chauffeured by a sergeant, while in the back sat the Colonel in charge of the operations centre.

Rimster, Jean and the Colonel got out of their cars and walked across to Duncan. The Colonel, long and lanky, wearing a thin sandy moustache, looked a wet, he thought. The woman was all right, dark-haired, good looking, a bit prim, not his type ... nice figure, though. One look at the man, however, and he knew that here was someone who outranked the Colonel on any point you liked to mention. Chipped from granite. If there was going to be trouble it would come from him. And all this high-powered police and army stuff? What was Charlie? A Russian spy in disguise?

Rimster, though he had had a briefing of a kind from the police, could have placed Duncan Sparrow at once. He had gone to school with people like him and even now had friends like him. They were all men who took things lightly even when things weren't going their way. He decided to handle him easily as a matter of policy because Charlie had to attract no undue importance and also because it would bring the right response from Sparrow.

He said easily, 'Mr Sparrow?'

'Yes.'

'Sorry to come down on you like a three-ring circus.'

'That's all right. I like circuses.'

'Where's Charlie?'

'In the barn. I picked him up yesterday morning, drenched to the skin. Settled him down in the barn. Thought he ranked a day's rest and feeding up before I turned him in. Here's the key. There's a light switch inside on the right of the door. He won't give any trouble. Happy chap. He belong to you?'

'I'm his owner's agent.'

Duncan, eyeing two helicopters which had appeared and were circling high overhead, said innocently, 'He must be someone who carries a lot of weight. Police, troops, helicopters? Just for nice old Charlie boy?'

'He could be dangerous if upset — particularly to a small child.'

Rimster turned to Jean.

'He's in the barn. Take a couple of bananas and go and have a look at him. If you think he's going to be awkward we can go in and net him.'

The Colonel said gallantly, 'Perhaps I should go in with Miss Blackwell?'

Rimster shook his head. 'There's no need. Charlie knows her. You might disturb him.'

Without thinking, Rimster took her by

the arm and walked towards the barn with her.

Feeling the light grip of his hand on her elbow, Jean realized that this was how George had so often steered her through a crowd, his big, warm hand controlling her ... hands which at more intimate moments so easily woke passion in her. What would this man's be like? She shook the thought from her, wondering what it was about him that awoke such curiosity in her. Well, thank goodness, she wouldn't have to wonder much longer. With the bait of a banana, Charlie would follow her like a dog and once he was in the truck she would be free to go her own and new way.

Rimster turned the key in the lock and pulled one of the double doors open just enough to let Jean slip in. He shut the door on her, saying, 'The light switch is on the right just inside.'

He stood outside and waited. The helicopters droned high overhead. Some loose hens scratched at the worn turf of a paddock beyond the yard. From the oak trees that lined the field at the top of the holding a pigeon sailed out lazily, clapped its wings, and slanted away on the light morning breeze.

Tonight, tomorrow at the latest, he thought, he would be back in London, the brief pastoral excursion over . . . And then what? Never again any real job which would give him the hard, callous satisfaction and lift which had become like a drug to him over the years. Grandison had already decreed the drying-out process.

The barn door opened and from inside Jean said, 'Come and have a look.'

Before he moved he knew from the tone of her voice that things had gone wrong. He went in. Naked bulbs on the cross rafters lit the place. It was untidy with old machinery, crates and loose hay and straw.

Jean pointed to the far roof corner of the barn above the wooden stall.

'He's gone.'

Sunlight streamed through a gap where the heavy slates and their battens had been pushed and broken away. It was easy to see how Charlie had reached the roof. An upright timber post from the corner of the stall ran upwards to a cross-rafter.

Jean said flatly, 'Once he wanted to get out it was easy for him. He's nothing like an adult yet, but he's very strong. I've looked around, he's nowhere in the barn.'

'Right. Well, that's that.' Rimster looked at his wrist-watch. It was half-past nine. 'Let's go.'

He left Jean at the car and went across to the Colonel and told him what had happened, finishing, 'He's probably had at the most somewhere around four hours' start. I'll check with our friend Sparrow in a moment, but you'd better let the chopper boys know. He could be six to eight miles from here by now.'

'Right. What are you going to do about this damned fellow Sparrow?'

'I'll deal with him.'

He walked over to Sparrow, knowing that there was nothing that could be done about him. He had done nothing wrong. Taken Charlie in, lodged and fed him, and had been going to inform the police — nobody could touch him. Any fuss or police action meant publicity — and that was out.

Sparrow spoke before he did. 'Don't tell me he's gone?'

Without feeling, Rimster said, 'Yes. He pushed a hole in the roof at the back of the barn. What time did you leave here this morning?'

'About half-past four, maybe a bit later. Gave him some grub. He was quite settled then. So what happens now?'

'Nothing so far as you are concerned. You had him and while you were making up your mind to let us know, you lost him.' His voice hardened. 'Now answer me one question — and I want the truth.'

'Fire ahead. And truly, I'm sorry about all this.'

'Spare me that. All I want to know is whether you told anyone else that you had him here? Did you?'

'No, I didn't.'

The lie came easily out of self-protection and fast thinking. By the time the press arrived these people would be away. There would be no story for them, no photographs. Charlie had gone. Anyway, he didn't like the look of this man — there was something odd going on about Charlie. He sensed it. If there should be trouble then the longer he put off meeting it the stronger might be his position.

Rimster said quietly, 'I don't believe you.'

Duncan Sparrow smiled. 'You can believe what you like. And I'd like to make an interesting little point of my own. I don't know you from Adam. If I've done anything wrong' — he nodded to the police car — 'those boys over there are the ones to tell me. What's more, if I should have happened to phone my mother or girl friend and told them about Charlie I'd like to know what law I was breaking? But don't worry' — he was enjoying himself now, sensing that, for whatever hidden reason, this man couldn't touch him — 'my mother's dead and I'm in the market for a new girl friend. Charlie's gone. That's the end of the business so far as I'm concerned — except it seems I have to do some roof repairs. That's what comes of being kind to animals.'

Rimster said quietly, 'Right. Well, thank you for your co-operation, Mr Sparrow.'

He went back to his car, wishing he were free to come down hard on Sparrow, but that was the last thing he could do. Keep it all in low profile. Orders. Charlie was an ordinary chimpanzee on the loose. Keep it that way. His own guess was that Sparrow might easily have already got in touch with the press. Well, that was Grandison's end of the affair when he let him know how things had gone at Westacott Bottom.

★　★　★

From fifteen hundred feet, Captain Stevens could see the cars in the yard of Westacott Bottom and the movement of people. He was flying in a great circle with two more helicopters.

His observer said, 'Looks like old Charlie's lodged up in that barn.'

'Not is. Was.'

The man and the woman who had gone into the barn had come out a little while ago and had left the door open. At this moment

152

fresh orders came over the radio for the helicopters, dropping them to six hundred feet and laying out a new search pattern.

'Was — yes,' said the observer. 'Here we go again.'

And all very monotonous it was becoming too, thought Stevens, and — seen from up here — not half as efficient as the operations centre people might think it was. Again and again he had watched a strung-out patrol line of soldiers move up a valley, or across a downland bowl, the search line, evenly spaced at first, soon becoming ragged and gapped because the men adapted their going to the easier contours and ground. Probably did it without knowing they were doing it. Six men across a half-mile front had to miss ground. Just as from up here his own observer couldn't keep everything under survey. The high crops, the summer-dry tall grasses, and shrub and tree shadows offered all sorts of easy camouflage to Charlie if he happened not to be moving. Add to that that most people now were getting bored with the whole thing, losing their first fine sharp-eyed rapture. The odds were swinging Charlie's way. The chaps who had drawn double figure numbers in the mess sweepstake for the capture of Charlie were beginning to rub their hands. Including himself. Into the sixth day now. Keep it up, Charlie boy. He'd drawn day fourteen. A big bunch of bananas if you make it, Charlie boy. There was a big kitty to be picked up.

The observer said, 'Hear that?'

Captain Stevens nodded. The call had gone out for a pair of handlers and their dogs to report to Westacott Bottom. Bloody great Alsatians or German police dogs. Well, if they picked up a line Charlie would have to do some quick thinking. Stick it Charlie, he thought, sympathy for the animal as much as the thought of his own gain moving him. Stick it, lad. Use your loaf. Give 'em a good run until day fourteen. Thirty-five quid in the kitty.

They moved slowly northwards and he watched the ground and the shadow of the helicopter racing ahead of him along the dried-up bed of a small stream, one of the bourns which flowed only in the winter. A handful of grazing horses moved away at a gallop as the machine passed over, their manes flaring as they dipped and swung their long necks, great scuds of turf kicked up by their hooves. They raced across the field to a hedge against which was a long concrete drinking trough, then wheeled abruptly and went down the slope to clatter across the dry gravel and stones of the stream bed.

Stevens watched them, enjoying the sight, imagining himself, if he won the kitty, riding one of them . . . not here though. Along some golden stretch of sand with a golden-haired girl on another horse alongside him . . . sunshine, salt breeze in their faces and a whole long, luxurious loving week-end before them.

If he had paid more attention to the hedge and the water trough he might just have caught a glimpse of Charlie sitting in the hedge shadow after drinking from the trough. He was grooming himself and hooing gently through pouting lips. After a while he got up and going to the trough rubbed his back against it as he watched, far to his right, a helicopter move across the sky. He watched it until it disappeared and then turned and climbed through the hedge into the next field.

The ground in the field was cut, furrowed and grubbed up from the rooting of pigs. A hundred yards away an old sow was feeding while six piglets moved around her. Erect, his long arms swinging, Charlie moved out into the field. He was almost up to the sow before she saw him. She lifted her head and grunted warningly at him. Charlie dropped to all fours and began to lope quickly around her. As he did so the piglets, squealing in noisy panic, broke away from the sow in all directions.

Suddenly excited by their movement and

squeals Charlie ran after one of them and caught it by a hind leg. The sow charged at him. Charlie moved away quickly, loping on his legs and one arm, dragging the screaming piglet with him. He reached a wooden fence on the far side of the field and climbed over it. Then he turned and screamed at the sow on the other side as he swung the piglet above his head and smashed it to the hard ground, breaking its neck and killing it. Maybe as he did so there was some memory in him of his far-off African days when, crouched against his mother, he had watched some adult chimpanzee male so catch and kill a young bushpig or baby baboon.

He screamed and chattered at the sow for a moment or two and then turned away, moving erect and holding the dead piglet trailing from one hand along the ground.

Twenty yards away was the fringe of a large oak wood, an outlying spur of the old forest of Chute. When he came to the first tree he climbed it and began to make his way into the wood through the upper branches of the densely packed trees. Behind him the noise of the sow and her piglets died away.

Holding the piglet sometimes in his mouth or one hand Charlie swung and leaped his way through the treetops. It was the first time since his escape that he had been in a large wood and could travel fast high above ground.

When he was well into the middle of the oak wood he found a wide crotch between branch and trunk of a tree and settled himself down. He ate half the piglet and then dropped the remainder of the carcass to the ground where it was found that night by a scavenging but not hungry fox who carried it away and buried it in a field beneath a large pat of cow dung to leave it until it should be high enough for eating.

Charlie slept for an hour and then moved through the treetops deeper into the wood, heading for its northern boundaries.

Almost three hours after Charlie had entered the wood the two handlers with their dogs and another soldier carrying an R/T pack arrived at the edge of the forest at the point where Charlie had entered. The dogs had taken Charlie's scent from the straw of his barn bedding and had picked it up at the back of the barn where he had dropped to the ground. There was little wind and the scent had held true along a haphazard line which had taken them generally in a northerly direction.

Now, at the wood's edge, the dogs stood balked at the foot of the tree which Charlie had climbed with the dead piglet. The handlers made them cast around, but they persisted in coming back to the tree.

Consulting their map the soldiers decided to split up and move left and right-handed respectively around the perimeter of the wood in the hope that, if Charlie had left the place, one or other of them would pick up his scent again. The fact that the total distance around the perimeter was something like ten miles gave them no pleasure at all.

A toss of a coin decided that the signaller should go with the left-handed perimeter dog handler.

Before moving off he reported their situation back to the operations room and from there two helicopters were ordered to move to the wood and cover it. In addition five patrols were detailed into the area to beat through the wood from different points so that the whole of it would be searched.

Captain Stevens, one of the pilots ordered to the wood, came to it from the westward side. Before he began to lose height he had the whole area of the wood spread out below him. He saw that it was in shape a crude, curving S, rather like a clumsy drawing of a green, rearing seahorse, and was about two miles in breadth at its widest point. It was cut by overgrown rides and paths and lying off it at intervals around its edges were isolated spinneys and copses. If Charlie was in there still it would take all day to beat the place properly and flush him out and unless there were men at twenty-yard intervals all around the wood he could easily come out unnoticed. From up here, of course, it was easier but still by no means a certainty that he would be spotted. The pilot flying the other helicopter he knew held day ten in the sweepstake.

He grinned to himself. If Charlie did make a break for it they would both be under the temptation of turning a blind eye. He dropped to searching height at the south end of the wood — marked on his map as Collingbourne Wood — and began to move along his patrol course up the western side of the mass of trees.

*   *   *

At Westacott Bottom, Duncan Sparrow had no trouble from the press when they arrived a good hour after the dog handlers had left and the police and other cars had driven off.

They were disappointed that Charlie had gone but they photographed the yard and the barn and the stall where Charlie had slept and also the hole in the roof through which Charlie had escaped. They then — there were three of them, a driver, a reporter and a photographer — adjourned to his kitchen for coffee and what was left of his brandy and had a long talk with him about all that had happened. Apart from the direct questions they asked him, they were good-naturedly interested in his opinions and speculations about the whole Charlie business.

Before they left they paid him well, more than he had expected considering they had not been able to photograph Charlie. Still it was, if not enough for a couple of weeks by the briny in company, more than enough for an extended week-end with ditto, he told himself as he poured himself another glass of brandy from a reserve store he had wisely resisted all temptation to broach in their company.

Driving off in the car the reporter said to the photographer, 'What do you think?'

The other shrugged his shoulders. 'That's your job. But for my money and the pricking in my thumbs something fishy this way comes.'

'You're dead right. It's not like the police to take a back seat to anyone. Nor the Army for that matter. I wonder who the two civilians were?'

'Well, he said the woman was called Miss Blackwell — she's got to rank somewhere. We've got a local bloke in Salisbury, get him on to it.'

'Okay. We'll stop at the next call-box and

I'll ring him. There's something in all this. Charlie's somebody's darling and the old man will want to know whose. The story's no good without a hook to hang it on.' He belched suddenly. 'God, that was pretty cheap brandy . . . '

'Well, he was a pretty cheap type. What a dump — no wonder Charlie skipped it.'

★ ★ ★

George Freemantle let himself into Jean's flat. He had over the last few days, whenever he had time or was in the neighbourhood, taken to going to the flat in the hope of finding her there. That she, or somebody else, visited the flat he was certain because the mail which he often found in the flat was always gone on his next visit.

He picked up now two letters from inside the door and carried them into the sitting room; both of them looked like bills. The determination to find her and have a straight talk with her was still strong in him. Boyson had refused to take any more letters for her and it had not been difficult to see that somebody had given the man a directive he could not dare to ignore.

Well, to hell with them, he thought. As the old song or proverb said, love would always

161

find a way. And love it was — if only he could get a chance to see her and prove it to her. She was the woman he wanted, the woman he loved and he was going to have her.

As he put the letters down on her desk the idea came to him that it would be the easiest thing in the world to write a letter and leave it with the rest of the mail to be collected. You're slipping, Georgie boy, he told himself. Should have thought of that days ago.

He took paper and envelope from her desk and sat down to write. It would be difficult to write what it would have been easy to say to her face ... watching her face and eyes he would have been able to pick up the slightest change in her feelings, see an opening and take it. He sighed as he set to the bleak task of composition. Women, they thought love was all up there in the clouds, rosy stuff. They never seemed to understand that, while a man would cut off a hand for them, work himself to the bone, give them the earth in a silver plate, and really mean until death us do part, against all that, the odd half hour when the old Adam in you trapped you with your trousers down was of no more importance than one drink too many. But how the hell did you get that down on paper? How the devil did he start? On the few occasions he had written to her before it was usually *My lovely lass,* or *Honey pot.* Didn't seem right somehow now. *My darling? My dearest Jean?*

He groaned. The door bell rang and with a sudden spurt of hope he got up quickly and went to it.

A middle-aged man in a crumpled fawn linen suit stood outside. He had a large, bland reddish face, sloe-dark eyes and a long, loosely assembled body.

He said, 'Sorry to bother you, but I'm looking for a Miss Blackwell.'

'So am I.'

'Oh . . . Well, I'm not sure that the one who lives here is the one. She's — ' He broke off, eyed George up and down and then went on, 'You're not the press are you?'

'No, I'm not. Are you?'

'Yes — Craister's the name. I've drawn three blanks so far. The one I want is thirtyish, tallish, dark-haired, good-looking and has something to do with this Charlie the chimp that's missing. You've heard about that?'

'Yes, I have. Come in. We may be able to help one another.'

'Ta.'

George showed Craister into the sitting room and waved him to a seat. He dropped into it, took out a handkerchief and wiped his face, saying, 'Bloody hot isn't it? Thirsty

163

weather, too. Not that I'm suggesting anything. Here's my card.'

George took it and glanced at it as he made his way to the kitchen. Press all right. Area representative Press Association so on and so on. What the hell was all this about? Charlie the chimpanzee and Jean? Well? Could be, of course. The Lord only knew what went on up at Fadledean.

He came back with glasses and four cans of lager. As Craister drank, George said, 'This flat belongs to a Miss Jean Blackwell. She's also my fiancée. She also fits the description you've given. And that's all I'm saying until you've spoken your piece.'

'Fair enough. But you did say you were looking for her?'

'Yes.'

'Since when?'

'Six days odd. And that's all you get, old man, until I know what makes you interested in her.'

'Fair enough.'

They talked, which was thirsty work, and finished six cans of lager between them.

* * *

Just before dinner that evening as Jean was sitting on the terrace, Rimster came out to

164

her and handed her the letters which one of the orderlies had been detailed to collect each day. He strolled away down the terrace while she read them. Two of them were bills, he guessed, but the other was unstamped. George Freemantle, he knew now, was the only other person with a key to her flat. George had been a little slow in realizing how easily he could communicate with her. Slow, but sure maybe. Perhaps in the end he would get the girl. The way life went turned on too many small things. Because of George, Charlie had escaped — and he was here doing a job which, significantly, for the first time in his career, was right out of his line. A rare spasm of anger flared through him. There was nothing to get his teeth into, nothing he could do to push things forward. He just had to sit and let other people do things. He was beginning to suspect, for all the men and machines the army had, they weren't making a very efficient job of things. The simplest and most effective way of scotching Charlie would have been to put out a public warning that he could be dangerous and offer a reward for him . . . a hundred pounds dead or alive. That way he wouldn't have lasted three days and Fadledean could have got another chimpanzee and started their experiment all over again and with much tighter security precautions.

But clearly someone, somewhere on the Olympian heights of Whitehall, had vetoed that.

Jean read George's letter after she had opened the two bills. It read —

My darling Girl,

Like the Irishman said if you don't receive this please write and let me know. Not that I feel flippant, just frustrated because it's hopeless to try and put things on paper. I've got to be talking to you — so please leave a note in your flat saying when and where. A little bird tells me that probably you're tied down because of this Charlie the chimp business. I say no more because I know how you are over Fadledean stuff. But there's nothing to stop you dropping me a note, and I know how to be patient. YOU ARE THE ONLY ONE FOR ME AND I CAN PROVE IT.

All my love and yours always —

George

P.S. I don't mind Charlie coming between us if that's urgent business — but nobody else.

Despite herself Jean smiled. George would promise anything to get what he wanted.

However, he was successful in business because he backed his promises with performance. How many other women, she wondered, were married to Georges and had learned to live with them happily?

Rimster came back and said, 'George?'

'Yes.' She held up the letter.

He shook his head. 'You don't have to.'

'I know. But I have to with this one. It concerns you.'

Rimster read the letter and then handed it back.

'How could he possibly have connected you with Charlie?'

'I can't think. I never discussed my work with him and certainly never mentioned Charlie.'

'Then I'd better find out.'

He drove down to Salisbury by himself. There was no reply to the bell of George's flat. In the lobby he asked the hall porter about him.

The man said, 'He left about four in his car. Had his big case with him. Probably means he's away for a few days. His works will know if you give them a ring tomorrow morning. You can leave a note here for him if you like, sir.'

'No, thanks.'

Rimster went back to Redthorn House and

rang his office. Grandison was not there but he left a message for him.

If George had coupled Charlie's escape with Jean's work at Fadledean then he had not snatched the idea out of the blue. Somebody had told him or suggested it to him. He could think of a dozen possibilities and of one more likely than any other. That stupid Colonel had used Jean's name in front of Duncan Sparrow and the man had been clearly lying when he said he had made no approach to the press — and there had been nothing he could do about it. That was the kind of stupid job this was. The odds were that when Grandison saw the papers tomorrow morning there would be fireworks because the over-anxious men above him had refused right from the beginning to couple Charlie's name with Fadledean.

He went in and joined Jean, who had already started dinner.

'You spoke to him?'

'No. The hall porter says he's gone away for a few days. Do you think George could just have made a wild guess?'

'I don't think so. He doesn't have that kind of imagination.'

'Well, somebody has. Damn that stupid Sparrow man.'

Jean said nothing. For the first time since

she had known him he was openly showing frustration. Even granite over the years slowly rotted away.

★ ★ ★

Charlie slept most of the afternoon in the northern part of Collingbourne Wood. He had made a nest up in the top branches of a beech tree. He slept fitfully, waking now and then to the noise of a helicopter and once to hear the voices of searching patrols beating northwards through the trees and under-growth, the sound of their sticks thudding at tree trunks and bushes twice passing quite close to his beech. Normally he might have been excited by this and have moved from his tree, but the unaccustomed pig meat which he had eaten had made him feel lethargic and ill. He just lay, holding his arms close around himself to ease the disturbance in his stomach.

Towards sunset the noise of the helicopters moved away and there were no more disturbances by the searching patrols which had moved to the southern part of the wood. As the day's fierce heat slowly leached away Charlie's stomach began to settle.

Just before sunset thirst grew in him and he dropped down from the tree and began to search for water. He found it a quarter of a mile away near the top end of the wood where a spring broke through the floor of an old stone working and formed a small pool fringed with reeds and a tangle of alder growths. Charlie drank his fill and, feeling more comfortable every minute, began to explore the edges of the pool and found a moorhen's nest with a late clutch of eggs. He gathered four or five of them in the crook of one arm and carried them into a patch of tall willow herbs. Pulling leaves from the willow herbs he chewed them into a thick wad and then began to eat the eggs by putting them whole into his mouth and crunching them so that their savouriness mixed with the mess of leaves.

He sat for half an hour contentedly mouthing on his egg and leaf wads, grunting and softly hooing to himself and enjoying the cooling evening air as the daylight faded to dusk. On the far side of the pool he now and then caught the agitated flick of a moorhen's white tail as the bird moved nervously among the reeds, too scared to return to her nest while Charlie was in sight. A tawny owl floated silently through the trees and banked softly away as it saw Charlie. Distantly there were the sounds of traffic on a road and once a jet fighter flew low over the wood, the sudden roar of its passing making Charlie jump to his feet and scream with fright.

Disturbed by the jet he left the pool and wandered aimlessly through the trees until he reached the edge of the wood. He climbed one of the outlying trees and made himself a bed. He twisted and turned on it for a while until the bent and broken branches were to his liking and then lay back on it and, long eased of all stomach discomfort, watched the darkening slope of the open rough land which ran down from the edge of the wood.

Two hundred yards away a light showed from the window of a small cottage and farther away Charlie saw the headlights of cars passing along a road. At the cottage a dog began to bark intermittently and was only stilled when a man shouted at it.

The stars brightened in the moonless sky as the night darkened. Charlie lay, watching the erratic flight of bats hawking above the trees, and finally slept. During the night the fox which had found the remains of the piglet and buried it came through the trees and winded Charlie's scent. It circled his tree, looking upwards, and then moved on out of the wood, passing the cottage and setting the dog barking again briefly.

At first light the next morning a game-keeper, who lived alone in the cottage, came out, carrying a shotgun. He released the dog from its shed and the pair moved away down the side of the wood.

Charlie, who had been awake some time, watched them go and then dropped down from his tree and ambled on all fours down to the cottage garden where he breakfasted on young pea pods for a while and then pulled the netting from a row of strawberries and ate his fill of the fruit while above him the larks filled the dawn sky with song as the daylight slowly strengthened on the seventh day of Charlie's freedom.

7

All the national daily papers carried the Charlie story that morning with photographs of the barn and the hole in the roof, and some with photographs of Duncan Sparrow to mark the interview with him. Without exception all of them wanted to know the truth about Charlie. Why were troops and helicopters being employed in the search for him — at the public's expense? Was his mysterious, unrevealed private owner going to foot the bill for the search? Or was he really privately owned? If so, why was a distinguished micro-biologist from the Fadledean Research Station, a Miss Jean Blackwell — not available for interview — taking a prominent part in the search? Had Charlie escaped while on his way to Fadledean? Or had he escaped from Fadledean? The public was entitled to know since a great deal of their money was being spent on the search for him; a search which did not appear to be particularly competent since Charlie had now been free for almost a week.

Many of the newspaper cartoonists, glad to forget political and international subjects, featured Charlie.

Grandison, standing in the window bay of the Minister's room while the Minister spoke on the telephone at his desk, knew that before the day was out all the radio and television networks would be hard at work on the story and Charlie would be a national figure. So long as there was an element of mystery, or a chance to embarrass officialdom, the media would not let go.

He turned as he heard the telephone replaced. The day's newspapers were spread over the great desk and the Minister sat behind them, a small, brisk man with a thin, tired face, his top teeth working nervously on his lower lip.

A rabbit, thought Grandison. They were all rabbits, though not all of them looked like them.

The Minister said, 'I'm seeing the P.M. in an hour's time. What do you suggest?'

Grandison let the monocle drop from his eye to clink against his coat buttons. Always this way, he thought. What do you suggest, as though they had no minds of their own. Politicians in office never went out on the ice until they had pushed others forward first to test it.

'What I suggested originally. Go as near the damned truth as you can. People these days know all about Chemical and Biological Warfare establishments. Fadledean, Porton, Fort Detrick in the States, and the Suffield Proving Grounds in Canada ... every country has them. The public know they have to be but don't want to think about them. If we'd made a simple statement at the beginning saying Charlie had escaped from Fadledean where he was the subject of, say, animal behaviour research or some such guff — then there would have been no trouble except for the cries of a few cranks who would have been ignored by the press because that kind of protest isn't news.'

'And now?'

'Do it now. It cuts out all the mystery. Charlie must be put in the bag soon. The story will die.'

'Mightn't it be better to say he escaped on the way to Fadledean?'

'No. Some bright newsman might ferret out that Miss Blackwell is out in front because she knows Charlie and she's the only one he'll come and take a banana from. If she's not that important why is she, a micro-biologist not an animal handler, in the picture?'

'I don't know. Charlie's bound to be picked

up soon. Why go nearer the truth than necessary?'

Grandison replaced his monocle. He said heavily, 'Because, Minister, truth walks on its own legs and often where it will — not where you want it to go. What happens if by a miracle Charlie stays out over twenty-one days? Then you'll be forced to tell the whole truth, unless you want people dying like flies all over the country and start pretending it's some natural disease brought in by an immigrant or visitor to the country.'

'He can't possibly last that long.'

'He might. Particularly if — not knowing the truth — the public treat him as a national hero on the run and stop co-operating. Plenty will begin to take that line now because of those.' He nodded at the newspapers. 'No, my advice is that we say he's escaped from Fadledean where he was being used for harmless animal behaviour studies. Then, if a miracle occurs and he stays out, you'll have a cast-iron reason for not having told all the truth right away . . . setting up a plague scare which would have caused panic and trouble all round unnecessarily.'

'Well, it's certainly a point. But it will depend on the way the P.M. sees it. And on what other advice he's had. He'll have had the Home Secretary's opinion and you know he's a great believer in playing these kinds of cards close to his chest.'

Bluntly Grandison said, 'You had some good cards a week ago and they were played wrongly. It's time some of the not so good ones left were laid on the table.'

'I don't agree. Not by any odds can this damned animal last another two weeks. In this country? With everyone on the look out for it?'

Grandison sighed aloud, indifferent to the quick frown the Minister gave him and said, 'On that particular point the real outcome rests with time and chance and the will of God. Nothing the powers and principalities have been doing for the last two thousand years could have over-disposed Him towards politicians. The most that can be done should be done to curry favour. You called me here for my advice. I give it again. Charlie has escaped *from* Fadledean where he was being used for ethological research purposes. If he goes the limit then you have a valid reason for not having given the full truth needlessly early and scaring the country into a panic because all the odds were that Charlie would be caught — as I believe he will — well within the crucial time span. I say again, the best form of lie is the one which stays closest to the truth.'

The Minister was silent for a few moments and then he said, 'I agree with you. But you know the P.M.'s thinking in this kind of situation where constituency, electoral and factional interests might be roused — do the least that you have to, because you may never have to do more.'

★ ★ ★

Two hours later there was an official government press release that Charlie had escaped while being transported to Fadledean to be the subject of a series of researches into animal behaviour. The animal was harmless unless angered or maltreated and any sighting should be immediately reported to the police. It was confidently anticipated that the chimpanzee would be captured within the next few days.

On reading this many an editor in Fleet Street realized that the Charlie story would be good, with luck, for some time to come.

In the search area, further troops and helicopters were deployed and police leave and rest days were cancelled so that more patrol cars could be kept on the roads.

In mid-afternoon, the vicar of a parish well to the north of Salisbury reported in great agitation over the Charliephone that even as he talked he could see the chimpanzee in his garden chasing his hens. When the police arrived the reverend gentleman had recovered his calm and lucidity. His back garden was littered with feathers, three of the hens were dead and the wire netting of the hen roost had been ripped away from one side. The vicar said that immediately after his call the chimpanzee had climbed the wall at the bottom of the garden and had disappeared into the trees that fringed a small tributary of the Avon river.

Helicopters were switched to the area and troops lorried to it to throw a ring around the district.

That evening before dinner, the vicar retired to his study — where he often held long and confidential talks with the Archangel Gabriel and the spirit of Karl Marx — to compose his sermon for the next Sunday confident in the knowledge that instead of the usual miserable handful of a congregation he would have a full house. The sermon when finished was a sane, well-ordered and pious one. Only his housekeeper, who had seen him twist the necks of the chickens with his own hands and prepare the scene, could have disproved his story but she did not choose to do so because she shared his bed twice a week and sometimes joined him in his talks with the angelic and spiritual world.

As the vicar finished composing his sermon, Charlie, who had slept most of the day through the intense heat in his tree, dropped to the ground, went down to the cottage garden for an evening meal of radishes, young peas and lettuces, and then wandered away northwards, keeping just inside the fringe of the wood.

Half an hour later the keeper returned with his dog and immediately noticed the state of his garden. At that moment he was still in a bad temper at the way his young pheasants in the woods had been disturbed by the searching soldiers and low-flying helicopters. He was a sensible, phlegmatic man who lived alone, and he was well used to keeping his eyes and ears open and drawing his own conclusions.

As his dog was clearly disturbed, running around in circles with its nose to the ground and barking, he shut it in his back shed and then returned to the garden. The pea vines had been pulled over and some were torn out by the roots. Here and there in the row lay, still fresh, the well-chewed lumps of the wads which Charlie had discarded after sucking all the juice from them. The strawberry bed had been completely stripped of its fruit and the loose net dragged half-way across the garden to a newly dug bed in which he was going to plant out more young lettuce that evening. In the friable, soft dry earth of the bed were the clear hand and foot marks which Charlie had made.

The gamekeeper who was a good citizen, though there had been times when he had taken the law into his own hands with poachers, had been well aware of the reason for the patrols and helicopter activity in the area. He debated for a moment or two whether he should — since he had no telephone — cycle to the nearest call-box or take the law into his own hands.

The sight of the havoc in his garden and the disturbance of his pheasant poults suddenly made him angry and he decided to go after the vandal on his own account. There was plenty of daylight left yet, but it would be dark before any help could arrive if he wasted time telephoning, and anyway he just didn't want any more damn soldiers tramping the woods and his coverts.

Taking his dog and his gun he set out after Charlie. The dog, a well-trained black labrador, was soon made to understand that this was no evening stroll but an extra work period.

It soon picked up Charlie's recent scent at the edge of the garden and headed up the slope towards the fringe of the wood, moving steadily.

After a few hundred yards the scent line led them into the wood and the keeper soon realized that Charlie, although the general direction he had followed was northwards and not far from the wood's edge, was really moving at random, wandering away to left and right as the mood took him. He found a young ash tree with the fresh scar where a leafy branch had been torn off and a little later came across the branch discarded on the ground. Ten minutes later he came upon a fresh mound of faeces at the foot of a rabbit warren.

He called the dog closer to him, making him work slower, and sharply curbed any noise the animal made in its excitement. It was a good dog, one of the best he had ever had. He had no time for any dog which could not be trained to work for its keep, and to work his way.

After an hour the keeper heard the sudden alarm call of a cock pheasant not far ahead. Looking up he saw the bird rocket out of the wood's edge a few hundred yards away and plane low down the hill slope to the cover of a field of corn.

He motioned the dog to his side and they went forward quietly.

Ten minutes later the scent trail took them a little deeper into the wood and to the edge of a wide clearing where a stand of chestnuts had been felled a year before. Only one tree still stood in the clearing, an old oak growing now in isolation, its far spreading branches a good fifteen yards from the nearest trees of the encircling wood.

Squatting at the foot of the oak was Charlie holding in his hands a dead hen pheasant which he had caught in the undergrowth when the cock pheasant had been disturbed. He had pulled off the wings, roughly scratched and torn away some of the breast feathers, and was contentedly chewing into the warm flesh.

Keeper and dog halted and the man slowly slipped the gun from under his arm and held it loosely ready for action. The cheeky little sod, thought the keeper, calmly sitting there eating one of my birds and not caring a damn even though he's seen me.

Charlie had seen man and dog. He had heard them coming the last few yards and when they halted on the clearing's edge he looked up, feathers sticking to his mouth and hands. He parted his jaws slightly, his lips still covering his upper and lower front teeth, and gave a soft warning bark. The pheasant flesh was good and it belonged to him. When neither man nor dog made any move their stillness disturbed him. For men he had no real fear, but dogs always unsettled him. He opened his jaws wider, drawing his lips back over his upper and lower teeth and suddenly uttered a series of loud barking *waa-waa-waas*.

The dog, for all its training, stirred and whined. The keeper spoke sharply and quietened it. He freed the safety catch on the shotgun. This would be one for the lads on Saturday night at the White Hart . . . half the bloody army and the sky full of racketing helicopters and they hadn't come within a mile of the chimpanzee . . . all they'd done was to upset every damned pheasant in his woods for miles around . . . and if anyone bellyached because he had blown its head off what could they do? He'd thought it was a stray dog, upsetting his birds and had fired — as he had fired and finished off many a dog before.

He brought the gun up slowly. As he did so his dog, over-excited, quivering with eagerness, began to run forward.

Seeing the movement of the dog, Charlie screamed in rage and slipped behind the tree as the keeper fired. The shot pellets blasted into the big trunk of the oak and a few of them hit Charlie in the lower part of his left arm as he disappeared. Charlie screamed with pain and went up the tree on the far side fast, climbing as high as he could.

The keeper, angry with the dog and furious at missing Charlie, went over to the tree and made the dog sit and be quiet. Then he walked around the tree, shotgun at the ready, looking up in search of Charlie.

As he stood there, Charlie, well hidden in the top of the thick foliaged tree, screamed loudly at him and released the pheasant. It fell from branch to branch and hit the ground at the man's feet. Incensed at the sight of the bird's body, mangled and torn, the keeper raised his gun and fired blindly up into the tree. Most of the shot was blocked by branches and leaves and the rest whistled harmlessly away to Charlie's left.

But the noise of the shot and the passage of the hissing pellets frightened Charlie into a panic. He ran out along one of the spreading top branches and launched himself on a great leap across the wide gap towards the nearest of the trees on the fringe of the clearing. He failed to reach the trees, dropping awkwardly to the ground, and rolled in three or four panic somersaults into the wood. He went rapidly up a tree and began to swing away, through the safety of the spreading canopy of the forest roof.

The keeper saw him land from his leap and spring to the nearest tree but, although he took little time in reloading the double-barrelled gun, Charlie was out of sight before he could use it again. Standing there, his anger still high, the dog whimpering at his feet, he heard Charlie crashing away into the wood at top speed.

For a moment or two he contemplated following but then decided against it. A quarter of a mile away in the valley was a farmhouse which he knew had a telephone. He would go down there and get in touch with the police.

Meanwhile Charlie, thoroughly frightened, kept going through the tree tops, whimpering and grunting to himself but slowly becoming less aware of the few shotgun pellets which had lodged shallowly in his arm and body through his thick pelt and tough skin.

Police patrol cars covered all the lanes and roads in the Collingbourne Wood area later that night, and early the next morning the army patrols and helicopters were back, but none of them found any sign of Charlie.

★   ★   ★

Rimster and Jean Blackwell were sitting late that night in the lounge of Redthorn House

186

having drinks after coming back from a conference at the operations centre. Just before they had left a report had come through that a gamekeeper had sighted Charlie in the northern area of Collingbourne Wood.

Accepting one of her now occasional cigarettes from Rimster, Jean said, 'Either the good vicar this afternoon was seeing things or Charlie can move faster than a normal chimpanzee. Even as the crow flies it's a good twenty miles between the two places.'

Rimster smiled. 'Don't forget the hens. They'd had their necks twisted. Perhaps there are two chimpanzees kicking about.'

For a while, thinking that this was the first time she had known him to be flippant about the search, she was silent. Then she said, 'There's only one Charlie. Whose word would you take?'

'Not the man of God's against a gamekeeper's. And you?'

'I think I agree with you.'

'You'll see — now that the statement has been made publicly that Charlie is connected with Fadledean we'll be tossed a lot of false information. It's a game the public like playing — the pub wits after a few drinks, the cranks, the quietly mad but apparently sane types like the vicar, the nice old ladies who genuinely think it's a shame to keep any animal shut up in a cage, and all those who for some reason or another have a grudge against the police, the army or the government. It's an easy game to play and a safe one. The only thing that would bring honest co-operation would be a frank statement of the truth. Tell them that if Charlie stays out for twenty days then this country runs the risk of a new form of plague and then, whatever they might feel about the ethics of the thing, nobody would care a damn for him except to get him back in his cage as soon as possible.'

'Would you do that?'

'If I were an ordinary citizen who knew the facts, yes. But if I were the Prime Minister or the Minister of Defence or somebody like that I don't think so. Not yet anyway — because like them I'm a gambler and for the moment the odds are on Charlie being picked up soon. But I would have stuck much closer to the truth right from the beginning. What about you?'

'I don't know.'

Rimster smiled. 'That's partly why I'm here. Left to yourself there would always have been the risk that you might be tempted to pick up the telephone and call some editor.'

Stirred, Jean said sharply, 'You think I'd do that?'

'Don't jump at me. My opinion doesn't count. I'm here because other people just want to have every safeguard they can. Emotion set Charlie free. Your emotion. That makes you a risk.'

'You still haven't given me your opinion.'

'No, I don't think you'd do it.'

'Well, thank you for that.'

Rimster shrugged his shoulders gently, and said, 'Would you like another drink?'

'No thank you. I'm going to bed.' She paused, and then, not knowing even what prompted it, she said, 'I get the feeling sometimes that you don't care a damn whether Charlie is caught or not, that the whole thing bores you.'

Rimster laughed. 'You've got it wrong. I do care that Charlie should be caught before the time limit. But you're right. The whole thing bores me.'

'Why?'

He was silent for a while, debating whether he should tell her. Unexpectedly he suddenly realized that he did want to tell someone. He was over the hill, burnt-out. Oh, yes, he knew he was just as clearly as Grandison did. Nerve, muscle and brain — maybe even conscience — had been tautly stretched over

189

the years. Now the slackness was beginning. Small things escaped him ... like not foreseeing that that damned Colonel might refer to Jean by name in front of Sparrow. Yes, Grandison was being kind in relegating him, otherwise some small thing, overlooked, might finish him off on one of his usual missions.

He said calmly, 'Because it's not my usual kind of job. And that's the reason I've been given it. It's the first step to easing me out. I've seen it happen before with other people like me. People who've been burnt-out doing what they have had to do in our service. It's a pretty common occupational hazard. And when the people upstairs, the bosses, see the signs there's a sort of kindness in them which makes them offer you a choice without putting it into words. You can either settle for a simple life doing jobs which don't set the adrenalin pumping, or you can sign the final document and retire to nurse your dirty memories dozing in a club armchair or digging your cottage garden.' Spreading his hands and smiling, he asked, 'Make sense to you?'

Shocked at the sudden nakedness of his reply, she said, 'What do you mean that you've done things? That you've — '

'Killed people? Of course. In many ways.

With these.' He spread his hands, palms up. 'Often without a weapon. Seldom from a safe distance. Shocked?'

'Yes, I am, though I know I shouldn't be.'

Bluntly, he said, 'No, you shouldn't. That's what you and the rest of the people at Fadledean have done and would do — but always from a safe distance. In a handful of days Charlie will be walking death. A whiff of his breath, a single droplet of his spittle, a flea bite from one of his fleas, a drink of water into which he's piddled — and bingo! And after Charlie the time would come when a few men could fly tourist to any country and plague would fly in with them. What difference is there?'

'None at all.'

'Full marks for honesty. But what happens to the Fadledean types when they get beyond it, when age or conscience unsteadies their hands or doubts fog their minds? A cottage with a garden and a fat pension? Or, more likely, a safe billet in some university, distinguished fellows or dons, with an eye open for likely graduates, the bright boys and girls, the potential Nobel prize winners, maybe? Looking through their microscopes, shaking up their test tubes and dreaming dark dreams. You and I and our kind are killers. The only point I would make — not a plea for mercy or mitigation — is that every man, woman and child I've killed has been killed quickly, not coughing up their lungs from some foul gas or lingering while a filthy disease eats them away. Crude, isn't it? But true — and I say it without anger or any personal condemnation of you. For us both the whole affair has long been academic. And now, for both of us, our masters have decided that our specific usefulness has gone. Nothing left but to be turned out to pasture . . . for me. And you?'

Jean was silent for a while. Every word he had said was true, the bleakness of spirit behind his talk unmasked almost totally. So what was there for her?

She said, 'I suppose I shall get married and wait for memory to fade enough to leave me comfortable.'

'Quite right. As my father's favourite poet said, time at last will set all things even.' He nodded at her left hand. 'Who will it be? George Freemantle? You still wear his ring.'

'So I do. And so I shall until I can give it back to him personally.'

'To run a risk that you really at heart want to run?'

Jean stood up, and he rose with her. She said evenly, 'I'm going to bed.'

'Why not?'

He walked up with her and at her bedroom he stepped past her and opened the door.

As she went in, he followed her and when she turned, facing him with a frown, he said, 'Children get scared by bad dreams at night and seek comfort. So do men and women, not because they're scared but sometimes because they want the comfort of forgetting their own identities.'

For a moment or two she was on the verge of rejecting him angrily, but the words died in her mind. She looked at him and the brown deeply creased face was impassive, the overhead light turning the grey thatching of his hair to silver, and his body was still, ready to turn to or from her with a calm indifference as to which it might be, so that she guessed that it was not only comfort he sought for himself but comfort for her if she needed it.

She said, 'Yes, I'd like you to stay.'

He walked to her telephone, called the switchboard, and said, 'If there's a call for me during the night ring this number.'

Then he went to her wardrobe and opening it took down the bottle of whisky from the top shelf.

As he turned and smiled, she said, 'You've searched this room before?'

'Naturally. But I'm off duty now. We'll have

to make do with the bathroom glasses for our nightcap. Minor comforts before the major ones.'

Waking during the night with him sleeping at her side she wondered how Charlie was passing this night . . . man, woman and ape all adrift.

★   ★   ★

Charlie, since the light never died completely from the sky of the midsummer night and the attack by the gamekeeper had disturbed him, wandered eight miles northwest along the line of a disused railway track. For most of its way the track ran through deep cuttings, their sides now thickly tangled with thorns and briars and the bed of the track carpeted with a flourishing growth of flowers and weeds. Hawking pipistrelle bats hunted the soft-winged moths and rabbits, hearing Charlie's approach, ran for their burrows, white scuts signalling alarm to others of their kind. The air was still and balmy. A plane went over with its navigation lights winking and Charlie sat down and watched it, chattering softly to himself. The few pellet shots he had suffered had long ceased to worry him. Finding an old tin can, he picked it up and moved on, throwing it ahead of him and then racing to retrieve it. He played with the can for a while as he progressed and then abandoned it as his eye was caught by the pale light of a glow-worm in a patch of weeds. He squatted by it and touched it with one finger cautiously. The light went out. He sat and waited and the light came on after a while. He touched it again and this time the light went out and stayed out. Charlie picked up the grub and ate it and shuffled away.

Half an hour later he came to a part of the track where it ran level with the surrounding fields. Close to one of the field fences a small bivouac-type tent had been pitched. Propped against the fence were two bicycles. The front of the tent was open against the warmth of the night and stacked outside it were two cardboard boxes.

Charlie sat down by one of the boxes and opened its cardboard flaps. Inside, among other things, was a wrapped loaf of sliced bread and a bottle of milk. Charlie poked a finger through the tin foil cover of the bottle and drank clumsily from it, the milk spilling over his chin and throat. Then he tore the wrapper from the loaf and stuffed three slices of bread into his mouth and sat quietly chewing.

Inside the tent a young man and a girl slept soundly in a large sleeping-bag. The girl mumbled something in her sleep.

Attracted by the noise and having no real fear of human beings, Charlie swallowed his bread and moved into the tent. He squatted by the girl. When in sleep she muttered again he put out a finger and touched the side of her face gently and gave a few soft pant-hoots. The girl stirred and turned her head away, her loose hair lying across her pillow close to Charlie's hand.

The young man at her side, disturbed by her movement, turned towards her and in his sleep threw out a bare arm across her shoulders and said from the depth of some dream, 'So I told him. Yes, I told him — and that was that . . . '

His words mumbled away into silence.

Charlie reached out and gathered up a thick tress of the girl's hair. For a moment or two he fingered it gently.

The girl shook her head in sleep.

The movement excited Charlie who drew back his lips and through partly closed teeth gave a friendly but loud series of *waa-waa-waas* and tugged at the long hair.

The girl woke suddenly, sat up, and found herself looking into the grimacing face of Charlie. For a moment the girl stared at Charlie, who pushed his lips forward in a great pout and hoo-hooed at her.

The girl screamed, a long, high-pitched scream, and the suddenness of the noise startled and panicked Charlie, and woke the young man. The girl screamed again and struck at Charlie who leaped away and ran in his sudden alarm towards the closed end of the tent. He hit the thin upright pole at the back of the tent. It snapped at his weight and the fabric collapsed over him in dark folds.

Thoroughly frightened now by the canvas about him and the screams of the girl and the shouting of the young man, Charlie fought his way free of the fabric and back towards the front of the tent. He jumped over the young man as he was struggling out of the sleeping-bag and somersaulted out of the tent, hitting the front pole with his full body force and snapping it so that the whole of the tent canvas slowly settled down over the two campers in an untidy heavy mantle from underneath which came the screams of the frightened girl and the angry swearing and shouting of the young man.

Moving quickly, upset and frightened, Charlie vaulted the field fence and headed straight across it, travelling fast on all fours and scattering a flock of sheep. It was some time before the alarm in Charlie died away and he slackened off his pace.

As the first larks began to rise to greet with

their song the strengthening return of daylight, Charlie came out of a small fir copse bordering a rough side road. He crossed the road and followed a narrow path which passed through a small water meadow. Beyond the meadow was a stretch of canal over which the path was carried by a humped-back bridge. Charlie crossed the bridge and veered away up the canal path. To his right a main railway line ran parallel with the canal for a while.

A few hundred yards along the line to the east was a small town and a railway station.

Charlie slipped through the wire of a fence at the canal side and crossed a piece of waste ground beyond which was a railway siding holding a goods train. Charlie climbed the siding wooden fence, calm now and drifting aimlessly.

But as he approached the trucks a dog came down the track, a large black-and-white mongrel. Seeing Charlie, the dog began to bark and headed for him. Frightened, Charlie ran for the nearest sanctuary.

He galloped to one of the carriages, climbed its side and dropped down into it, and stayed there hidden.

The dog stood by the side for some minutes, barking and running around and then, since Charlie did not reappear, finally moved off down the line, wormed its way under the fence and headed canalwards in search of rabbits.

At ten o'clock that morning the Charliephone rang in the Salisbury police station. It was from the Newbury police station. A sergeant reported that they had had a call from one of their local constables that a young newly-married couple camping out on their honeymoon by the old railway line near West Grafton had told him that during the night they had been attacked by the escaped chimpanzee, Charlie.

'Attacked?' queried the Salisbury man.

'Well, that's what the girl says. Says she woke up when Charlie began to get familiar with her as she slept. She screamed and, Charlie did a bolt for the wrong end of the tent and one way and another the whole thing collapsed on them. But her husband thinks Charlie wandered in looking for food and when his wife woke and screamed he just panicked.'

'That's more like it. Well, let's have all the details. Time, names and address and so on. Where are they now, anyway?'

'God knows. They just reported it and cycled off.'

But the young couple did more than that. Their story was too good to keep to themselves. At a café where they stopped for coffee they told it to the owner and in the public house where they had a beer and a lunch snack they told it, and since the publican was often in a position to pass titbits of news to the local press he passed the story on. It reached Fleet Street in time to make the last editions of the evening newspapers.

But long before all this, Charlie, who had dropped off to sleep in his railway truck, was awakened by its jolting as it moved away from the siding, being drawn westward in a string of container vans and trucks along the main line running down from London to Exeter.

8

After breakfast that same morning as Charlie moved westwards, Rimster motored down to Salisbury to Jean's flat to collect her mail and also to pick up some personal articles which she wanted.

Ever since George Freemantle had left a letter for her at the flat he had kept her away from the place in case she should run into the man, making his intention quite clear to her. This morning, anyway, Armstrong, the Scientific Co-ordinator of Fadledean Research Station, was coming to Redthorn House to discuss certain technical details with her which had to be cleared up from the work she had left behind. Although she knew quite clearly that she would never go back to work there, he guessed that Armstrong would probably make this announcement officially to her at the meeting. Well, she would not be over-concerned. The best thing she could do, anyway, when this was all over would be to go back to George. Retire, if not immediately gracefully, at least with confidence into marriage and let time dull her memories.

When he let himself into the flat, Rimster

found George sitting in the lounge, reading a newspaper and drinking coffee. George showed no surprise at seeing him. He lowered his newspaper and said, 'Who are you?'

'My name's Rimster. I've come to collect Miss Blackwell's letters and a few of her things. You're George Freemantle?'

'Right. The letters are there.' George nodded to the table. 'Including another one from me. I don't suppose you've brought anything from her to me?'

'No.'

'Where is she?'

'I can't tell you that.'

George stood up. 'Can't or won't?'

'Both. But I can give you some advice.'

'I don't want advice. I just want to know where she is so that I can go and talk to her. Today's Monday, a flat day at the works, so I got here at seven and decided to sit it out until someone came. And here you are, though you're not quite the type I expected. I was looking for some army type or a pimple-faced boffin.'

For a moment Rimster said nothing, eyeing this big, amiable man, sizing him up . . . easy-going with people, except in business, and probably very much in love with Jean even though he found himself stepping over the side lines at times.

202

Match-making wasn't in his brief, but he felt that Jean could do far worse. Marry George and have his children, run his house and overlook his occasional excesses of the spirit and flesh, and Fadledean would soon fade from her memory. In bed she had come alive with him, and clearly had with this man — but this was the man who would warm her to life during the day as well. Happy couple, like thousands of others. Lucky George and lucky Jean.

He said, 'My advice to you is to sit tight until she's finished the job she's doing and you'll find that things will work out.'

'Where is she, Mister Messenger Boy?'

'Carrying on with her work — and she's not allowed visitors.'

George shook his head. 'Not good enough. Not for me, anyway. So I'll tell you what I'm going to do. Either you tell me where she is without trouble, or I'll make you tell me. And don't think I'd worry about an assault and battery charge or any damn thing like that. Understood?'

'Perfectly, but I'd advise against it.'

George shrugged his shoulders. 'You're a cool number, aren't you?'

'Just sit down and finish your coffee while I collect a few things.' Rimster began to move across the room.

As he did so, George reached out and grabbed him by the shoulders from the back to spin him round.

Rimster coming round easily, not wanting to do what had to be done, kicked George's feet from under him and pushed him backwards so that he fell sprawling into the armchair.

Rimster said, 'If you get up from that chair before I leave here, I'll have to start being rough.'

For a moment or two George looked up at him, anger working across his face. Then suddenly he smiled and shook his head, saying, 'Funny thing, isn't it, but I had a feeling right from the start that it might happen this way. Okay — I'm not the type who goes bashing his head against a brick wall. You know what happened between Jean and me?'

'Yes, I do.'

'Bloody fool I was, but there it is . . . the old Adam.'

'I wouldn't worry too much about it.'

'You think that, really think that?'

'Yes, I do. Once she's finished this job she's on I'd bet on it. But until then just be content with writing.'

'What's it all about — this Charlie the chimp thing?'

204

Rimster smiled. 'I can't discuss Miss Blackwell's work. But when her present job is finished I can tell you that she will be resigning from Fadledean. And now you can help me.' He took a list from his pocket and handed it to George. 'You know her things better than I do. Just get these packed up into a case while I help myself to a lager from the kitchen.'

George stood up. 'I'll be glad to.'

Standing at the lounge window with his glass of lager, looking over the roof tops, at the tall spire of the cathedral and the distant greenery of the poplars and willows by the river, Rimster was caught by a rare passage of regrets. George was all right and he would get his Jean . . . nice house, children and all the trimmings . . . all the things he would never get because he had never wanted them before and it was far too late now to think about them. And he knew too that he would never sleep with Jean again, not now that he had met George. He had gone to her bed, he saw now, far less from a need for comfort than conventionally — as so often before — because it was a fringe benefit of the job. And she had let him come because . . . well, probably because she was humanly calculating enough to want to even the score with George. Love might make the world go round, but anger and injured pride too often led to a loveless sharing of beds.

George came back with a small suitcase. Handing it to Rimster, he said, 'Give her my love.'

'I will. And in return if the press come poking around you just say she's away on a job. You don't know where.'

'Will do,' said George, and added as Rimster went towards the door, 'And give my love to Charlie as well when you find him.'

★   ★   ★

Charlie at that moment had been in his moving carriage for about ten minutes as the train moved westwards down the line. The truck was empty except for a folded tarpaulin cover in one corner. Standing on this, Charlie could look over the side. At first he had been frightened by the movement of the train, but by now he was becoming used to it and was hooing and waaing to himself gently. The sun was shining from a cloudless sky on the eighth day of his freedom.

After a while Charlie, bored with standing, watching the countryside roll by, squatted down on the tarpaulin. He began to groom himself, his body swaying gently to the movement of the truck. Then finding a tear in the tarpaulin he amused himself by tugging at it until he pulled a piece off. He put it in his mouth and began to suck at it contentedly.

Meanwhile the goods train rolled on, passing through small stations . . . Pewsey, Woodborough, Patney and Chirton Junction and, a little after mid-morning, through Lavington. Two miles beyond Lavington it slowed up and finally halted in a deep cutting where the signals were against it.

When the train jolted to a halt, Charlie was dislodged from his tarpaulin seat. He rolled over lithely and then stood up on the folded canvas and looked over the side. A few yards away on the track side was a small hut and standing outside it were three railway gangers who were working on the line. Charlie swung himself up on to the edge of the side and dropped to the ground.

Seeing the men he ambled towards them, holding on to the piece of torn canvas as he sucked it.

The three men saw him at the moment he jumped from the truck. Without moving they watched him come along the track side.

The head ganger, Bill Springer, a middle-aged man, stocky, hard-bodied and slow to show emotion of any kind, pushed the peak of his cap back, pulled at the end of his nose, and said, 'You see what I see, Ron?'

Ron Squires, a lean, equally phlegmatic type, who was rolling himself a cigarette, said, without interrupting the process, 'Yes, I see what you see, Bill. Come off the train — riding without a ticket and now he's walking up the track without a walking permit. Cheek.'

The third ganger, Tom Burke, a young, long-haired and far from serious or sensible youth said, 'That's a chimpanzee. That's that there Charlie. What do we do?'

Bill with a wink at Ron said, 'What do you suggest, Tom? Hoist him back aboard again?'

'Better ask him first,' said Ron.

'Hey,' said Tom, 'if we caught him we could get our names in the papers.'

'You'll do that one day anyway without catching any chimpanzee,' said Ron.

'Well, one thing's for sure,' said Bill as the goods train began to move off, the couplings banging and rattling as it gathered speed, 'Charlie's not going back aboard.'

Charlie meanwhile came slowly up the track towards the three men. He had no fear of them and from the low serious of pant hoots he gave it could have been that he was glad to see them.

When he reached the men he sat down on his haunches by Ron and, with his great lips pouting, his brown eyes shining, he watched

208

with interest the completion of the rolling of the cigarette.

Bill said, 'Looks like he's dying for a smoke.'

'Chimps don't smoke,' said Tom.

'How do you know what they do when no one's lookin'?'

Charlie, attracted by the smell of tobacco, reached up a long arm towards the cigarette which Ron had finished rolling.

Obligingly Ron gave it to Charlie who promptly crammed it into his mouth and began to chew it.

'Old-fashioned sort,' said Bill. 'Baccy chewer.' He turned and went into the hut and came out with a thick bread-and-cheese sandwich from his lunch pail. He handed it to Charlie who hoo-hooed with pleasure and then stuffed the sandwich into his mouth with the cigarette. The three men watched him. The noise of the departing goods train died away into the distance.

'Seems friendly enough,' said Ron, beginning to roll another cigarette for himself. 'Could be cupboard love, though.'

'What do we do with 'im?' asked Tom.

'You could take him home for a pet,' said Bill. 'Put some clothes on him and nobody would notice the difference between you. You've both got the same hair style even.'

'Same look about the face, too,' said Ron.

'Oh, very funny,' said Tom.

'That's what we aimed to be,' said Bill.

'Poor little bugger,' said Ron. 'Papers said he was off to some place for experiments on 'im. Can't think why. They want some types to experiment on I could give 'em a list of chaps as long as my arm — and not one would ever be missed.'

'We got to report 'im,' said Tom. 'Hey, maybe there's a reward!'

'You'd sell your mother for the price of a beer,' said Bill. 'Still we can't have him hanging around here all day interfering with our work or getting cut up by some express train. So I tell you what, Tom. You walk down the line to the signal box and get them to phone the police.'

'That's over two miles away.'

'Won't take long if you trot. Meanwhile Ron and me will try and get Charlie into the hut and shut him up. Go on — get moving.'

Grumbling, Tom began to move away down the line.

Ron said, 'Wonder what kind of experiment they aim to do on 'im?'

'None of our business.'

'That's the trouble these days — there's too much kickin' around that ain't none of our business. Like all this newclear fishing

— blow the bloody world up one day.'

'Nobody'd miss it. Come on, let's try and get Charlie into the hut.'

Bill went back into the hut and reappeared with another sandwich.

Ron said, 'You won't have any grub left the rate you're going.'

'Don't worry. It's from Tom's pail.'

Bill went up to Charlie and held out the sandwich. When Charlie reached for it he stepped back towards the hut door.

Charlie followed him but when Bill stepped inside, Charlie halted on the threshold.

'He knows what you're up to,' said Ron.

'Get behind him and give him a shove.'

'No thanks. It said on T.V. he's harmless unless interfered with. I'm not the interfering kind. Besides I'm on his side.'

'So am I — but we got a duty to help the authorities.'

'Since when?'

'Since never — but I don't want the poor little bleeder out there when the Cornish express comes slashin' through. Just crowd him a bit from behind.'

Reluctantly, Ron moved up behind Charlie, who turned and, raising his head, drew back his great lips and gave a friendly grin, showing his strong teeth. Then he bent forward and somersaulted slowly past Ron

211

and came to rest in a patch of ragwort at the side of the track path. He lay there contentedly chewing while with the fingers of both hands he slowly scratched his scalp.

Coming out from the hut, Bill said, 'A chimp with a mind of his own.'

'That's right.'

'Well, we tried.'

'That's right — but not too hard.'

'Well, suppose he might as well have Tom's sandwich to go with the other.' Bill walked over to Charlie and held out the sandwich.

Charlie lifted a foot and took the sandwich from him.

'Neat,' said Ron. 'Not a man living could do that.'

Bill walked back to the hut and sat down on the small bench outside it and began to fill a pipe. He said, 'That express is due up in ten minutes. We'll keep an eye on him until it's gone past.'

'And after that there's another one due down in half an hour. Looks like we've got a tiring morning ahead chimp-sitting.'

Ron went to the bench and sat down beside Bill and lit a cigarette.

Charlie lay in the patch of weeds and slowly masticated his wad of sandwiches. The sun was warm on his body and he was feeling sleepy after his restless night. When he had finished eating he began to make low, chattering noises to himself and then fell asleep. Above him flies and bees worked around the ragwort blooms and a robin that nested behind the railway hut came and foraged close to him for the sandwich crumbs which had fallen to the ground.

'Sleepin' like a babe,' said Ron. 'Wonder what he thinks about it all? Half the bloody army after him.'

'They don't think,' said Bill. 'Not like that.'

'I don't know. That's too easy to say. Why I've had some dogs in my time that could think faster and better than . . . than, well, that stupid Tom for instance. I had a dog once — '

'Not again, Ron,' Bill sighed. 'It's too good a morning for any of your dog stories.'

'Well, all I know is I've had some dogs that I've liked and respected better than a lot of men I've known. And I'll tell you something else, something I read a bit about in the paper yesterday about chimps.'

'Yes? Well — if you're going to tell it now you'll have to shout your head off, 'cause here comes the express.'

Ron looked at his watch. 'Three minutes ahead of time.' He stood up and walked over to the sleeping Charlie and stood between him and the track. A few seconds later the express came roaring up the line and went past the group in a thundering surge of sound.

In his light sleep Charlie heard it, woke and was suddenly full of alarm and fright at the noise and the sight of the long line of coaches speeding past. He gave a loud scream of fear, rolled to all fours and began to gallop away from the sight as fast as he could go, calling and waaing wide-mouthed as he had often done when in his earlier days in Africa he had offended some large male and had been chased after in a sudden display of rage from the adult.

He went up the slope of the embankment, jumped the wire fence, crossed a small field where a man on a tractor was cutting the tall grass for hay and then burst his way through a hedge into a large piece of waste ground studded with young osiers which sloped down to a marshy bowl through which a sluggish stream ran to disappear into a tangle of old trees that fringed a series of shallow ponds.

Behind him, as the noise of the express faded, Ron went back to Bill and sat on the bench with him and began to roll a cigarette.

He said, 'Poor little bleeder, he won't stop running for a while. I quite took to him.'

Bill said, 'They'll come and ask us about it.

214

I kinda liked him too. Think we ought to give him a sporting chance when they ask which way he went?'

Ron shook his head. 'Can't do that. Must tell the police which way he went.' He nodded across the railway lines to the opposite embankment to the one which Charlie had taken. 'Just tell 'em the truth. Saw him with me own eyes. Took off that way. We couldn't stop him. Agree?'

'Of course. That's the way he went, swear to it. Anyway, they're goin' to get him some time, but I don't see — if he's enjoying himself, nice weather and all — why we should be on their side against his. Good luck to him, I say.'

Ron nodded.

★   ★   ★

Rimster came out on to the terrace to join Jean in a drink before lunch.

He said, 'When I fetched your stuff this morning George was waiting in the flat. We had a chat. I calmed him down about your not being around. He's a likeable man, I thought.'

'That's his greatest asset. Everyone likes George. That's what he trades on. Has there been any news of Charlie this morning?'

Knowing the subject of George had been dismissed, Rimster said, 'Only the report of the two campers. That means he's shifted north of Collingbourne Wood. The helicopters and patrols have moved up there. How did you get on with Armstrong?'

'We cleared up various things. I told him that I was going to resign as soon as I'm free of this place. He was nice enough not to make the point that if I didn't I would be dismissed . . . retired. The station are fitting up a special truck to put Charlie in when he's caught.'

'What happens to him when he is caught? Will they carry on with the project?'

'Oh yes. They'll have missed a lot of interim facts, but there's plenty of valuable research data to be got after he reaches his infective stage at twenty-one days.'

'How long after that does he stay a carrier?'

'That's one of the points to be checked. From our earlier work we reckoned about a month.'

'Long enough — when a handful of men take Charlie's place to do a real job if needed — to be effective. Nice thought. But how do you know that Charlie won't always remain a carrier?'

'Well, we've established that already on some of the lower primates, lemurs and capuchin monkeys. When I say we, I mean it's been done at other stations. People who get plague, you know, don't all die.'

'And what happens to Charlie when Armstrong and his boffins have finished with him and he's got a clear bill of health?'

'When it's absolutely certain he's clear he'll go to some zoo or wild-life park, here or abroad.'

'Honourable retirement?'

'That's right.'

'Well, if the press and so on work up enough publicity he'll be a draw anywhere.'

Through the open doors of the lounge behind them came an announcement over the Tannoy.

'Mr Rimster to the signals office please. Mr Rimster to the signals office.'

Sitting there, waiting for him to return, Jean realized that, despite her dismissal of the subject, she would really have liked to know all that had passed between Rimster and George. Her feelings about George, she acknowledged, were slowly changing. From the first shock, which had led to Charlie's escape and to the present situation, she had passed through anger into indifference, and now that she had made love with Rimster — partly an act, she knew, of redressing some emotional balance — she found herself able to think of George more easily in the way she had once done. Nice George, blunt, unexpected, full of life and large appetites, but with his own robust and rough kind of loyalty. When Charlie was eventually caught and she left Fadledean behind her she knew that she would be moving into the bleakness of making a new life, and the prospect was unattractive. If she had any sense, she would go back to George. Be practical, admit that she had evened the score, she told herself. That's what human beings were like. Love and marriage had their rough and smooth sides — but happiness and a deep content were the true elements that held people together. Suddenly there was an ache in her for all this Charlie business to be finished. To get up now and be able to go back to George seemed the most sensible and desirable thing in the world for her. Too much pride was a stupidity. She should be glad that George was there, wanting her still. Nobody, she guessed, waited for Rimster. There was no passing shadow like hers over him. He lived in shade and could never escape it. She remembered the thin twist of his mouth when speaking of Charlie he had said, 'Honourable retirement', and she knew that honour was something he had lost long ago. No matter under what authorized human mandate he had operated — as in fact she had been doing at Fadledean — there was a higher conscience in him and all people which had to be acknowledged.

There was no escape from the sentence which in the end you passed on yourself.

Rimster came back and said, smiling, 'Our friend Charlie dropped off a goods train truck on the main Exeter line the other side of a place called Lavington this morning. Two gangers tried to hold him while another went to report. Tried to get him into their hut with the offer of food, but he wasn't having any. He finally took off northwards towards Devizes. The army people are covering the area as fast as they can. He's quite a travelling gent, isn't he? And having the luck of the devil.'

'Devil?'

He shrugged his shoulders. 'Depends on your attitude to theology. My old father used to say that God couldn't get along without the Devil, and vice versa. Now and again I have an idea that they work together. Perhaps God has decided that this country deserves a plague, and the Devil, naturally, is going along with him.'

'Is that what you would like?'

'No. In my book, plague is not selective enough. Still it could happen. I expected him to be put in the bag in a few days. He's been out a week now.'

'And he's due for his second vomiting attack. It will be much more severe than the first and he won't be able to move around much. Somebody's sure to find him.' Jean stood up. 'Shall we go and have lunch?'

'Why not?'

* * *

Three miles north of the main railway line, Captain Stevens brought his helicopter round in a tight curve at the end of his allotted sector and began to make a new line back towards the village of Lavington. Since mid-day somebody had been gingering things up from the operations centre. The roads below were busy with police cars and army trucks, and patrol lines of troops were combing through the area on a two-mile front northwards from the line. If Charlie were anywhere around down there he would be lucky not to be found.

His observer said, 'You think he really took a fancy to that girl in the tent?'

'Dunno and don't care. I'm bored with the whole bloody business. I came down here for an advanced training course. Not for this kind of lark. I'm beginning to think that if they just let the little chap alone he'd wander into some farm or village and would sit tight until the recovery truck turned up. But with troops bashing about below and us buzzing around above he's probably scared stiff and keeping well under cover. Those railway gangers as near as a touch got him.'

The observer was silent for a while, and then said, 'I think there's more to Charlie than meets the eye.'

'Marvellous. Of course there is. But you won't know and I won't know, whatever happens. And what's more we're not expected to know or to ask questions.'

'Other people are beginning to. You know, the press and all that. Fadledean's a rum place.'

'Maybe that's what Charlie thought.'

'You know, I'm on his side really. I don't know but that if I spotted him down below somewhere I wouldn't keep my trap shut. Why shouldn't he have some fun and games?'

'You do that and I'll have your guts for garters. And not because I'm on his side, but because I'm more on my side.'

Coming to the end of their southward leg, Captain Stevens took the helicopter up above patrolling height and began to head back to base for refuelling.

Five minutes later, moving south-east, the helicopter passed directly over Charlie.

Charlie had followed the line of ponds southwards over marshy ground which was rank with high yellow flag growths and sedge and tangled with a sprawl of low willows and old decayed trees which had fallen from age and rot until he had come to the edge of a long, narrow lake at whose head, overhung by a large ash tree, was a boathouse with a narrow landing stage.

Far down the lake a punt was anchored and a man sat in it fishing, his back to Charlie.

Charlie sat down on the landing stage, watching the distant man and enjoying the sunshine. Coots and moorhens foraged and fussed along the line of tall reeds fringing the lake. Dragonflies hunted for gnats. Swallows and martins dipped to the water, making rings which matched those of the rising fish. From the roof of the hut a wren suddenly filled the summer air with brief, sharp song.

After a while, Charlie stood up and went into the boathouse. Along one side ran a narrow shelf on which the punt fisherman had left a small wickerwork basket. Charlie lifted it down and sat holding it between his legs. The lid was closed and held by a small

222

length of cane which ran through loops on its side.

Boxes with lids were nothing new in Charlie's life. He lifted the box and shook it and something moved inside. Hooing and grunting to himself, he smelt the basket and recognized a familiar and exciting smell. Holding it between his legs again, he tried to open the lid and when it refused to move he struck it sharply two or three times with his right hand. Then, seeing the holding piece of cane, he began to fiddle with it. Door handles he had long learned could be turned to open a door and he had once had a box with a spring clasp which had to be pressed to release the lid. In a very short while he had pulled the cane free from its loops and had the basket top open.

Inside were a packet of sandwiches, a paper bag which held two bananas and an apple, and a bottle whose top was corked. Charlie ate the bananas and the apple and one of the sandwiches. Picking up the bottle, he shook it once or twice and then pulled the cork free with his teeth. Bottles, too, he had dealt with before. He raised the bottle, which held a cheap white wine, and poured some into his mouth. Almost at once, not relishing the taste, he spat the wine out and threw the bottle through the open boathouse door, chattering quietly to himself.

An hour later when the fisherman, who had been having good sport, came back for a late lunch, Charlie was half-a-mile away, lying full length on his stomach along a stout branch almost at the top of a tall elm in a spinney at the foot of a long rising sweep of bare downland. He lay there watching the traffic moving along the broad curve of a stretch of main road that climbed the downland a quarter of a mile away, the sunlight flashing on windscreens as the cars and trucks turned into the beginning of the curve.

Charlie lay there all the afternoon, disinclined to move and aware of a slow growth of uneasiness in his body.

Now and again he whimpered, and once, when he pulled himself leaves to make a wad in his mouth, he held it only briefly and then spat it out.

Towards evening his head began to ache and a thirst grew in him so strongly that he finally climbed listlessly down the tree and set out in search of drink.

He found it in a water tank at the back of a small cattle shed in a field that lay alongside the road. The water came from the roof guttering and the tank was still half full from the past week's storm. Charlie leaned over the edge of the tank and drank his fill.

Feeling better, he moved across the field and climbed up on to the hedge which bordered the road. The hedge was an old one made of beech which had been layered years before and now was thick with new growth. Charlie pushed his way through it and then sat in a tall patch of hogweed and thistles that fringed a small lay-by. It was seven o'clock and broad daylight, but the traffic along the road had thinned. The few cars that passed came fast around the bend and none of the drivers or passengers saw Charlie, whose dark coat merged into the shadow cast by the hedge.

Feeling more at ease, but disinclined still to move much, Charlie lay back among the weeds and watched the traffic. Ten minutes later, Harry Swinton came slowly round the bend and, seeing the lay-by, pulled into it.

Harry Swinton was a commercial traveller who worked for a Southampton firm of sweet and chocolate manufacturers. He was a middle-aged man, short and far too much overweight from lack of exercise and an over-fondness for food and drink. Not being a family man he felt that what he did with his own body was nobody else's concern and, since he was a jolly and a kindly man as well as a fat one and loved a joke and good company, he was well liked in the trade and very successful. At this particular moment he was recovering very slowly from the effects of a heavy lunch with plenty to drink with one customer and also the cumulative effect of an hour's drinking that evening with another customer. The years had taught him just how much he could drink with safety and still drive, a criterion strictly his own and not likely to be recognized by the police.

He switched off the motor of his station wagon, unclipped his safety belt for comfort, and leaned over and opened the passenger door to admit more air into the car. Fresh air, though it was still damned hot with the day's heat, Harry boy, he told himself, and half an hour's shut-eye would do him the world of good.

He eased himself back in his seat comfortably, lit a cigarette which he did not want, took two or three puffs and then threw it out of the window and shut his eyes. A good day, Harry, he mused. A damned good day. Nice fat order book, good company along the way, maybe just a few more drinks than usual over the odds, but what the hell? If you didn't drink with them when they wanted to it showed up in the orders they gave. There was, the Lord be praised, no nagging or anxious wife waiting at home. Not that he was against women, and many barmaids' eyes lit up when he bounced into a pub and, now and again, lit up even brighter when he bounced into bed with them. No regular attachments, though. Not for you, Harry boy. A canary and a cat in his flat and a landlady to look after them while he was away were all he wanted in the way of company for the short hours he was at home. Pity about kids, of course — but then you couldn't have everything, and anyway, Harry lad, you've got plenty of nephews and nieces to spoil. So what . . . so what? Snoring gently, he drifted into sleep.

As he slept, cars now and then passed along the road but the people in them had no chance to see Charlie because he was shielded by the bulk of Harry's car, which was standing only a few yards from where he lay.

Not feeling well, Charlie was disinclined to move. He sat with his long arms wrapped around his legs and his chin resting on the top of his knees and watched Harry's cigarette slowly burn itself away on the gravel of the lay-by. A squirrel came out of the hedge, tail arched, ran to the lay-by waste bin and climbed it to forage for food scraps. Beyond the road on the down slope a colony of rooks began to return to their roosts in some tall trees, cawing and wheeling. From somewhere in the distance came the drone of a helicopter and once an army truck came up around the bend, carrying soldiers who had been out looking for Charlie. A few moments later, a wood pigeon flew from the field to the top of the beech hedge and, seeing Charlie, flighted away across the road.

As the bird disappeared, Charlie eased himself forward on to all fours and went slowly across to the open door of the station wagon. Harry was snoring loudly.

Charlie hesitated for a moment and then climbed up on to the empty seat alongside him. Harry stirred and muttered something in his sleep. Charlie replied with a soft and friendly pant-hoot. Then he reached out and rummaged with one hand in the shelf of the facia board in front of him. Lying on it were road maps, a packet of cigarettes, a crumpled paperback book and a few bars and packets of Harry's confectionery wares. Harry seldom ate his own wares, although he could extol them with convincing fervour and sincerity. He kept the sweets there to give away.

Charlie took a crimson-wrapped bar, smelt it, and then slowly began to tear away the paper wrapping. A few seconds later he was munching on a round length of milk chocolate studded with chopped walnuts. Charlie ate half of it and reached again to the shelf. Within the next five minutes, Charlie, without any real hunger, but unable to resist the feast although he was not his normal self, sampled four of Harry's most popular lines. The last of them was a bag of soft-centred boiled sweets of different flavours, and it was as Charlie was listlessly sucking one of these, his big lips pouted, that Harry woke up.

And Harry woke as he always woke from his short naps. Fifteen minutes or half an hour was enough to bring him awake, alert and unfogged by any residual sleep. Though this time, because of his good day, he still retained a slight suggestion of a headache but not enough to impair his usual good humour and aplomb. He grunted, opened his eyes, and pulled himself upright in his seat.

At the movement, Charlie turned to him, hoo-hooed softly through pouted lips and touched him on the arm.

Harry turned his head and saw Charlie. The fading euphoria of past drink still mellow in him, he showed no surprise. It took a lot to surprise Harry and a lot to frighten him, and his reaction to the unusual was usually humorous and quick-witted. He knew all about Charlie. The shops and public houses he had covered that day had been full of talk about the Fadledean chimpanzee.

After a moment or two, he said, 'Well,

Charlie, old boy, nice to see you.' Then, seeing the scattered wrappings and half-eaten chocolate and sweets, he went on, 'Sampling the wares, eh? Well, nothing like trying the goods before you buy.'

Charlie, who could sense friendliness in humans, hoo-hooed a little louder and beat gently with one hand on the shelf in front of him.

'What's that mean?' asked Harry. 'You want to get moving? And so you should. You stay loafing around here and some stupid bastard will run you over as you cross the road. But you don't have to worry. Harry'll look after you — though Harry didn't mind admitting that right at this moment you're a bit of a surprise number. Have to think you out.' He reached for his cigarettes and lit one.

As he did so Charlie gave a quick grunt and reached for the packet. Harry pulled out another cigarette and gave it to him. 'Shouldn't use 'em at your age, but if that's what you want.'

As Charlie put the cigarette into his mouth and began to chew on it, Harry got out of the car without hurry, closed his door and walked around the car and closed Charlie's door. Back in the car, he gave Charlie a grin and fastened his seat belt, thinking to himself, Harry boy, you've had a few odd turn-ups in your mis-spent life but this is the oddest and, Harry, you can't say it's unwelcome. Seems a nice friendly chap and what a story . . . Oh, yes, Harry, what a story for customers and friends — and the publicity! Here he comes, Harry the big white hunter, doing what half the bloody army and air force couldn't do. Every customer will want to hear that one — and that should push up sales. Still, only problem is — will Charlie boy sit there and be good while I drive him?

Without hurry he switched on the engine and let it idle for a while. Charlie appeared unconcerned. Have to watch him when I start, thought Harry. If he starts jumping about frightened I'll have to stop, slip out and flag a car for help. Whatever happens I'm not letting this one go. Harry Swinton rides into town with Charlie the most wanted chimpanzee in the country. They'll have me on telly and in the papers. Tough on the little fellow though. Back into the cage. Still, let's face it, we all live in cages of some kind or other. Well, here I go.

He put the car into gear and began to move slowly off. Charlie drew his lips back tight, grimaced and called softly *waa-waa-waa*. But he made no attempt to move.

'That's a good chap,' said Harry. 'And don't worry, we'll take it easy. Have you in

Salisbury under the hour.'

Harry moved out on to the road and began to go easily up the curve. Charlie squatted on his haunches on the seat and held the front of the dashboard shelf with one hand. In his time, Charlie had driven in enough trucks and cars not to have any fear of them. In addition, his slowly rising feeling of unease probably made him unwilling to take any action unless it were forced on him.

So with Charlie sitting quietly beside him, Harry began the drive to Salisbury — which was on his route back to Southampton. He drove carefully, chiefly not to disturb Charlie and also partly because the effects of the day's business drinking were still with him. And as he drove he chatted gently to Charlie, fancying that his talk would help to keep the animal calm.

Talking to Charlie was no strain because Harry in his long hours on the road had years ago developed the habit of talking aloud to himself. Some of his best ideas had come to him while driving and talking. Within ten minutes of leaving the lay-by one of the best ideas Harry had ever had came to him.

Consolingly, he said, 'You got to look at it like this, Charlie boy. While in principle I'm all in favour of freedom, for everybody and every damn thing . . . well, freedom's got its dangers for the likes of you . . . Oh, yes it has. It's all right in the good old summer time, easy pickings in every garden and warm days and nights. But what about when winter comes? Thought of that yet?'

Charlie suddenly belched loudly.

'Pardon?' said Harry. 'Well, perhaps you're right. But think about me. Do me a lot of good taking you in will. Things are keen in my business, you know. Cut-throat. Anything that gives you an edge must be considered, and I've already considered it. Put it up to the boss as soon as I get back. We'll put out a new line . . . let's say *The Charlie Bar*. Milk or plain chocolate with a nut-and-cream filling. Nice wrapper with a jungle background and your beautiful old face stuck right in the middle. I tell you, Charlie — it can't miss. Not with all the free publicity to go with ours. The old man will wet his pants with excitement and yours truly will get his in the form of a damn big pay rise . . . Oh. Charlie boy, I can see happy days ahead — '

At this moment Charlie gave an anguished grunt, gaped his mouth wide, and was violently and heavily sick. The vomit spurted across Harry's lap, distracting his attention from driving.

The car swerved to the left and, before Harry could correct it, Charlie was sick again and began to swing his arms about wildly. One hand accidentally caught Harry heavily across the face making him lose control of the wheel. His car slewed off the road, bounced across the sun-baked grass verge and the front hit the bordering hedge with a crash. Harry's seat belt saved him from going through the windscreen, but the impact of the crash made the door on Charlie's side fly open.

Before Harry could do anything — though he was capable of little — Charlie gave a loud scream of fright and jumped out of the car. Screaming he ran up the grass verge, swerved across the road and disappeared down a narrow footpath which ran alongside a plantation of young spruce trees.

Very slowly Harry freed himself from his seat belt, got out of the car and examined it. It was damaged but not too badly. He stood there shaken, his jacket and trousers covered in vomit. Then bracing himself together he took a series of deep breaths and, since he was a quick-witted man, rapidly assessed his personal position.

It was the firm's car. The firm did not like its cars knocked about — especially by travellers who might have been drinking too much. Though you tell me, Harry asked himself, how you can do business without being sociable? But there it was, good-bye to the *Charlie Bar* available with five different fillings.

A car turned the far corner and as it came towards him he stepped into the road and began to flag it down, rehearsing his story . . . *Bloody motor cyclist came down like a bat out of hell on his wrong side. Forced me over . . . Could have killed me . . . Look at the state I'm in — shook the guts out of me with fright.* Yes, that was it. And no mention of Charlie. That would only lead to more trouble, and trouble enough, Harry boy, you've already got plenty of. Nobody — least of all his boss who knew how he liked his drop — was going to believe any story about giving a chimpanzee a lift.

The approaching car drew up, and Harry Swinton braced himself staunchly to begin his story.

9

On the morning of the ninth day of Charlie's freedom the publicity about him began to build up rapidly. All the papers carried the story of his supposed attack on the two campers and most of them had also the story of his dropping off a goods train and the attempt of the gangers to detain him, all with photographs and personal interviews with the people concerned. It was a good story for the press because Charlie was a sympathetic character, the public immediately siding with him against authority, and delighted that he had evaded capture for so long. There was editorial comment, some of it humorous and some of it serious. Why, it was asked, was such a large operation being mounted to capture him and get him to Fadledean? What was going to happen to him when he got there? Was there a possibility that the authorities might be being less than frank and that Charlie had really escaped *from* Fadledean? One paper carried a popular article by a well-known ethologist on chimpanzees, and two others had articles discussing Fadledean and the ethics of using animals for experimental purposes. On radio the disc jockeys made jokes and puns, and there was an interview with a Fellow of the Royal Zoological Society outlining the biological similarities between men and the higher primates, and two manufacturing firms began to put in train the production of Charlie sweat shirts with a grinning chimpanzee face on the front.

The correspondence columns of most papers carried readers' letters — astutely held over from the first news of Charlie's escape — which echoed the editorial comments and the public feeling.

It was commented that no further statement had been available from the Ministry of Defence about Charlie's role when he should eventually be taken to Fadledean and that calls to Fadledean had been met with a refusal to discuss Charlie. A Liberal Member of Parliament, prominent in his support for the Royal Society for the Prevention of Cruelty to Animals, announced that he was putting down a question in the House of Commons and would be satisfied with nothing less than a personal answer from the Minister of Defence.

Spurious or mistaken sightings of Charlie

began to come in on the Charliephone at Salisbury and to other surrounding police stations. The noble owners of two wild life parks announced that they were only too willing to buy Charlie from the government to save him from going to Fadledean.

There was mad comment and glad comment, humorous and wise and crank comment on the air, in print and on television. Charlie had arrived as a national figure.

Captain Stevens, reading his morning newspaper at breakfast, pursed his lips cynically at the thought of all the fads, cranks, and genuinely concerned people who would jump on the Charlie bandwagon.

Rimster and Jean reading, too, at breakfast knew that no editor was going to let the story die while Charlie remained free, and Harry Swinton, setting out on his day's round in a borrowed car, switched off the radio news in disgust as he savoured the bitterness of the loss of publicity to his firm and the fading vision of the Charlie Bar in different flavours.

Grandison, in an early-morning interview with the Minister of Defence, eventually got him to agree to press the Prime Minister hard for an official statement to be made that, while Charlie was harmless, unless frightened or cornered, there had been, unfortunately,

some official confusion over the first statement covering Charlie's escape. He had
broken loose from Fadledean, not while being
transported there.

'You've got to cover yourself on that point,
Minister, as I've said all along. The papers
and the media will ride it hard for a day or so
and then it will be accepted. Once you've got
that, you're on solid ground if Charlie should
ever look like going the limit.' For a moment
or two he was tempted to go further and say
to the Minister that if the government refused
to do this, then he should back up his
insistence to the point of stating that he
would resign otherwise. He decided against it
because by now he was pretty sure that the
statement he wanted would be made. He
went on, 'Also, I think you should settle a
date by which — if Charlie by some miracle is
still free — the first of a series of warning
announcements should begin.'

'How can he possibly stay free up to
anywhere near that point? With all this
publicity he's got to be spotted and caught.
Damn it, he's not loose in some great jungle
— this is England.'

Grandison, tempted to indulge himself in
the comment that England, too, was a jungle
of a kind, said, 'Because it doesn't need a
miracle now to keep him free. Just consider it

this way — religion, politics and a love of animals produce more fanatics in this country than anything else. In any body of dedicated people there's always some who go over the limit. Somebody may pick Charlie up and keep him hidden, thinking they are saving him from a fate worse than death. That's why right from the start the truth should have been told, that Charlie's a potential plague or, at least, a serious disease carrier. There'd have been a terrific outcry — but, by God, you'd have had the public on your side and against Charlie. High principles, cocking a snook at authority, fanaticism would be forgotten. Not a soul in this country would risk plague on Charlie's behalf.'

In the House of Commons late that afternoon, a junior minister for the Ministry of Defence made an announcement that unfortunately, owing to an administrative misunderstanding, it had been stated that Charlie had escaped while on his way to Fadledean whereas, in fact, it now transpired that he had escaped from Fadledean where he had been the subject of a routine series of studies in animal behaviour.

Every press agency, every news editor of newspaper, radio and television knew then that the Charlie story was not just a summer gift from the gods to wither in a few days.

Charlie was hard news, a rich vein that could be mined, perhaps, even after he was recaptured, and knew also that it was far too late for any government interference to hamper them in their duty to the public, their papers' circulations or their audience ratings.

★   ★   ★

When Charlie woke that morning it was raining softly and steadily. After leaving Harry Swinton he had wandered along the smooth flank of a long line of down-land feeling ill and occasionally attacked by bouts of shivering until he had come to a large, horseshoe-shaped chalk cutting which bit back into the slope of the hill. Chalk had long ceased to be taken from the cutting and along its top curve had grown up a tall standing of beech trees.

Thick thorn growths matted the sides of the great pit and between them grew a thin covering of rabbit-bitten grass, bright now with flowering scabious, milkwort and yellow bedstraw. The floor of the quarry was littered with abandoned junk, old prams, bicycles, derelict motor cars, broken boxes, rusty cans, twisted sheets of corrugated iron, piles of builders' plaster, brick and stone clearings, old sacks, old clothes, all the sad and sorry and ugly cast-offs of careless mankind which, as it crumbled, rotted and rusted away, was being slowly mantled by a tall growth of hog-weed, nettles, thistles, burdock and wild mallow.

His head aching, whimpering to himself in his distress, Charlie had, with the last light, clambered into the body of an old saloon car and curled up on the ripped leather of the back seat. He had shivered and complained his way through a night of constantly broken sleep and two more attacks of vomiting.

Waking, he found his throat and mouth dry and the need for drink urgent in him. He clambered weakly out of the car, drank from a scum-covered pool in a choked ditch just outside the quarry, and then sat in the rain. Listlessly with his fingers he combed and groomed at his pelt but soon gave up and wandered back into the quarry. His natural instinct, ill though he was, for cleanliness and dry bedding took him away from the car in which he had passed the night to find another. He finally bedded down in the body of a wrecked van which held a litter of old newspapers and paper sacks which were dry. He slept on and off, shivering but no longer vomiting, chattering and moaning to himself in his sleep as well as his waking periods. He lay there all day, undisturbed, while the soft rain moved away to the east and left the skies clear. Then at night, with the new moon passing now into the thinnest nail-paring of its quarter, Charlie left the van, still far from well, but moved by the stir of a faintly reviving hunger.

He worked his way weakly up the side of the cutting, pulling at the hawthorn leaves to make a wad on which he chewed without relish. Under the row of beech trees at the top of the quarry he found a growth of puff-balls and one or two wrinkle-topped morel fungi and ate them. Then, crossing the crest of the down, he found in a field bordering a small road a crop of cabbages. He squatted among them and ate for a while without appetite.

He crossed the small road after midnight and, climbing through a gap in the broken-down wall which had once been the boundary of a large estate, moved downhill through rough pasture land to find himself in the bed of a twisting valley through which ran a small stream. He drank his fill and, beginning to feel better, waded across the shallow stream and curled up in a patch of tall new bracken on the far side. Two hundred yards down the valley, the stream flowed into a small lake, its surface plated with water-lily growths, its verges flanked by tall banks of meadowsweet, mace reed and yellow irises.

Looking down over the lake and separated from it by a rough sloping lawn was a large, red-brick Tudor house, called Deanfinch Hall, the family home of the holders of the once large estate through whose broken wall Charlie had scrambled, and the home of a member of that ancient family — Lady Cynthia Chickley, who now occupied one wing of the large, rambling mansion.

At eight o'clock, Lady Cynthia was having breakfast in the morning room, whose mullioned windows looked down across the rough stretch of lawn to the lake. The lawn was rough and starred with flowers not because Lady Cynthia was so hard up that she could not afford a gardener. She had plenty of money, far more than she needed, in fact, but she hated trim, barbered lawns and she acclaimed the beauty of flowering weeds with the same delight as she did the splendours of the blooms at the Chelsea Flower Show.

Except for the Deanfinch walled fruit and vegetable garden, the rest of the nine-acre estate had been allowed to grow more or less naturally into a path-cut wilderness of rhododendron thickets and copses of specimen and wild trees. No more than a little light pruning and the removal of dead or fallen trees and shrubs was ever done. In the lake at the foot of the lawn, twenty-pound mirror carp and great golden orfe would come to her hand to be fed. She loved cats for their individuality and self-reliance and kept six of different breeds. But she would tolerate no dogs on the estate, considering them to be sycophants and disturbers of the peace.

She was a charitable, far from gullible, unmarried lady in her late forties, who spoke her mind and had no fear of defending her principles with vigorous action. She had been in love once, when she was thirty, but her fiancé, a titled barrister of great promise, had slipped to his death while climbing in Switzerland. She was a tall, rawboned woman with straight, pale straw-coloured hair, soft grey eyes and a long, plain face with a slightly hooked and prominent nose. The clothes she wore tended to be plain, durable and many years out of fashion. She liked good plain food which was provided by her good, plain and elderly cook, kept a good cellar, had a knowledge and appreciation of wines and port which had come to her from her noble father, and she drank her whisky straight and enjoyed a good cigar or cheroot.

Finishing her breakfast, she poured herself another cup of coffee, lit a cheroot and went on reading the *Daily Telegraph*.

After a while, her cook, Mrs Paget, came

into the room. Lady Cynthia had three servants, Mrs Paget and her husband, Tom Paget, the gardener, and also Lily Harkness, a quiet, efficient widow of fifty, childless, who had been at Deanfinch Hall for fifteen years. All these were devoted to Lady Cynthia and lived on the estate, the Pagets in their cottage close to the drive entrance and Lily in her own rooms at the top of the occupied wing.

Mrs Paget, a round-faced, plump woman of sixty said, 'If you please, me lady, Paget says could he have a word with you?'

'Of course. Tell him to come in.'

A few moments later Paget came in, a hard-bodied, round-shouldered, elderly man who, like all good gardeners, never hurried, never got flustered and matched his rhythms to those of nature.

'What's the trouble, Paget?' asked Lady Cynthia.

'Well, ma'am, I don't rightly know as it's trouble, but there's a kind of monkey thing in the walled garden.'

'Monkey thing?'

'Yes, ma'am.'

'I see. Well let's go and have a look at it.'

Lady Cynthia walked down through the shrubberies to the high-walled garden. The iron-barred gate of the arched entrance was closed.

'When I saw 'im in there, ma'am, I shut the gate and come right up to you.'

Lady Cynthia opened the gate and went into the garden which Paget kept immaculately, sublimating here the instinct for order and neatness denied him in the rest of the garden. Each plot was edged with low, neatly trimmed box edging, the dark soil showed no weeds.

Charlie was sitting in the middle of a strawberry bed next to a large netted section under which grew raspberries and gooseberries. He had eaten his fill of strawberries and sat now sucking at a length of corn stalk which he had taken from the straw layering which Paget had put around the fruit plants. Although he looked bedraggled and unkempt, he was feeling much better and recovering fast.

Seeing Lady Cynthia coming towards him he raised his head, thrust out his chin and gave a few friendly pant-hoots. Charlie liked company. Slowly he rose to his feet and waddled upright across the bed to Lady Cynthia.

Lady Cynthia knew all about Charlie. She had followed the first news of his escape with interest and, only a few minutes before, had been reading the latest information about him in the *Daily Telegraph*. She knew a great

247

deal, too, about places like Fadledean and had little tolerance for such establishments.

As Charlie came up to her, she bent and reached out a hand to him and said gently, 'Well, Charlie — fancy you coming here.'

Charlie, sensing her friendliness, took her hand in his as he had often done with Jean Blackwell and many of his other keepers, and drawing back his lips gave a soft *waa-waa-waa*.

'He seems friendly enough, ma'am,' said Paget.

'Of course he is. After all we are distantly related.'

Lady Cynthia turned and began to walk back towards the gate and Charlie, holding her hand, went with her.

Paget, following behind, knowing that even after all his years of service with Lady Cynthia he could never be sure what she might or might not do, said, 'What's to be done about him, ma'am?'

'That's a good question, Paget, and I'll have to think about it. But for the moment he's our guest and must be treated as such. He looks as though he's spent a few rough nights out.'

'Papers were full of him this morning, ma'am. I suppose we ought really to let someone know.'

Over her shoulder, and a little flattered at the friendly way in which Charlie seemed to have taken to her, walking along at her side chattering happily to himself, Lady Cynthia said, 'It's much too early to start supposing anything, Paget. For the time being we'll put him in the old billiard room.'

Half an hour later Charlie was installed in the old billiard room in an unused wing of Deanfinch Hall. The room, an Edwardian addition to the house, had been built originally as a conservatory projecting from the side of the wing into a small, yew-hedged garden and had later been converted into a billiard room, leaving only the glass roof intact. The place now held only broken furniture and packing cases and a miscellany of the odds and ends of household junk which had accumulated in a family with a reluctance to throw things away which might at some time or other come in useful.

Paget brought in two bales of straw and broke them open to cover the floor and make a bedding place for Charlie. A large tin bowl was found for water and an old feeding trough for food.

While Paget prepared the place, Lady Cynthia brought Charlie fruit to eat and when he had taken some of it, she squatted alongside him and, talking quietly to him, she gave him a good grooming with an old hairbrush, a service for which Charlie showed his appreciation by chattering and calling, beating his hands together and occasionally rolling away from her to do a quick somersault before returning for more brushing.

When she had finished she sent Paget to the kitchen to get a bowl of warm milk, saying, 'Tell your wife to put a few drops of her cooking brandy in it.'

Coming back with the bowl, Paget said, 'Well, me lady, he certainly looks a different chap from what he did a little while ago. Seems to have a nice nature, too.' Then, as he watched Lady Cynthia hand the bowl to Charlie, who took it and drank, pausing now and then to grin at her, his lips rimmed with a white beard of milk, Paget — who after years of service could read his mistress's mind sometimes faster than she could make it up — said reflectively, 'Course, if he was going to be staying a while, I could clear this place out and rig it up proper. Hang a few climbing ropes from the roof beams and get in a few bits of old dead tree like for him to scramble about on. That's if he was going to be here any time.'

Lady Cynthia, watching Charlie who was now moving around in a tight circle in his loose straw to make a bed, smiled to herself and said, 'I don't know that we could do that, Paget. He's government property.'

'So he might be, ma'am. But he wasn't anybody's property but his own when whoever it was pinched him out of his jungle. So I think he's — '

'Paget . . . ' Lady Cynthia shook her head at him. 'So you think he's nobody's chimpanzee but his own?'

'In a way, yes.'

'Well, I'll think about it. In the meantime I'd like you to stop trying to make up my mind for me.'

'Yes, me lady.'

When Charlie had settled down and showed signs of going to sleep, Lady Cynthia went to the drawing-room, poured herself a large glass of dry sherry, lit a thin cheroot, and settled down to think about Charlie. God, she thought, in Whom she believed but with Whom she had only an irregular nodding acquaintance in any formal way through the offices of the Church, would instruct her in her proper duty. But first He would expect her to try and sort things out for herself before He made any clear sign. So while she smoked and sipped her sherry she considered the case of Charlie.

Outside, while she considered, Adonis blue

and large white butterflies moved across the rough lawn, a spotted flycatcher that nested in the thick virginia creeper tangle that grew up the face of the house made darting, hovering forays to take flies for its young, the mirror face of the far lake was shattered by the sudden leaping of a shoal of young dace as a pike chased them, and the kitchen tabby cat moved up the gravel path carrying a young rabbit in its mouth.

Birth, life and death, thought Lady Cynthia, the lot of all God's creatures. But of all God's creatures only man had developed the habit of imprisoning his own kind and the rest of God's kind. Maybe, she thought, this was what God intended should happen. Well, if he did, then it was up to Him to tell her so because she couldn't believe that he really approved of places like Fadledean and the way — if all the stories were true, and why would there be smoke without fire? — they used animals and had used or intended to use Charlie. She gave the matter a great deal of thought and had another glass of sherry and another cheroot. Then with her own mind quite firm decided to refer the judgment to a higher authority.

From the walnut bureau at the side of the window she fetched a well-thumbed pack of cards which she had used many times before for the same purpose. She shuffled the pack well and then began to deal the cards out before her face upwards.

If God wanted her to save Charlie from Fadledean all He had to do was to see that a red ace turned up before a black one.

And it did. The ace of hearts.

Ten minutes later she stood in the kitchen addressing her staff who, knowing her so well, and having already discussed the matter between themselves, were not surprised when she told them that she was going to keep Charlie until she had decided the right thing to do with him to make sure that he never went back to Fadledean. Until then they were to tell no one that he was at Deanfinch Hall, and if there should be any subsequent trouble about this she would accept full responsibility.

Each of them readily gave their word.

After she was gone, Paget said, 'I could have told you this would happen the moment Charlie took her hand and began to trot alongside her.'

Mrs Paget said, 'She should have married — no matter the first upset — and had children.'

Lily, whose mind often worked obliquely, said, 'You don't always have children even when married — and not from want of trying because if anyone was a real trier, my dear old Fred was. Nothing wrong with either of us, too, the doctor said.'

Mr and Mrs Paget said nothing. They had had three children and they had all emigrated to Australia which, they often felt, was the same as not having children.

Meanwhile in the morning-room Lady Cynthia was speaking over the telephone to Horace Simbath in his London flat. On the telephone her voice — particularly when she spoke to Horace — tended to become a shade imperious and commanding.

'Horace,' she said, 'I would like you to come down as soon as you can to discuss a very important matter with me . . . No, I can't discuss it over the telephone, but I can say that it is something which will be very much to your advantage. When can you come? . . . Tomorrow — that's good. And drive carefully. No daydreaming.'

★ ★ ★

That night, before going to bed, Jean sat at the small table before her open bedroom window and re-read the letter from George which Rimster had brought her the day before. The night was still, the air warm and heavily scented with the perfume from a bed

254

of stocks which grew along the inner edge of the terrace below. Now and again a little owl screeched down by the river and once a falling star scored a slash of pastel blue and gold across the pale midsummer sky.

George wrote as George spoke and, re-reading the letter, she was conscious of the feeling that he was here in this room . . . bluff, cheerful, earthy George with all his faults and all his robust affection and enthusiasm. Compared with George, Rimster was a ghost. Although nothing had been said between them she had guessed that he would not come again to make love to her. That had been as transient as the shooting star, a brief flare and burning up of desire born from impulses on both sides of little value and certainly no virtue.

She decided to write to George and have the letter sent down by the daily courier the next day. That Rimster might insist on reading it was unimportant.

She wrote:

Darling George —
Not that I particularly think you deserve the 'Darling'. Still, since I have now got over my anger with you it would be ungenerous of me to withhold it. Oh, Lord, I don't seem to be writing at all the kind of

letter I meant. It's all coming out so bloody stiff and prim which is perhaps a bit what I am. But I know you will read between the lines.

All I want to say is, please don't fuss and worry about me. I really have been put in purdah over — you must have long guessed — this Charlie business. But as soon as I can I will be back and we can sort things out. So be patient.

Love,
Jean.

Having written it, she was dissatisfied with it and for a moment was tempted to tear it up. Then she thought, Oh, what the hell. The letter was, in a way, how she was, and George was how he was, and it would have to do. And George, she knew, would make do with it because George, ever the optimist and catcher of stray gleams of hope, would read between the lines and be content. Please God, she thought, let Charlie be caught soon so that she could go to George and really find herself and a life which didn't give her bad dreams at night.

And Rimster, in his room, put down the telephone after talking to Grandison, fixed himself a large whisky and sat drinking and smoking, realizing that he was getting bored with this Charlie business, bored to death with it because there was nothing for him to do except drive around the countryside with Jean Blackwell, imagining that the thousand-to-one chance might come up that they would spot Charlie and he could reach for the car microphone and make the call that would set him free from this job. But, he mused, only free from this bloody job . . . merely, some time or other, to be shuffled off into another job equally unfulfilling. He had come to the end of the road — no longer finely honed, no longer able to sustain the high pitch of cruel efficiency and frozen feeling which were demanded of his kind. He had seen it happen to others, and now it had happened to him. When it happened to footballers, and athletes . . . aye, and music hall comedians . . . they retired, took a pub, and risked growing fat and boring everyone with tales of their past glory. Even that was denied him . . . no enthralling his cronies with the tales of the past twenty years of high-level murder, brutality and callousness, a life — the echo from some past reading beat into his mind — *simpliciter sanguinarius atrox*. Where the devil did that come from? What did it matter? Where did he come from anyway? Not from a high-perched limestone Yorkshire rectory with decent God-fearing

257

parents, surely? Somewhere along the line some stupid nurse must have slipped a changeling into the cradle.

Suddenly angry with himself, he said aloud, 'Oh, for Christ's sake, shut up.' He poured himself another whisky.

And Charlie, lying back comfortably on his bed of straw, well-fed and content, but not feeling sleepy, slowly rose to all fours and began to amble round his quarters in the pale light that came through the glass roof from the strengthening moon in the early stages of its first quarter. He found an old tennis ball and, throwing it from him and seeing it bounce, was soon happily engaged in playing with it, bouncing and throwing it and chasing after it. When he got bored with this, he took the ball back to his straw and sat chewing at its cover until he had torn it to pieces.

As he sat there, a distant church clock struck midnight. Charlie's eleventh day of freedom — Thursday, the first of July — had begun.

10

Lady Cynthia's warning to Horace Simbath not to daydream while he was driving was very justified, for Mr Simbath, without his dreams — all of them optimistic — would have been a very unhappy man.

Driving now on his way to Deanfinch Hall, his mind was flighting wildly into the future. Mr Simbath, a man of fifty, a man who dressed impeccably — thanks to a long-suffering tailor — in sober, slightly old-fashioned cut clothes, was a round, roly-poly of a man, short, and with a habit of walking with his toes turned outwards. His dark hair was needle-pointed with grey, his eyes dark and seldom still because he was always apprehensive of missing some golden opportunity, and his smile was amiable and always on show. He was a rogue, but a kindly one and, indeed, had moments of mild conscience when he genuinely grieved at the gullibility and vanity of the general public.

In his time he had failed at many enterprises, but had succeeded in enough to keep his optimism buoyant. It was through vanity that he had met Lady Cynthia, while he had been running a small publishing firm which specialized in inviting the public with poetic ambitions to submit their verse which he published — at their expense. The world was full of unsung and unpublished and unpublishable poets. Mr Simbath had done his best to redress this unhappy state — at a gratifying profit to himself. He had produced a slim volume of verse by Lady Cynthia — which privately he thought awful. But it had been the start, first of a correspondence and then an odd friendship which had equally oddly endured beyond the life of his publishing firm, beyond the realization by Lady Cynthia that her stuff was rubbish, to grow into something like affection on Lady Cynthia's side and love — with financial overtones quietly and privately nursed — on Mr Simbath's. He was tired of dreaming up new ventures — presently he was running a one-man mail order business in high-class art books specializing in the erotic temple sculptures of the East — and longed genuinely for marriage and the comfort of a wife who could substantially provide for him.

This morning, his hopes were high as he remembered Lady Cynthia's words that she wanted to discuss with him a very important matter which could not be trusted to the telephone. He knew Lady Cynthia well enough by now to realize that — although he had made his feelings obliquely felt — any proposal of marriage would come from her — probably quite baldly and out of the blue.

A remarkable woman, he mused to himself as he drove. Mildly eccentric, of course, but then so was he. Not good looking, but then the pleasures of the flesh meant little to him, companionship and a true communion of spirit, backed by a freedom from money cares, were all. No trouble with the staff at Deanfinch, either. They liked him. Bloody great ruin of a place, of course. And the gardens were terrible, but still, once he had the rights and cares of a husband, he could quietly begin to alter things. Dear Cynthia was not as strong-minded and inflexible as she imagined she was. Somewhere in the heart of her must lurk, as lurk it did in all women — no matter all this tommy-rot about liberation — the need to be cherished, loved and managed.

So, driving, he day-dreamed, but cautiously, over the joys of marriage, a minor squirearchy and the bliss of perhaps one day being able to look his bank manager fairly in the eyes without a single qualm. But don't build too high too soon, Horace, my dear chap, he told himself. She may only want you to help her compose some scatty letter to the

261

press about some hare-brained cause she's just espoused. Espoused. He smiled. It was a good word. Espousal, betrothal . . . and do you, Horace Macintyre Simbath, take this . . . He whistled gently to himself.

He arrived at Deanfinch Hall an hour before lunch, was greeted with a chaste kiss from Lady Cynthia and a glass of sherry, and ten minutes of unrevealing and every-day chat. Not for him to make the first move towards the heart of the matter, he warned himself.

When their sherry was finished Lady Cynthia stood up, tall, and possessed, he could sense, with some inner excitement, and dressed in a loose blue-and-purple smock that almost reached her ankles and reminded him of a bedspread in the past which had covered his parents' bed.

'Horace, my dear,' announced Lady Cynthia, 'I want you to come with me and see something. And I want you to promise not to say anything until we come back here again. Oh, and you'd better have this, too.'

From a bowl on the table she handed him a banana, which Mr Simbath took, smiling doubtfully.

A few moments later he was led into the old billiard room which that morning Lady Cynthia and Tom Paget had converted into more amenable quarters for Charlie. Two thick ropes, knotted at intervals, hung from the roof rafters. A long length of dead beech tree had been fixed so that it ran from the floor to half-way up one of the walls. Much of the old rubbish had been removed from the place and the floor was strewn with straw and sawdust. Five or six packing cases had been arranged to make an open pen in one corner of the room to serve as sleeping quarters for Charlie.

When they entered, Charlie was sitting low down on the dead tree length. Seeing Lady Cynthia he raised his head and gave a series of friendly pant-hoots.

Lady Cynthia went to him and gently scratched the top of his head and Charlie, enjoying the grooming, dropped from the tree and, while she still scratched him, buried his face in the loose folds of her smock and began to suck at the material.

Over her shoulder Lady Cynthia said, 'Come and be introduced, Horace.'

Horace, banana in hand, hesitated for a moment. Animals were not his strong point. Cats and dogs he could just take, but horses, cattle, anything of a larger and less amenable nature he avoided whenever possible. And as he hesitated, the day-dreams of his drive down evaporated a little, but not entirely.

Cynthia could, as most women, be oblique and devious in arriving at some wished-for position or desire. Knowing what was expected of him, he played his part obligingly.

He walked over to Charlie and held out the banana. Charlie took it quickly, chattered with a moment's excitement and reached out and pulled at the smartly creased run of Mr Simbath's dove-grey trousers.

'He's thanking you, Horace. In fact — isn't that good? — I can see he's taken to you.'

Mr Simbath, keeping to his oath of silence with difficulty, smoothing his trouser leg, said nothing, but thought — For God's sake, a hairy great monkey . . . Well, well, you never knew with Cynthia. Take a deep breath and keep your aplomb.

Charlie climbed back on the tree and began to eat the banana.

Lady Cynthia turned and took Horace by the arm, leading him towards the door. She said warmly, 'That's what I like about you Horace, my dear. What I know I can always depend on from you — an unshakeable calm no matter what the circumstances. That's your great, but not only gift.'

Horace gave her a little bow of his head, patted her hand on his arm, and felt the warmth of hope return to his heart. She wanted something from him . . . there would be time enough for the quid pro quos and the gratitude, no doubt.

As Lady Cynthia closed the door of the billiard room, Horace noticed that a good strong hasp and padlock had been fitted to it. And — knowing the billiard room's usual state and the way it had now been more or less cleared — he realized that the new inmate was not to be a temporary guest. What, in God's name, was his beloved Cynthia, his bright hope for the future, up to now?

Back in the large sitting room which commanded a view over the tangle of shrubberies and trees westwards, Lady Cynthia poured two glasses of sherry and lit a cheroot for herself. Horace, who never smoked himself, wondered if in time it might be a habit he could break in her, and then dismissed the thought as trivial in the present circumstances.

With a large, big-teethed smile, Lady Cynthia said, 'Well, Horace, I must say you took it well. And without a word. You really are a treasure of a dear man. Of course, you know who he is?'

Horace, whose day would have been out of joint without a newspaper to read at breakfast, said, 'I do indeed, my dear. The much-wanted Charlie.'

'The poor, innocent harmless creature, raped from his native forest, caged for life and, as we know, vilely used by places like Fadledean. One of God's creatures tortured and manipulated by Man for the most, I am sure, ignoble of purposes. Doesn't that make your blood boil?'

'It does indeed, my dear Cynthia,' said Horace without strict truth but with great conviction.

'I knew it would. And that's why I called for you, a man whom I respect and trust and for whom I have, not only the greatest fondness, but in whom I have the most absolute faith. Now, tell me, what are we going to do with him?'

Horace would have liked to say that they should inform the authorities about Charlie right away, but he knew what was expected of him, and what was to his advantage, and he guessed too, that Cynthia had long by now got some wild idea or half-formed plan of her own.

He said easily, 'I'm sure, my dear, you must have given that a lot of thought already . . . a woman of your warmth of heart and deep love of all God's creatures. Ah, Cynthia, more than any other man I know the way your mind and your generous heart move. So — since you know without me telling you

— that in any resolve, out of my deep affection and regard for you you can always command my support, I suggest you reveal what it is in your mind to do and we can discuss it sensibly and consider all the practicalities.'

'Well, Horace, that's really the trouble. Lots of things have occurred to me. But the problem is to decide which one would have the maximum effect.'

'The maximum effect in what way?'

'Why, to raise public opinion and outcry against places like Fadledean and, of course, to make sure that he never goes back to the horrible place.'

For a moment Horace was silent. He had not quite expected such a dramatic suggestion.

Then, seeking for thinking room, he asked, 'You think something like that can be done?'

Vigorously, Lady Cynthia said, 'I don't think. I know it must and will be done. You've seen the papers. There's enough public sympathy for Charlie in this country to save him from Fadledean — a great reservoir of it. The only problem is how to harness and control that force and make it work successfully. Horace, my love . . . ' she smiled at him warmly, ' . . . that is why I immediately called for you. You understand the press and

267

the media, as they call it, and the way they all work. I want you to devise a scheme.'

Horace sipped at his sherry, glad that the motion partly covered the smile about his lips. Never before had she called him 'my love'. My angel, my pet, my dear, yes. But not my love. Rosy visions and a rising heartbeat temporarily put him off his stroke.

'Well now, um, that's a . . . well a . . . quite a nice little matter of, shall we say, tactics.'

'Naturally, Horace — and you're the man for it. I could think of no one else. The maximum effect and the maximum publicity.'

'Um, well, let me think.' Absently he reached for the sherry decanter and helped himself, a thing he had never done before and one which, he noted, dear Cynthia accepted clearly, he hoped, as a well-deserved new privilege. It was true, of course, that he knew the ways of the press and the media. He had worked on a provincial newspaper in his callow youth and some years ago had managed the publicity for a pop group which had been highly profitable for well over a year until certain little transactions of mild peculation on his part had come to light. But, yes, he knew the press and the media and, what was more, he was aware of Charlie's potential. If he handled things right for Cynthia surely the wedding bells would ring?

'You don't,' said Lady Cynthia, 'have to settle anything right away. There's plenty of time. And let me say, Horace, and I hope you won't take offence, that I don't expect you to do this just out of affection and friendship for me. I shall pay you generously. And, what's more, you must stay here as long as you wish until we have the whole campaign worked out.'

'Well . . . yes, well.' Things were running a bit fast for him but Horace forced himself to push aside his rosy dreams and appear serious and concerned. 'What I suggest is that after lunch you give me an hour or so on my own and I'll prepare a programme for discussion.'

'Excellent!' Lady Cynthia rose, bent over him and kissed him on his broad, bland brow. 'You are a dear man . . . the dearest. I never cease to be thankful that I wrote that dreadful poetry and so came to meet you.'

Horace Simbath blushed, which was something he had not done for over thirty years.

After lunch he went up to his room and sat down at the small desk in the window overlooking the front of the house and began to work on the Charlie problem. He worked efficiently, with complete dedication and with shrewd intelligence and sustaining happiness.

It was just like one of the many times when he had decided to pull out of a failing venture and to plan another.

When he had finished he was confident that Cynthia would accept the plan. He knew her well and her love of the dramatic combined with noble impulses. In some ways, he could admit to himself, they were different sides of the same coin.

Then as he looked out of the window he was surprised to see Cynthia walking across the rough lawn with Charlie lolloping around her playfully. My God, he thought, what a woman! Was she mad? Any kind of larking around outside like that must stop or his whole plan would be ruined!

For a moment he was tempted to open the window and shout down to her, but quickly decided against it. If the gods smiled, then one day he would be master in this house, but until then he must tread softly and talk sweetly. Love in its early stages was a tender plant, to bring it to full bloom was the craft of a master gardener. Mr Simbath's emotional thoughts often still reflected echoes of the bad vanity verse which he had once so profitably published for people.

★ ★ ★

At dinner that night Rimster said to Jean, 'Grandison is coming down tomorrow.'

'Grandison?'

'My master.'

'Oh, yes. Why is he coming?'

'Because he's worried.' Rimster smiled. 'He didn't say so, of course. But I know him well enough to tell that he is. He has a sixth sense which warns him of trouble no matter how distant it is. Like some people can tell two or three days ahead that rain is coming. Charlie's been out eleven days — that's just over the halfway mark. Would you ever have thought that possible?'

'No, I wouldn't.'

'Nor would I. But Grandison would. That's why he's where he is and does what he does. He has a gift for sensing the arbitrary stir of the Fates. You know . . . the rare moment when they get bored and decide to stir things up a little.'

'Do you believe in Fate . . . I mean a direct, positive interference in human affairs?'

'Yes, I do. I have to. Otherwise how could I have been and be what I am.' He grinned. 'But, of course, they don't muck around with everyone. They just pick someone now and then to experiment with. Like your Fadledean crowd picked Charlie. Could have been any other of dozens of chimpanzees. But they fingered him as the one, the prototype of the plague carrier.' Suddenly, his voice full of quiet force, he added, 'What if Charlie stays out over the limit and this country has an outbreak of plague? People dying . . . children, babes, going down like flies?'

Angrily, Jean said, 'What are you trying to do? Why talk like that?'

Shrugging his shoulders, casual again, he said, 'I'm not sure — unless it's to point out that we . . . you and I, Armstrong, Boyson, all the Fadledean gang and similar gangs in other countries are brothers and sisters under the skin. Murderers, actual or potential — the sin's the same. Only the weapons vary, sword, gun or bacillus.'

Jean stood up and without a word walked from the dining room.

Watching her go he felt no shame or comfort, no release or pity. He had spoken, without thought, unable to control himself. And he knew that in doing so he was justifying Grandison's sending him here, confirming in himself what others who had worked with him for years had known long before him. He was past it, over the hill, his poise and control seized now by the shakes without warning like the hands of a heavy drinker. Well, he had to accept it. This was his last job. All he had to worry about now were the terms and the mode of his retirement. That Jean Blackwell was probably up in her room having a good cry left him untouched. The terms and mode of her retirement would be generous and progressively more placid. Her letter to George, which he had censored, made that clear.

★ ★ ★

Mellowed with a good dinner and now a little flushed over coffee and then port, Horace Simbath was in an expansive mood, a state which always made him a little pompous. Additionally, he was well pleased with himself and the way things were going and — he was sure — would go.

Lady Cynthia had accepted his plan for Charlie. She had been so pleased with it that, impulsively, she had put her long arms around him, giving him a brisk hug and a quick peck of a kiss on his brow.

They sat now in the late evening dusk in a small arbour at the end of the terrace which overlooked lawn and lake. The smoke from Lady Cynthia's cigar — she only smoked cheroots during the day — drifted in a slow, listless trail in the almost still, warm air. A silver tray of liqueurs rested on a small cane table between them. Dusty-winged moths moved clumsily over the flowers of the tangle of clematis growth which covered the arbour and a hatch of golden-eyed lace-winged flies danced in a cloud above the rough lawn grasses, harried now and then by the forays of bats. The moon shadows were beginning to darken and a faint mist was rising from the surface of the lake.

Horace said smoothly, 'The essence of good publicity — particularly in a case like Charlie's where he has already attracted a great deal — is suddenly to cut off all hard news. That is to say, to create, my dear Cynthia, a vacuum in which speculation, rumour and suspense will breed. This we can do easily by holding him here without anyone knowing about it. No more sightings for days on end. Where's Charlie? What's happened to Charlie? The press won't be able to resist the challenge of solving that mystery. That's stage one.'

He reached for the Drambuie and poured himself another glass.

Already he was feeling his way towards the pleasing liberties and prerogatives of his new status.

'And how long should that go on, Horace?'

'Well, I would say right up to the point where the press show signs of dropping the story. From my experience I would say that

274

might be six or seven days.'

'And then, we do as you suggest?'

'Quite. We revive the press and public interest with a bang. I've been thinking more about that. I think we should take a photograph of Charlie — against a suitably anonymous background — holding a newspaper so that its date shows clearly. Charlie is alive and well, in good hands, reading a copy of *The Times*. You, of course, will have to write the statement of your intentions so far as Charlie is concerned, but anonymously naturally.'

'Indeed I will. And I know exactly what to say.'

'Of that I am sure, my dear Cynthia.' Though, Horace thought to himself, he would do a little discreet sub-editing because, good-hearted and well-intentioned as she was, dear Cynthia was inclined to ramble when it came to composition. 'We'll send the photograph and statement anonymously to a press agency. What a scoop for them! And then — hey presto — the publicity will all start up again with renewed force. Animal lovers and every humanitarian organization and society in the land adjured to stand up and demand freedom from Fadledean for Charlie. And they will . . . '

Oh, they would, Horace knew, because all

such organizations, despite their worthiness and complete sincerity, welcomed any publicity which pulled in new members and donations. The Save Charlie Fund. There, too, was sure to be some noble lord or high churchman who would eagerly offer himself as President, with luck even some minor royalty. In the gloom he smiled to himself at the rich future which loomed before him. He, Horace Simbath, would be known to have masterminded the whole campaign. A national figure. And then, a little later, the announcement of the forthcoming marriage of Lady Cynthia Chickley and Mr Horace Simbath.

Lady Cynthia's voice called him back from his contemplation of paradise.

'And for the final move, Horace, my love? Have you thought further about that?'

'Indeed, yes. Two days later, say, another photograph and the announcement that, on such and such a date, all interested parties, organizations and the general public are invited to a great rally in, say, Hyde Park — or perhaps better still, because of its zoological connections, Regent's Park — where Charlie will be produced. Thousands of people, demanding Charlie's freedom, cheering him and you. The police, the government authorities, will be powerless and bow before the storm.'

Excited, seeing herself in the role, standing on a platform holding Charlie's hand, Lady Cynthia found herself near to tears.

'It's wonderful, Horace! Wonderful! Brilliant! I knew that I could rely on you. What a treasure of a man you are.' She reached out and held his hand in the gloaming.

Indeed, indeed, thought Horace, a treasure of a man, and a man with the doors of a treasure house already slowly swinging open before him. He sipped his Drambuie and then said very seriously, 'But Cynthia, my dear' — not yet did he feel it the moment to say, my love — 'this whole thing will fail unless Charlie is kept strictly incommunicado. No more walking him around the garden. He must stay in the billiard room until the great day comes. After all — if we are to work for his freedom it is no cruelty to keep him confined until that moment comes.'

'You're quite right, Horace,' said Lady Cynthia meekly. 'Now tell me — how long do you think all this will take?'

'Well . . .' Horace paused, not to consider the time factors, but to relish the meekness she had just displayed. She was coming to hand nicely. In a crisis she had turned to him and he was not going to fail her. Gratitude and admiration were the outriders of love, of the chariot of matrimony. His tailor would be paid and all the others. No more schemes to milk the gullible public. *Do not miss this unique opportunity* — how often had he used that phrase in scores of advertisements? Well, here was his unique opportunity coming up and he was certainly not going to miss it.

He said, 'I should say about five days to the first press release, perhaps two more before the second with the announcement of the great rally, and then the rally itself — we must give people time to get organized — in another three. Now, let's see — where would that take us?'

'Up to . . . ' Lady Cynthia began to tick off the days silently on her fingers . . . 'up to Sunday, the 11th of July. Is Sunday a good day for a rally?'

'The best, my dear. People are free. We shall get the maximum attendance. Couldn't be better.'

★   ★   ★

The eleventh of July would be the day, since his vomiting attacks had run true to course, that Charlie would be fully infective.

Charlie at that moment was sleeping in his packingcase quarters buried deep in clean straw, nursing to himself an old tennis racket

278

with broken strings which he had found.

He was snoring a little and, now and then in his sleep, he scratched himself to ease the biting attacks of the fleas he had picked up on his travels.

A barn owl, perched on top of the glass roof under which had long ago been stretched a safety layer of stout wire netting to hold any glass breakage, looked down through the webbing of mesh at Charlie, holding in its beak a long-tailed field mouse which it had taken in the rhododendron shrubberies. After a moment or two the bird spread wide, silent wings and drifted through the summer air high across the lawn, over the walled garden and came to rest on the tall, turreted tower of the seldom-used private chapel of the Chickley family.

Slowly it began to tear at the body of the mouse and finally swallowed it.

The red glow of a cigar end caught the bird's eyes. Swivelling its head it watched Horace Simbath and Lady Cynthia move out of the arbour and walk slowly along the terrace. Horace had his arm through Lady Cynthia's and the sound of their voices drifted across the night.

★　★　★

For two days press, radio and television had played the Charlie story hard. Charlie was well established as a national figure and a very popular one . . . far more than he would have been had he merely escaped from a zoo or a wild life park because everyone realized that he was an embarrassment to the Government, and that there was more to Charlie than met the eye. No one believed that the first communiqué saying he had escaped on the way to Fadledean had been a departmental mistake.

On the morning of his twelfth day of freedom when there had been no sighting or news of him, the press radio and television proceeded to demonstrate that even no news was good news. Where was Charlie? What had happened to Charlie? Perhaps he had been quietly captured and was already back at Fadledean. Perhaps some hasty gamekeeper had shot him in some covert and his body lay there waiting for vermin and birds to pick it clean.

By this time, too, the correspondence columns of the papers were drawing their full weight of indignant letters from individuals, societies and institutions — indignation evoked not always by humane feelings and a righteous readiness to champion the cause of conservation, preservation or abhorrence of the improper use of any animal for scientific purposes but with a sharp eye on publicity, personal, or for their particular organizations. Even at the best of times Man's noblest emotions were not entirely purified by the sharp fires of humane protest.

When Grandison came down to Redthorn House that morning he was in a dour, far from loquacious mood. Taking Rimster and Jean Blackwell with him he went to the operations centre. By the Colonel in charge he was given a detailed description of all the search moves which had been made so far, and copies of all the statements made by people who had actually seen or met Charlie. He made no comment on them, which Rimster knew — though other people did not — was more to be feared than any suggestions or criticisms. He examined the special van which had been provided by Fadledean, the protective clothing and masks, and the two rifles which were specially adapted for firing the nembutal darts to immobilize Charlie when they found him.

Driving away from the operations centre to go to Fadledean to see Armstrong he said to Rimster, 'At close quarters a rifle could be clumsy or even useless. I'll have two long-barrelled pistols sent down this after-noon.'

At Fadledean he grilled Armstrong with a sharp politeness. He asked him, 'Assuming everything is progressing as you planned with Charlie he will become infective on what day?'

'At the earliest on the nineteenth day, that's Friday the ninth of July.'

'At what time?'

'I don't know.'

'And the latest day?'

'The twenty-first, that's Sunday the eleventh.'

'If he's not infective by then does it mean he never will be, that the process has gone wrong?'

'I don't know, but the odds — '

'I'm not interested in the odds. You don't know?'

'That's correct.'

'Once he's a carrier how long does he remain one?'

'Between thirty to thirty-five days.'

'And you can make tests which will establish without doubt when he is clear?'

'Yes.'

'All right. Now suppose he's lying dead, shot or killed by some accident in a wood right now — would he be a danger at this moment?'

'No.'

'So if a rat or a fox had a go at his body they wouldn't become eventually infective?'

'No.'

'Say he dies or is killed any time on the nineteenth, twentieth or twenty-first day and rat, fox or crow got at him or his fleas hop away and find another host — do they become infective?'

'Yes.'

'For how long would his body be virulent?'

Armstrong hesitated and then with a little shrug of his broad shoulders, said, 'I don't know, but ultimately — '

'I'm not interested in the ultimate. You don't know.'

'No, I don't know.'

With sudden, surprising mildness Grandison, putting his monocle into place, said, 'In your position I can assure you that it would have been something I would have wanted to know before going to the starting post. Anyway, that's all. Thank you for your co-operation.'

When Grandison had gone and Armstrong was alone, although it was only three o'clock in the afternoon, he went to his cupboard and poured himself a large whisky. It was the first time he had ever met Grandison and he sincerely hoped that it would be the last.

Before Grandison left Redthorn House,

alone with Rimster he said, 'When they find Charlie — no matter where it is — I've left orders that you are to go in and do the job. I don't want any damned stupid waving of bananas or cajoling. You take the pistol and knock him out. Everyone else down here may be behaving like a bunch of bloody amateurs but I want the job finished professionally.'

'Yes, sir.'

Grandison smiled. 'In the meantime, enjoy the country air. You're looking well on it. Better than I've seen you for a long time.'

Not knowing what prompted it, except that it was there suddenly in him and nothing could stop it coming out, Rimster said, 'When this job is over, I don't want to come back. I want to pack it all in. I'm eligible for retirement.'

Grandison stroked the silk cord of his dangling monocle for a moment or two, then nodded, and said gently. 'I think that's wise. Your record is one of the best. Just get this Charlie thing wrapped up and we'll go into it.'

Going back into the house, Rimster thought, *Your record is one of the best.* By God, it was — and putting it down must have made the recording angel's hand shake from time to time.

Seeing Jean sitting on the terrace he went

out to her and said, 'I'm sorry for slashing out at you as I did last night. It was unforgivable. I hope you can overlook it so that we can have a drink together and then dinner?'

She looked at him for a moment or two, then smiled and nodded her head, saying, 'There's nothing to forgive. It was the truth.'

★   ★   ★

That evening Horace Simbath drove back to London in a state of steady euphoria. He would be returning to Deanfinch Hall in two days' time to take photographs of Charlie for the press. In his time Mr Simbath had been an amateur of many things, including photography. It would be no problem for him to set up a dark room in his flat where he could develop and print his film. The whole campaign lay clear in his mind and he could see no problems.

But more than the Charlie campaign he was concerned with the Lady Cynthia campaign. At one time his biggest hope had been that he might talk her into making a loan — repayable, of course, at a good rate of interest — for one of his ventures. But before he had reached the point of making any move in this direction the idea had blossomed in his mind of marriage. Marriage, in a sense, was the biggest loan she could possibly make him, and there would be no interest, hypothetical or otherwise, to pay.

Daydreaming as he drove, he began to go over the various little improvements he would make at Deanfinch when they were married. It would, at first, be a question of going softly softly, and always of choosing the right moment. Dear Cynthia, as he had learnt early on, could — if approached wrongly — be not only arrogant, intolerant, and stubborn, but also bloody bad-tempered. At the moment the biggest problem which exercised his mind was the right moment to pick for making his declaration of love. If he waited until the whole Charlie campaign had been carried out and she had become a public figure he realized that he might easily lose her. Publicity, as he knew only too well, did strange things to the ego. She might be off on lecture tours, in demand at meetings, find herself surrounded by new friends — and well-heeled ones at that — and he could be hard put to claim her attention in the intimate surroundings needed to suit his proposal. No, he decided, the best way was to set all the Charlie publicity going and, once it snowballed, to lay bare his soul and love for her before the mass meeting.

Leave it beyond that peak and, he knew, he

might find himself wallowing in the trough of that very high wave whose crest she would be riding.

He began to whistle gently to himself as he drove through the dusk along the motorway . . . seeing himself as master of Deanfinch, its rough acres and well-stocked cellars. Would he ever, he wondered, be able to break her of the habit of smoking cheroots and cigars? Detestable habit, smoking. But still, no marriage was absolutely perfect. A man could learn to forgive and endure for the sake of love. And to think that it had all started when she had sent him a crumby poem about a nightingale . . . *Swart bird of sable night something something all delight. Song that fills the heart with love while the something moon hangs high above.* Lambent moon, that was it.

At that moment in the billiard room, unlit except for the light from the thin sliver of moon above which shone through the glass roof, Lady Cynthia, sitting on an old milking stool by Charlie's pen, was saying goodnight to him.

Handing him an onion, which she had discovered was a favourite food, she said. 'No more Fadledean for you, Charlie. Horace and I are going to see to that. But you mustn't mind if we have to keep you shut up in here for a few days.'

Charlie, well fed, tapped the top of his head with the onion and, pouting his great lips, breathed soft pant-hoots at her as he walked around her, upright, swinging his shoulders from side to side. Then he reached out and fingered the long string of china beads she was wearing and gave them a tug.

'You like them? Then you shall have them.' Lady Cynthia unclasped the beads and Charlie walked into his pen, swinging the beads and chattering to himself. He sat down and began to eat his onion.

Lady Cynthia lit herself a cheroot and sat watching him and her thoughts drifted away. She saw herself standing, holding Charlie by the hand, with a great crowd, all Charlie lovers, spread before her, a crowd which she would sway, captivate and compel with an impassioned speech. In her time she had championed, but only in a minor way, many causes. But this time it would be a cause which she would lead . . . her cause to which in the full blaze of publicity she could give herself wholeheartedly. When dear Horace came down next she must talk to him about the speech. He had a way with words which, she could confess, she lacked. He would write the speech for her. What an angel man Horace was. Dear Horace . . . a true friend indeed.

11

On Saturday, the third of July — Charlie's thirteenth day of freedom — the papers were still keeping his story alive. On that day, too, there were no valid reports of any sightings. But there were plenty of calls on the Charliephone at Salisbury and the men on duty realized at once that the nature of the calls had changed. Flippancy and flights of imagination were few, but abuse and indignation had grown.

'Why don't you let the little bleeder alone and get on with your proper job? What about hooliganism and all this bloody thieving and it not being safe for a man to take his wife out for a quiet drink without some drunk causing trouble?'

'I would just like to say that I consider all the time and money being spent on this search for an innocent animal is a wicked waste. Thousands of pounds being squandered by the army and the police which could be put to a far better use like, for instance, better housing and more police patrols around where they are really needed.'

'No, I haven't seen him, and if I had I

wouldn't be telling you. All I want to say is that instead of carrying out experiments on animals why not use Members of Parliament of all parties? They'd never be missed. Try grafting another head on the Prime Minister — though even with two he'd still be half-witted.'

'Why use Charlie for experiments? Our comprehensive school system is turning out hundreds of chimpanzees every year. Use some of them. They'd never be missed even from their own homes.'

And quite a lot of them — anonymous telephone calls being a convenient release for the libido of many — were frankly blasphemous.

Captain Stevens, piloting his helicopter that morning, was in a light-hearted mood. Charlie had been out thirteen days now, and he had drawn the fourteenth day for his capture in the sweepstake. If he spotted him now it would be a great temptation to say nothing, though it would mean cutting his observer in on some of the money. Whoever the man was who had come down from the Ministry he must have distributed a few rockets. His superior officers were all now barking and bullying around giving a great display of efficiency. Flight plans and ground patrols had all been reorganized, and the search area now covered a circle with a radius of twenty miles centred on Salisbury. All the new plan meant was that men were thinner on the ground and the flight schedules made longer so that you got bored sooner than before and almost forgot what you were looking for as you went off into some daydream . . . Saturday night tonight, and thank God he was going off duty until Monday. Saturday night and Sunday, a sleeping-out pass and all the delights of amorous dalliance. Lovely phrase. Wonder where Charlie would be sleeping tonight? He knew where he would.

A few seconds later he passed over Deanfinch Hall. Damn great place, he thought, going to rack and ruin. He watched a pair of swans, wings beating, feet churning the water, take off heavily from the surface of the long lake below. On the far side of the house a small saloon car was moving up the driveway, hidden at times by the overhanging foliage of the trees which lined it. Shabby old car, shabby old house, he thought. The landed aristocracy were hard put to it these days to keep going. Sic transit gloria mundi. Nothing more certain than death and taxes.

Driving the saloon car was Horace Simbath who had left London early that morning. A few minutes later he walked in unannounced and unexpected by Lady Cynthia who was having her mid-morning coffee and cheroot and reading the *Daily Telegraph* announcements of forthcoming marriages.

Seeing him a frown creased her high forehead momentarily. 'Horace — what are you doing here?'

Horace beamed. 'Don't worry, my dear Cynthia. Nothing's gone wrong, and nothing will. But when I woke early this morning I had an idea. I realized that if I had to come all the way down here to photograph Charlie and then go all the way back to London to develop and print the film it would take up a lot of time. And timing is important. Now tomorrow's Sunday — so I can take a photograph first thing of Charlie with a Sunday paper and have the prints off to a press agency the same day.'

'How can you? There no postal collection on Sundays.'

Her voice was a little sharp. She felt that Horace was taking a little too much for granted in making arrangements which concerned her and her household without consulting her first.

'Oh, I know that, dear Cynthia. I shall motor to Oxford, ring the agency and tell them that the prints are being put on a train. Don't worry, I've already checked that there is a train. That means — with luck — we shall catch the Monday papers. I've brought all my dark room stuff. All I need is a little attic to work in.'

'Well, that's no problem. There are dozens to choose from. And then you'll go back to London from Oxford, I imagine.'

Horace hesitated for a moment. He had sensed and indeed had expected that she would be a little unsettled by his unexpected arrival, but it was a risk he had decided to take because he saw it as a small test of the bond between them.

Shaking his head gently, he said, 'No, my dear Cynthia. And I do beg of you to be patient with me while I explain. I have given this matter great thought because I know how much its success means to you. If I don't have to go back to London between photographs it means that we can send off four or five over the days instead of just two or three — and that means we build up bigger publicity. Don't you agree?'

'Well . . . ' Lady Cynthia prodded the cold skin which had formed on the top of her coffee with a spoon. 'Well . . . yes, yes, I suppose I do.'

'I knew you would. I just knew it. The more we feed the press the better. And besides, my dear, it might happen that circumstances could arise when you really needed me — say, for instance, Charlie got out and was loose around the house? Or you had some new idea you wanted to discuss. We can't trust the telephone, you know. Not these days. Just one crossed line and somebody overhearing our talk . . . Oh, dear, can you imagine? I really do think that I should be here with you to give you all the help and advice I can. Remember, you conceived this brilliant idea of the mass rally for a great cause. It would break my heart if anything went wrong. I should blame myself bitterly for not having seen that we should be together in order to maintain security and secrecy. My respect and affection for you and my appreciation of the nobility of feeling which prompted this desire in you to have Charlie know no bounds . . .'

He stood, his eyes on her, warm with admiration, and knew that his sudden impulse had been right, that he must have a positive sign of real hope from her. All his life he had been inclined to rush things and regret it, but with Cynthia the circumstances were different. He didn't want to get involved in this Charlie business unless it would give him what he wanted. He waited now anxiously for her reaction. It came slowly.

Letting the coffee spoon drop into her cup,

Lady Cynthia slowly stubbed out her cheroot in the saucer and rose. She came to him, her long face solemn, framed in the lank fall of her pale hair. Taller than he was by far, she slowly stooped a little, raised her hands and placed them on his cheeks and then kissed him, briefly and dryly on the lips.

She said, smiling happily, 'Horace, my dear, darling Horace, you are absolutely right. Absolutely. In this thing we must be together, close together. One heart, one mind and one resolve. You were absolutely right to come. You have a kind and generous heart, but more than that you are a man of initiative and understanding. Bless you, my dear.'

For a moment Horace thought she was going to kiss him again, but she contented herself with giving him a slight caress on the cheek with one hand and then went back to the table to help herself to another cheroot.

Horace, as he went outside to unpack his dark room paraphernalia, trod on clouds. By God, he had taken a risk, impulsively, daring all, win or lose, and it had paid off. He was as good as permanently installed at Deanfinch Hall. Touch and go it had seemed for a while, but it had come right for him. Faint heart never won fair lady. Nothing venture, nothing win, and a tip of the hat for bouncy old Charlie who, bored with having syringes stuck into him at Fadledean, had wisely scarpered and made it all possible. In return he really would do a good job on the photographs. At last life was going to give him a real reward for all the years of bad luck and failed ventures ... Horace Simbath, Esquire, Deanfinch Hall, Deanfinch, Wilts.

★　★　★

On Monday morning all the papers carried the press agency photographs of Charlie and the story was given new vigour and even wider coverage.

Jean read the story in her paper over breakfast. There were two photographs of Charlie. One showed him squatting on a pile of straw, the background taken up by the side of a packing case. There was a big, happy grin all over his great face and he was holding — though upside down — a copy of a Sunday newspaper with its front page well displayed. The second one had Charlie standing, holding the paper so that it covered the lower part of his body like a pinafore with the back and front page spread wide He had his head raised, looking towards the camera, and his big lips were drawn back over his teeth, his mouth wide open as though he was roaring with laughter. In the body of the printed story was also a blown-up facsimile of a note which had accompanied the photographs.

Printed in ill-formed capitals, it read:

DEAR PEOPLE — THIS IS TO SHOW YOU THAT I AM ALIVE AND HAPPY AND STAYING WITH GOOD FRIENDS WHO FEED ME WELL AND SAY THAT IF I AM GOOD I WONT EVER HAVE TO GO BACK TO THAT HORRIBLE FADLEDEAN PLACE. I WILL WRITE AND SEND SOME MORE PHOTOS SOON. LOVE CHARLIE.

As she finished reading the story, Rimster came in and joined her at the table.

She said, 'You've seen the paper?'

'Yes. And I've just had a call from Grandison. The agency had a phone call yesterday afternoon from a man. He told them what he was sending and asked them to have a man collect it at Paddington Station from an Oxford train. The guard had all the stuff and handed it over. He said it was given to him, with a substantial tip, by a well-dressed, plump shortish man with a moustache and a little goatee beard. He couldn't remember much else about him. Is there any doubt that it is Charlie?'

Jean shook her head. 'None.' She pointed to the picture on the front page. 'You can see the big nick in Charlie's left ear clearly. What does it all mean?'

'Well, first of all that someone's got Charlie. Grandison has people working on that already. There may be prints on the writing paper or on the photographs from developing and printing. They'll get anything they can from the guard, but my guess is that the beard and moustache were probably false.'

'And whoever's got him is against giving him up to go back to Fadledean?'

'Sure. This publicity is just the beginning.' He frowned. 'But the real problem — and they can't know it — is that they could hold him too long for their own safety. Today's the fifth of July — by the ninth he could just possibly be infective. That's in five days' time, counting today. What's your reaction to that?'

'That it mustn't be allowed to happen. There's only one way to stop him, isn't there? The truth.'

Rimster pursed his lips and shook his head. 'They won't do that yet. Not from what Grandison told me. Shove it out over radio and television and in the press that all this time Charlie has been developing into a potential plague carrier ... that that's what the Fadledean studies in animal behaviour really were? There's not a politician or government official who would put a light to that fuse until the very last moment.'

'Then why not name some other disease or fever he may be incubating. There are plenty that wouldn't scare people as plague would, but it would make them turn Charlie over.'

'Just as bad. If it were something not too serious like that, why haven't the public already been told? There'd be a big back-lash just the same. The animal lovers and all the fringe organizations now would be up in arms against the use of Charlie. I tell you, politicians and government officials are scared stiff of any kind of half-truth about him. The Opposition in Parliament would have a field day. People would be quick now to realize that the half-truth was only hiding a real truth, a dangerous truth, and one that could destroy reputations and political careers — and even bring down the Government.'

'I don't care. It should be faced,' said Jean forcibly.

Rimster said quietly, 'You wouldn't escape, you know.'

'Then I would have to live with it. What does your Grandison say?'

'Probably what you're saying. But even he

can't twist the arm of a Prime Minister — not this one, anyway, who has a genius for making pompous excuses rather than hard, unpleasant decisions.'

'So?'

'So — now it's a police and CID job, plus Grandison and our people. Somebody's got Charlie. Clearly, I'd say, in the South of England. There'll be more photos and messages — and with them at some time a slip-up or clue which will betray them. I'll bet you that no truth or half-truth will be issued until the last moment if they don't find Charlie. I can hear it now, coming from the Prime Minister or some other minister on television and radio . . . *I am speaking to you tonight because, through a combination of circumstances, chief of which are the misguided and erroneous good intentions of certain individuals, a situation of grave potential danger to the people of this country has risen. Time is short and swift action is imperative to combat the threat which hangs over us all* . . . Oh, it'll sound good, and it will work only if the people holding Charlie believe it. But whatever happens, heads will roll. You know what I've done and been — the name of that game frankly was Murder. The name of this game is Chemical and Biological Warfare — but both games are the same.'

Rimster poured himself some coffee and lit a cigarette. As he did so, Jean reached out to his still open case and helped herself.

He lit it for her.

She said, 'How did I ever get into this? A bright girl at school, science and biology. Scholarship to university. Research, wanting to do something good for mankind, fighting disease, and then one day I find myself at Fadledean . . . '

Rimster, with a shrug of his shoulders as he closed his cigarette case, said quietly, 'Snap.'

★   ★   ★

Horace Simbath, after a photographic session with Charlie, sat on the sunny terrace with Lady Cynthia, having a glass of sherry before lunch. A pile of daily newspapers lay on the wrought-iron garden table. He had done well, and dear Cynthia was delighted with him. She had particularly liked his idea of wearing a false moustache and beard and had been almost girlishly excited when he had insisted that she should write the first Charlie letter.

Sitting across the table from him, she was engaged now in writing the second — which would be posted off with the new photographs later in the day — at his dictation.

This time, at his suggestion, she was using a different coloured ink and writing on different paper, and accepting the form of his dictation without question. His influence over her was fast blossoming. With every hour that passed a new link was forged between them.

Blinking his eyes from the sun glitter on the lake below, he spoke slowly, watching her lean, bony fingers moving the pen. No beauty, his dear Cynthia, but who wanted beauty? Not he at his age. Security . . . blissful security . . . ' . . . today I had raw onions and bananas for breakfast and then a jolly good romp with my friends. They tell me they have great plans for making sure I don't go back to Fadledean. But until I know them I can't tell you about them. However, they have promised that in my next letter I shall be able to tell you . . . ' Breaking off for a moment to refill his sherry glass, Horace went on to Lady Cynthia, 'The heart and strength of all good publicity, my dear Cynthia, is to create suspense, to tickle the fancy with intriguing hints. Curiosity, an itch to know, is the only one that you can't get rid of by scratching.'

Lady Cynthia looked at him, smiling, her eyes bright with admiration.

'Oh, Horace — what a joy that I have you to help me with all this. You're a man in a million.'

Horace gave a little sigh of thanks and nodded his head in agreement. He said, 'This afternoon I shall drive down to Southampton and post the stuff. It'll miss the morning papers but all the evening papers and radio and television will have it. Then, let me see, in the next lot of photos we must hit the dailies with the message about the great rally. Which means . . . ' He leaned back, sipping his sherry and thinking, ' . . . that I must take fresh photos tomorrow morning and then I'll drive up to London with them and deliver them to the agency by hand.'

'But you can't do that, Horace. It would be too risky!'

'Not at all. I shall just slip the envelope into their letter box and walk away. No risk. I'll do it in the late afternoon and be back here in time for dinner. All the big dailies will carry the story of the coming rally on Wednesday morning. Then we'll post another lot on the Thursday repeating the call to the rally to make the early editions of the evening papers and television and radio on Friday and the dailies on Saturday — and that should do it. What's that now? Friday the — '

'Ninth,' said Lady Cynthia. 'Then on

Saturday we can rent a van to drive Charlie to London on Sunday. Splendid!'

Friday, the ninth of July, was the earliest day on which Charlie could become infective. Charlie, himself, as the two talked on the terrace was swinging idly by one hand and one foot high up on a climbing rope and beating an intermittent tattoo on the stout roof netting with the old tennis racket, enjoying the noise he was making. Then, tiring of this, he linked his fingers through the strong mesh and, feet dangling, worked his way across the full length of the room hand over hand and dropped to the ground near the closed door. He stood up and twisted idly at the heavy, round bronze handle. Many a time he had played with door handles and catches and knew that sometimes the doors would open. But no amount of twisting and shaking opened this door because it was secured by a strong padlock and hasp on the other side.

Bored after a while with twisting the door knob Charlie turned, gave a scream, and then rolled himself in a series of somersaults across the floor and into the straw of his sleeping pen. Picking up a newspaper which had been left there after the last photographic session, he tore it in half and began to chew some of the pages into a soft wad, his forehead furrowing with ridges as he worked his big jaws slowly.

That afternoon Horace drove by himself to Southampton and posted the new photographs and the message. The first editions of the evening papers carried them the next morning and both radio and television were soon following them with the news.

While Grandison was reading the papers that morning the Minister walked into his room, a surprising event, but even more surprising to Grandison were his first words.

'Well, I think you're right. God and the devil are working against us. What's the answer?'

Grandison picked up a sheet of paper from his desk and handed it to the Minister. 'This. For radio and television presentation not later than midday on this coming Thursday — if not sooner. That's the last day before Charlie may become infective.'

The Minister read the announcement which Grandison had drafted earlier that day.

When he had finished, he asked, 'And who's to read this?'

'You, Minister — or the Prime Minister.' His face expressionless, he added, 'Since you now accept that the powers against us are so high ranking it would be courtesy, of course, for it to be the Prime Minister.'

Deciding to make no comment on this point the Minister asked, 'Haven't your people been able to pick up anything from the photos or the letters?'

'Fingerprints on the envelope and the writing paper. The guard's, those of the man who opened the letter at the agency and on the letter some others — all identifiable as agency people except one set. The unknown set are not known at Scotland Yard. And I didn't expect them to be. We're dealing with cranks and/or God-fearing people, not criminals. All we have is a short, plump, well-dressed man wearing gloves — a bit late in the day since he forgot to wear them when writing the letter, if he did write it. And, for my money, wearing a false moustache and beard.'

'Where the hell would anyone be able to hide a chimpanzee for any length of time?'

'Plenty of places, particularly as it isn't for any length of time. To do a house-to-house search over an area with a fifty-mile radius based on Fadledean would take weeks and — like it or not — unless you declare a state of emergency, you need search warrants.' He nodded at the paper which the Minister still held. 'That's the only answer. The truth.'

Giving way to a rare moment of emotion, the Minister said, 'For God's sake, what a mess!' Then with a shrug of his shoulders he said bitterly, 'Well, if it's agreed I know who it will be reading this to the country. And that'll be the end of me. I shall have to resign.'

Quietly Grandison said, 'It's no less than I expected to hear from you. Even so, it's an honourable move which, sadly, has long been out of fashion with other Ministers in recent years.'

The Minister smiled wearily and said, 'And all because Miss Blackwell fainted at the shock of discovering that her lover had gone to bed with another woman. God and the devil. I presume that was the devil's contribution?'

'Undoubtedly.'

★　★　★

At lunchtime that same day, Horace left Deanfinch Hall to drive to London with the third batch of photographs and letters announcing the rally in Regent's Park.

Horace, no fool when it came to protecting himself — he had operated many times just outside the fringes of the law without being caught — had decided that there might just have been a watch set up outside the agency building to catch him. After all, despite the false moustache and beard (which the police could well assume to be false), the train guard had given a fair description of him. So, in his own interests and approving his impartiality, he chose a different agency just off Fleet Street and pushed the large envelope into their brass letter box. In order that its importance should not be overlooked he had written in red ink on the cover — *Urgent. Charlie photos and message.*

He drove back to Deanfinch, reaching it in time for dinner. After taking their coffee and liqueurs on the terrace, the weather still set fine, the great blaze of the June heat-wave moving unchanged into these early days of July, Lady Cynthia and Horace took a stroll through the gardens, the aromatic trails of Lady Cynthia's cigar smoke coiling lazily in the air behind them.

As they moved alongside the lake, the long skirts of her evening gown brushing the tall grasses and picking up their seeds, Lady Cynthia stumbled a little on the rough path. Horace instinctively put out a hand and steadied her by the elbow.

Casually, though his intent was deliberate since Horace never was slow to improve on any opportunity, he kept his hand on her arm and, since she was chattering away about her plans for the mass rally, he slipped his arm through hers and they walked on linked together. Just as, Horace now was certain, they would soon be moving through life, linked together. *Love is the link that binds us together . . . Uncorrodible, sun-bright, no matter the weather . . .* He frowned a little at the odd memory of a snatch of bad verse from his publishing days. If he remembered rightly it had been written by a bank clerk from Glasgow.

Moving away from the lake through thick shrubberies they came out on to a weedy stretch of drive that ran up to the front of the family chapel. A mass of Virginia creeper covered the front of the chapel and reached in a thick, overhanging growth almost to the top of the high square bell-tower.

A little bored with Lady Cynthia's talk about the mass rally, Horace nodded towards the chapel and said, 'Do you ever use the chapel now, dear Cynthia?'

She shook her head. 'Not very often. But Lily keeps it clean and in order. Generations of Chickleys are buried there in the family vaults. One day I shall rest there too. We are an old family, you know, Horace, and although I will admit to being somewhat unorthodox in many ways I still cherish the family traditions. We came over, you know, with the Normans.'

'How wonderful to have such a lineage,'

said Horace, not really caring a button about lineage at all since he had been brought up in an orphanage, never knowing who were his parents or ever being able to stir up any great curiosity about them. Still, one day, when he became master here he decided that he would have to invent a good family background for himself. And what was more, if eventually he was going to take his place in one of the family vaults, he'd make sure that all that damned creeper stuff which was rotting away the stonework was cleared and the place generally tidied up. *Ah, death* . . . he checked the emerging memory of another snatch of bad verse, and said solicitously, 'I think it's growing a little late, my love, and I can see that the midges are worrying you. Let's go back and I would suggest' — he beamed at her through the gloaming — 'a leisurely nightcap to settle our excited minds before bed.'

Lady Cynthia patted his hand on her arm and said, 'A good idea, Horace, and we shall drink a toast to Charlie and to the success of our venture. I can see the rally now . . . a great spread of people and there I am, standing on the platform with Charlie at my side, his hand in mine and my voice ringing out . . . Oh, what a moment!'

'I can't wait for it, my love,' said Horace,

though he had a poor opinion of the ringing tones of her voice. High-pitched, yes, and loud, but without magic or music in it to charm crowds. Still . . .

* * *

Charlie lay on his back, chewing at the handle of his tennis racket and staring up at the glass roof of the billiard room. The moon, now full in its first quarter, was within a few hours of setting. Hidden by the trees low in the west, its light still flooded the sky. Charlie watched the owl which nightly came to roost for a while on the roof.

If he had any desire for freedom, or felt any resentment at being caged once more, he showed no obvious signs of this. To be caged had been his lot for so long that he probably experienced some kind of comfort and a sense of security from it. He was well-fed, well-groomed by Lady Cynthia with an old hair brush, his quarters were kept clean, and fresh straw brought in by Paget — who had taken a fancy to him and chatted to him as he worked — and he had plenty of room for exercise on his climbing ropes and the long length of old tree trunk. When the owl had gone he heard the sound of a mouse scutter across the floor and saw it move up the tree trunk.

Charlie knew the mouse. He had watched it on previous nights and once or twice had chased after it but never been able to catch it. He lay there watching it and then suddenly called loudly *waa-waa-waa* and threw the racket at it. The mouse ran up the trunk to the wire netting and disappeared along it.

Charlie walked over to his drinking trough and drank. When it had first been placed in the room he had amused himself by tipping it over, but now it had been securely screwed to the floor by Paget. The immoveability of the trough frustrated Charlie. He sat by it now, gripping its edges, pulling and tugging at it, his lips drawn back to expose his strong teeth in a vigorous grin. But Paget had done his work well and the trough would not budge.

At that moment in London, the newspaper presses were rolling, leafing out the morning papers and on the front pages of all of them the face of Charlie, grimacing vigorously, as he did now, was featured.

The next day, Wednesday, the seventh of July, and the seventeenth day of Charlie's freedom, the daily papers carried the story of the rally. A Charlie fever began to spread through the country. It was a great story, a comic story, a sad story, a crusading story and a cock-snooking-at-authority story. Slogans appeared on walls and hoardings. *Save Charlie Now! Good old Charlie! Freedom not Fadledean for Charlie! Who's Making a Charlie of Whom?* — this dauber a grammatical purist from the London School of Economics, a rarity. *All Out Regents Park Sunday. Charlie is Our Darling* . . . *Charlie for Prime Minister* (and under it *Why? We've got one already!*) . . .

Dozens of organizations began to make preparations for their members to attend the rally. Discussion groups were quickly organized for television appearances. Gag writers went into action for the comedians they serviced. Newspaper editorials varied from the light-hearted to the over-pompous. Various Save-Charlie-Funds were started, not all of them altruistic. The habitual letter-writers to the newspaper correspondence columns took again to pen and typewriter. Some Churchmen scrapped the tired old sermons they were going to use on Sunday and took up the theme of Charlie and man's inhumanity to animals, and — since it was the season of summer fêtes — scores of mothers began making Charlie outfits for their children in the hope of winning first prizes at the fancy-dress parades. Manufacturers rushed to the stores their first consignment of Charlie sweat shirts.

Harold Swinton, doing his commercial round, felt like committing suicide and consoled himself with drink to the extent that he was picked up that evening for drunken driving and, subsequently, had his licence suspended for a year. Captain Stevens had long kissed his chance of winning the Charlie sweepstake good-bye. The young married couple who Charlie had assaulted in their tent were signed up to appear as celebrity guests on a television show.

In the Whitehall corridors of power and the beehive of New Scotland Yard the reaction was different. Charlie was no joke.

Under conditions of the utmost secrecy the Minister of Defence recorded for television and radio an address of national importance to be held ready for release at the moment when the Prime Minister became finally convinced that the Almighty (or His temporary partner) was not going to vouchsafe any miracle to save his well-known, rather puffy Honest Joe face. The statement would be made at midday on Thursday, the eighteenth day of Charlie's freedom, giving the full facts and urging the people who held Charlie for their own and the country's safety to report their whereabouts immediately to the nearest police station.

That day Horace posted another batch of photographs to London from Portsmouth. With them was a message from Charlie which read:

DEAR FRIENDS I AM GLAD TO SAY I AM FIT AND WELL AND HOPE IT FINDS YOU THE SAME AND LOOK-ING FORWARD TO MEETING YOU ALL ON SUNDAY WHERE I KNOW YOU WILL ALL BAND TOGETHER TO SAVE ME FROM GOING BACK TO FADLEDEAN. LOVE CHARLIE.

Horace returned from this mission in a rising state of confidence as he considered his future. He basked in a climate of bliss which had only one small cloud on its horizon. He realized that the moment the rally was held, his and Lady Cynthia's names would be nationally known and they would be swept up into a round of public appearances and demonstrations, fêted, lionized, elected to dozens of committees, wooed and courted by all sorts of organizations, and sought after and taken up by many famous and well-connected people. He was not against that — but he could see the danger it held. Inevitably Lady Cynthia would have so many distractions, and be so pleased with herself and her achievements, that she would be in no mood to consider a marriage proposal. He was fast beginning to realize that to be absolutely certain of his future he should ensure it before the rally by asking her to marry him.

He considered the pros and cons of this as he drove back to Deanfinch Hall and finally decided that he must strike while the iron was hot, while dear Cynthia, welling over with gratitude and affection for him, was his to handle without the complications and distractions of fame. He made the decision to do this, but knew that the moment and the mood must be right. And, being the man he was, he felt well capable of creating the mood which would give birth to the moment. And he did — that evening after dinner.

They dined well by candlelight in a room where time-darkened oil paintings of past Chickleys looked down on them. The food was excellent, for Mrs Paget was a first-class cook. They had an excellent bottle of Meursault-Charmes with their Dover sole, almost the whole of a bottle of Château Latour 1965 with their roast leg of lamb and some glasses of excellent port before moving to the terrace for coffee and liqueurs.

The two of them, Horace, with his arm through Lady Cynthia's, paused for a moment to inhale the cooling air of the growing evening, air heavy with the heady scent of the phlox which filled the terrace beds.

'Dear Horace, dear Horace,' said Lady Cynthia, 'how happy I am. I look forward to Sunday as I've never looked forward to anything before.'

'The future, my love,' said Horace expansively, 'glows with a golden promise. How happy I am to have been able to act as your humble squire in this great crusade.' He led her to the wrought-iron table on which rested their coffee and liqueurs, held the chair for her to sit down, and then lightly touched the side of her cheek with the back of his hand as she looked up at him and smiled and nodded her thanks.

Sitting with her, he served her coffee and a glass of Grand Marnier and then did the same for himself. His natural euphoria enriched by wines and her tender regard promoted in him the thought that surely now, trembling on the lip of the immediate future, was coming the moment when he could elevate himself from squire to knight and claim the right to ride into the great tourney of the future wearing the silk of her colours knotted around his arm. Although he hated bad verse, drink always evoked from him

317

highly coloured but somewhat tarnished romantic speech forms, but never dimmed his appreciation of the right moment to make an approach of importance. He identified it now unerringly as the moment when she should have finished her second glass of liqueur.

While waiting for it, he lightly held her hand, talking easily and enduring the drift of her cigar smoke into his face.

Then, as Lady Cynthia finished her second glass of liqueur, as though it were a sign from the gods that they were on his side, she gave him the perfect opening.

Sighing and leaning back in her chair, her long legs thrust inelegantly out before her, drawing at her cigar and, momentarily, with her free hand scratching the top of her head to ease the mild irritation of the biting midges, she said, 'Horace, my love, what would I have done without you? You have been my mainstay and my prop. I can think of no other man I know who could have served me so well and so truly. I cannot imagine what I would have done without you. I repeat it and I mean it.'

Bracing himself, emboldened by hope and drink, Horace went in at the deep end. When the moment was right, there was no profit in shilly-shallying.

He said gently, 'How generous of you to

say that, Cynthia, my love. But what I have done is nothing beside what I would like to have the privilege of still doing for you ... that is to make you as happy as you are now for the rest of your life. We have both known our sorrows and our joys. Fate brought us together and Fate has joined us in this enterprise. But when that is won there still lies before us the great enterprise of life ... of a full, rich and rewarding life which we could make together. I feel for you, my dear Cynthia, a closeness which Elizabeth Barrett Browning spoke of when she wrote — *What I do and what I dream include thee, as the wine must taste of its own grapes.* Do I need say more?'

Lady Cynthia turned her head towards him, wrinkling her brows, and said, 'What are you talking about, Horace?'

Horace took her hand and pressed it gently, 'About love, my dear Cynthia. I love you, my dear one, and there is no greater happiness you could bestow on me than to hear you say that you, too, love me and will be my wife.' He raised her hand and kissed her bony knuckles warmly.

For a moment or two, Lady Cynthia was silent and then with a shrill laugh, almost a sharp whinny, she said, 'My dear Horace — what an extraordinary man you are! Why I never dreamt for one moment that you felt like this! Oh, dear Horace, I don't mean to be unkind' — she leaned towards him and kissed his cheek, her breath rich with the aroma of cigar — 'and in many, many ways I am deeply flattered. But, my dear Horace, the thing is utterly impossible.'

The world began to collapse slowly around Horace, fragmenting silently through the mild purple light of the summer night, but as it fell he made a desperate attempt to stay the catastrophe.

'Why, my dear Cynthia? Why is it impossible?'

Lady Cynthia, in the kindest way, told him, and he was man enough to accept it philosophically, which as he knew full well was a far different thing from taking it lying down. A distinction which when he lay in bed later he pondered with a meticulous concern, remembering the details of Lady Cynthia's reasons which could be summed up as the opposite of those inherent in the lines — *Kind hearts are more than coronets. And simple faith than Norman blood.*

He woke once in the middle of the night and suddenly said aloud angrily, 'What's bloody wrong with being Anglo-Saxon and an orphan?'

12

Tragedy and comedy sometimes share the same bed. Both are restless sleepers.

Horace Simbath rose early. The latter part of an almost *nuit blanche* had confirmed in him the resolution to have no more to do with Lady Cynthia's plans for Charlie. If she were so aristocratically blue-blooded, so conscious of her family and its traditions, so — no matter how regretfully expressed — concerned about the social gulf between them and — not positively expressed but hinted at — so sensitive of the view her friends and relatives would take of her marrying a commoner, then she could carry on with the rest of the Charlie project herself. He had done all the donkey work so far. Now she could do the rest.

Anger and injured pride smouldering in him like a slow peat fire, he packed up his case, dismantled his dark-room and collected his photographic equipment, and drove away in his shabby saloon car. The only person he saw was Paget, coming up the drive from his cottage to begin work.

He stopped the car and said to the

gardener, 'Paget, my dear fellow' — he was tempted to add 'as one serf to another', but decided against it — 'when you see Lady Cynthia, will you be kind enough to tell her that I have had to go back to London on urgent business?'

'Yes, sir, certainly.'

'That's a good chap.'

For a moment he was tempted to mark his going with a moment of panache by handing the man a five-pound note as a tip, but as he had only fifteen pounds in his wallet and petrol and lunch to buy, and a bank overdraft much larger than usual, he decided against it.

He drove off into the strengthening blue of the morning, the air full of bird song and the scent of the lime trees along the driveway, unmoved by the beauty of the day, aware only of the slow smouldering of the volcano within him.

Paget went up to the house and about his business. One of his first tasks since Charlie had arrived was to go to the billiard room to clean it up and to water and feed Charlie.

When he let himself in this morning, Charlie was swinging happily from one climbing rope to another, chattering to himself.

Seeing Paget, he raised his head and greeted him with a succession of noisy hoots.

Paget saw that during the night Charlie had

been tugging and pulling at his water trough again and this time had finally managed to break it free from the holding screws in the planks of the floor. Paget put fresh food in Charlie's feeding box and then went off to get his tools and new screws in order to fix the trough in a different position.

Charlie dropped down from his ropes and, squatting by the box, began to make a breakfast of fresh carrots and slices of cut melon.

When Paget came back and began to fix the trough, Charlie ambled over to him and, squatting on the floor, watched him.

Paget, who liked Charlie, said, 'Aye, you can well watch, Mister Charlie. These 'ere be three-inch screws — not like them others — and going into solid oak what was a growing tree a hundred years before you was just a gleam in your old monkey father's eyes. You pull them out and I'll call you Mister Samson in future.'

Charlie blew gently through pouted lips and nuzzled his head against Paget's.

An hour later, Lady Cynthia, never a late riser, strolled out on to the terrace to smoke a cheroot before breakfast.

Paget, who had been surreptitiously levelling mole hills in the rough lawn, walked up to her.

'Morning, my lady.'

'Good morning, Paget. Lovely morning. Is Mr Simbath about yet?'

'Aye, my lady. He was up early. Met him going down the drive in his car, I did.'

'In his car?'

'Yes, my lady. All packed up. He said would I tell you he'd had a call to go back to London on urgent business.'

'Business?' Lady Cynthia frowned. 'What business?'

'He didn't say, my lady, and I didn't think it was my place to ask.'

'No, of course not. Is Charlie all right this morning?'

'Yes, my lady, though I've just had to fix his trough. He got it loose during the night.'

Going in to her breakfast, Lady Cynthia was a little concerned at the baldness of Horace's message. But then you never knew with Horace. Probably something had occurred to him during the night, some new angle about Charlie and their crusade, perhaps. Yes, that could be it, and the dear man had been too considerate to disturb her so early.

Lifting the silver cover from the eggs and bacon on the sideboard, she took two eggs and four rashers of bacon and, as she began to make a hearty breakfast, smiled to herself at the thought of dear Horace. How delightfully quixotic he could be at times. Where on earth had he got the idea that she might marry him? Oh dear, she had had to be very tactful in refusing him, and she must say he had been most understanding. As a friend, companion and a wonderful help in this Charlie project, she could have wished for no one else. But marriage — even if she could remotely contemplate it after the tragic loss of her first and only love — would have been quite out of the question with Horace. After all, the Chickleys were a family who had always married their own kind, people of rank, wealth and good blood. Snobbish it might be, in this day and age. But high standards had to be kept.

Spreading marmalade thickly on her toast she considered what on earth would her county friends have said? She could hear them . . .

She must be going loopy . . . Couldn't she see the man was only after her money? . . . And have you seen him? A glib little, quite impossible man . . . Common as dirt, my dear . . . Poor Cynthia.

Taking an apple from the bowl on the sideboard she went along to the billiard room to make her morning visit to Charlie. He greeted her with an excited dash up his ropes and down the tree trunk and then galloped to her, calling, and holding out his hand for the apple.

She gave it to him and he went swiftly up the tree trunk, perched at the top, and began to eat it.

Watching him, Lady Cynthia saw herself in four days' time, standing in Regent's Park, the green of the grass obliterated by the crowd, an ocean of heads all turned her way . . . Charlie at her side, a stout leather belt around his waist with a chain attached to it which she would hold (dear Horace had thought of that) . . . and her voice ringing out, stirring the crowd to an emotional fervour that would sweep through them and spread over the whole country like a forest fire. Her eyes dimmed a little with tears at the thought as in her mind she began to go over the words of the great speech which Horace had already written for her.

She turned away, her mind rioting with the vision and sound of those moments to come, and let herself out of the billiard room.

Then — as she closed the door behind her — a sudden dark thought struck her.

Horace! Oh, no — it couldn't be. But could it? Suppose he had been more upset than he had shown? What call could he possibly have had so early? No, Paget must have got it wrong. He'd had an idea, something brilliant and which needed action at once, and the dear man had hurried away.

She looked at her wristwatch. Ten o'clock. He'd been gone four hours. Any moment now, perhaps already, he would be back in his London flat.

With a sudden resolve she began to move quickly towards the morning room to telephone Horace. In her agitation she forgot to padlock the billiard room door on the outside.

A little later, Charlie, who tended to become bored and mischievous towards mid-morning, made an attempt to pull up the newly fixed water trough without success. Waa-waa-waaing with frustration, he scooped his hands through the water and sprayed it all over the floor and then wandered to the billiard room door, where he began to play with the bronze door-knob.

A few seconds later the door was open and Charlie ambled out into the corridor which led to the main part of the house. A few yards along it was a sash window which had been left partly open at the top against the summer heat. Charlie climbed on to the window seat, reached for the top of the lowered window pane and swung himself up and over it.

★ ★ ★

At that moment, Grandison was in the large, wainscoted room of the Minister of Defence. It was ten minutes past ten, almost the same time, seventeen days before, when Charlie had been given the plague injection. At twelve o'clock all radio and television programmes would be interrupted and the secretly prepared announcement by the Minister would go on the air.

The Minister, smoking, and absently stirring the cup of coffee in front of him, looked across at the broad back of Grandison, who stood staring out of the window. To himself, as much as to Grandison, he said, 'Mankind has a genius for getting itself into a mess. That's the real lesson of history.'

Grandison turned, shrugged his shoulders, and said, 'I wouldn't argue with that philosophy. But it doesn't help at the moment to know it. What would have helped would have been to tell the truth days ago. Politics and philosophy never did run in harness.'

'You think that whoever holds Charlie will come into the open when the broadcasts go out?'

'Yes, I do. Unless they are raving lunatics — and their press campaign disproves that. Nobody's going to risk getting plague. But that will only be the beginning.'

'And then the heads will begin to roll.

Mine first.' The Minister pursed his lips ruefully. 'Nothing can stop it.'

Grandison polished his eyeglass. 'Prayer might. A miracle.' He nodded at the telephone. 'Pray hard enough and that phone might ring and Rimster or the police could be saying that they've located Charlie, even caught him.'

'You believe in that kind of thing?'

'No. But if I had my back against a wall facing a firing squad I think I would give prayer a try. God, so I'm told by modern churchmen, has a sense of humour and also of drama.'

'And what has the Devil got? It might be his doing.'

Grandison grinned.

'Little hope there, I'm afraid — unless he's in a good mood and is just going far enough to scare hell out of us, but not let all hell loose.'

While they talked, Rimster and Jean were having their mid-morning coffee at Redthorn House.

Rimster said, 'Don't look so glum. It'll work, you know. The moment that announcement goes out whoever has Charlie will start shouting for us to come and get him.'

'God, I hope so. They couldn't possibly think it was a trick just to get him back, could they?'

329

'Not a hope. Anything that comes over the radio or the television officially interrupting all programmes, the Minister sitting there behind his big desk looking grave and solemn, is gospel. No, I'm certain that within half an hour of the announcement we'll be on our way to pick up Charlie. Everything's all ready outside, the van, the protective clothing — even if it is only the earliest infection day minus one I'm taking no risks. In a few days you'll be able to go back to your George and live happily ever after.'

'I wonder.'

'Don't. Given time the human mind has a wonderful capacity for forgetting unpleasant experiences, and the human conscience renews itself every few years, shedding all scar tissues.'

Although he spoke lightly Jean was sure that there was no lightness in his heart and she wondered exactly at what point in his career he had given up being a man without a conscience . . . a walking, talking, cynical zombie of destruction.

★　★　★

Horace reached his flat at eleven o'clock. Long before that, as he had driven along the motorway, he had reached a decision. Life was a matter of balance and when the scales tipped unevenly one just had to do something to bring them level again. Leaving Deanfinch Hall he had known more disappointment than anger. By the time he reached London he knew more anger than disappointment.

Without hesitation he picked up his telephone and called the Salisbury police. Refusing to give his name or any information about himself, resolved only that Lady Cynthia Chickley should have her fair share of disappointment, he told the constable on duty the whereabouts of Charlie. When he put the telephone down, he turned to and began to pack his few belongings into a suitcase. He had no intention of hanging around and waiting for the possible consequences to himself.

Fifteen minutes later he was driving away in his car, heading north and feeling relaxed. In the art of going to ground he had long graduated. He had a good wardrobe in his suitcases and a few pounds in his pocket. He owed a month's rent on the furnished flat, had already begun to forget about his overdraft at the bank and was happily considering the future and a change of name. Scotland seemed a good bet. There was a big oil boom going on there, men with plenty of money, and firms who did not ask awkward questions about identity or national insurance numbers and ... surely ... somewhere maybe a wealthy widow or spinster he could charm who was entirely free of Norman blood or aristocratic snobbery.

Charlie, meanwhile, was happily wandering around the thickets and woods of Deanfinch Hall garden. He climbed a large tulip tree and, sitting in its top branches peered out through the leafy canopy. He had in view a corner of the walled garden where Paget was working, and a glimpse of the long lake where the duck, coots and moorhens foraged and fought. Away to the left, part of the tower of the Chickley private chapel showed above the trees. A pair of jackdaws circled over it.

Charlie leaned back, plucked a handful of leaves and began to chew them into a wad. Three hairy tiger caterpillars crawled within reach on a twig. He plucked them off and added them to the leaves for flavour. As he lay there, Charlie saw Lily Harkness come from the house and walk down the rough path beside the lawn and disappear into the dense shrubberies on the far side of the walled garden.

Still chewing, Charlie dropped down through the tree and ambled aimlessly away. He picked up a dead branch and threw it ahead of him. He raced after it and threw it again but it lodged in the top of a tall thicket of rhododendrons. Charlie abandoned it and moved on hoo-hooing gently to himself.

In London the report of Mr Simbath's message to the Salisbury police had reached Grandison and his Minister. It was decided to delay the public announcement until confirmation was received from Deanfinch Hall that Charlie really was there. Already Rimster and Jean were on their way there in the special van, led by a police car. Three helicopters had been detached from the day's search pattern to cover the area and a party of troops were on their way by lorry to throw a cordon around the place.

One of the helicopters was flown by Captain Stevens.

Flying high, as instructed, over the old Tudor manor house he and his observer had a good view of the burgeoning activity below.

'Hoax or the real thing?' queried the observer.

'Don't know and I don't care,' said Captain Stevens. In the early days of searching it had been fairly interesting, hoping he might be the one to spot Charlie. Later there had been the growing chance of winning the sweepstake. Now there was only boredom and some irritation because all this lark had meant the postponement of the advanced training which had brought him down to the Army School of Aviation.

'Police car and that special van thing,' said the observer.

The two vehicles had come up the tree-lined drive and stopped at the main terraced entrance to the house. Close behind them came an army staff car.

As Rimster, Jean and a police inspector and the army Colonel got out of their vehicles, Lady Cynthia came out of the house and stood at the top of the steps. The four of them moved towards her.

The Colonel and the Inspector gave her a brief salute and then the Inspector said, 'Lady Cynthia Chickley?'

'Yes. What can I do for you?' She knew what she could do, for she was no fool. For the last half hour she had been trying to reach Horace Simbath on the telephone without success. Seeing all these people here now only confirmed what she had already more than half-guessed might happen.

'We have been given information,' said the Inspector, 'that you are holding here an escaped chimpanzee named Charlie, the property of the Ministry of Defence. Is that so, Lady Cynthia?'

'No, it is not so, Inspector.' She stood tall and composed. After all, the Chickleys had faced adversity and disappointment many, many times through their long history only to triumph in the end. And triumph of a kind she had because only a few moments ago she had discovered that Charlie — through her own carelessness — had escaped.

God speed you, Charlie, she told herself, and may the gods lead you to some other safe haven.

'I should point out, my lady,' said the Inspector, 'that I have with me a sworn search warrant and, while I don't doubt your word' — she was well known in the county and not without influence so he trod carefully — 'we shall be obliged to search the house and all the outbuildings.'

'You are very welcome to do so. But it will be a waste of your time. It is true that I had Charlie here, and kept him here for good and humane reasons for which I am ready to answer to anyone. But Charlie has gone. When I visited him this morning I stupidly, when I left, forgot to lock the padlock on his door.'

Not to any of them would she have dreamt of saying why she had had this lapse. They were here clearly because Horace Simbath had betrayed her. The man was contemptible. Never would she ever mention his Judas name to anyone.

Rimster moved forward, and said, 'Lady Cynthia, I can assure you that none of us doubt your word. But would you be kind enough to tell us how long ago it was that you left the door unlocked.'

'Around nine-thirty this morning. He must have climbed out of the open window in the corridor outside the billiard room in which we . . . I was keeping him.'

'All right, Rimster,' said the Colonel, turning to move to his car, 'I'll get my men around the place and call the helicopters down.'

Lady Cynthia said, 'You have my permission to move about the grounds as much as you like. The only thing I would like to say to you is that I have nothing but contempt for people like you who wantonly and cruelly use God's innocent creatures for wicked and evil purposes. You are all beneath contempt!'

It was said proudly and with sincerity and, although it was far, far from being the long and noble call to the conscience of the nation which she had seen herself giving in Regent's Park, the few words were a balm to her disappointment and gave her the strength to stem the movement of tears into her eyes.

As she began to turn away to enter the house, Lily Harkness came around the corner of the terrace and said, 'Oh, my lady, there you are. Could I have a word — '

'Not now, Lily.' Lady Cynthia waved her away.

'But, my lady, that there Charlie's down in the chapel. He came in while I was cleaning and dusting round like I always do once a week. So I shut him in and came up here to tell you.'

Lady Cynthia said, 'Thank you, Lily. I'm sure these gentlemen will be delighted to hear that.'

She went into the house to the morning room. Without even a glance out of the window at the activity beginning outside, she poured herself a large glass of sherry, lit a cheroot, and then sat down to read the *Daily Telegraph*. One thing the Chickleys had never lacked over the centuries was dignity in defeat.

* * *

Three helicopters, flying low, circled at a few hundred yards' radius round the chapel. On the ground, soldiers at close intervals were posted around the outside of the overgrown churchyard. By the entrance lychgate, the special van was drawn up and close to it stood an army radio truck in touch with the operations centre and through it to London.

Rimster, wearing white protective overalls, a close-fitting hood and gloves, adjusted the goggles over his eye slits and then checked the nembutal pistol. It held three darts which could be fired rapidly. The moment Charlie was hit it would take anything from five to ten seconds to knock him out, according to which part of his body the dart struck.

Nobody, he thought wryly, knew for sure about these things. What the books and the boffins said could always be conditioned by Nature. He had used poison, the same poison on more than one man, and some died fast and some died slow.

Behind him, Jean reached round to adjust his mouth mask and said, 'You don't have to worry. All the odds are that Charlie won't be infective until tomorrow.'

Rimster made no answer. She was the same as the rest of them. Oh, they knew . . . they'd worked it all out, formulae and calculations, millions of bacilli and what-have-you growing to maturity in the blood stream. Science was their god — but they could never be sure whether heaven or hell was their destination, so they put the thought from their minds. Well, his face hidden now from them all, only his eyes showing through the goggles, he knew his destination and, no matter how long the years might stretch out before he died, knew that he wouldn't be the first parson's son the Devil had made warmly welcome.

He walked up the path towards the closed church door. Dense growths of hemp agrimony made a dusty pink border for the weed and moss-patched path. They let the outside go to hell, he thought, but tidied and cleaned the chapel once a week. No escape for Charlie now. No sanctuary for him within the altar rails.

He pushed the door open, slipped through quickly and shut it. He stood with his back to it and let his eyes grow accustomed to the gloom.

A simple chapel. Four rows of short pews on either side, big flagged paving stones running between them up to the raised altar. A door to the right, the vestry; a door to the left leading up to the tower. Behind the altar was a narrow stained glass window carrying the Chickley arms at the top and below a seated Madonna with the Child on her lap, bearded saints on either side. The blue of her robe was as clear as a cloudless cold spring sky. On the far side of the pews, against the thick, stone walls were the Chickley tombs and memorials. Knights lying in armour with their toes turned stiffly up, mailed hands crossed . . . one of them had a woman, long robed and kirtled, lying on either side of him.

Two wives . . . would that, he wondered, ensure discord in the hereafter?

He reached out to his right and found the switches. Pale yellow tongues of light came from the imitation candles on their hanging roundels, and the Madonna's gown lost some of its cerulean glow.

He began to move slowly forward, checking the rows of pews and the hidden spaces behind the standing catafalques and memorials. No Charlie.

The bust of a high-coiffured, eighteenth-century woman stared down at him from a wall niche, long-nosed, horse-faced, she looked just like Lady Cynthia. A woman of character . . . standing at the top of the steps and speaking her mind and the truth. What had gone wrong there? Had one of the servants betrayed her? Hardly likely. But something had gone wrong. Betrayal . . .

In tall brass holders a pair of half-burned candles flanked the altar, guarding the tall black marble cross from which hung the ivory-carved Christ. He went round behind the altar to check the space there. Dead leaves and dust on the ground. Lily clearly had her lapses.

He opened the vestry door. The room was bare except for a small table, a little hanging cupboard and a row of hooks down one wall.

The small window was barred and festooned with old cobwebs.

He came out and, seeing the door to the tower partly open, he checked the main body of the chapel again in case Charlie had come down while he was in the vestry. Meticulous. Take no chances. Years of special training — with Grandison unforgiving over the smallest mistake. One moment of stupidity and you were killed instead of killing. How much, he wondered, had his father guessed, before he died, of the real nature of his son's career? Something in the Ministry of Defence . . . a lot of travel and a lot of secrecy.

Inside the door he had expected to find the bellringers' floor and hanging ropes, but there was only a wide, circular wooden stairway that coiled around an immense solid pillar of stone. No bells to ring out for the Chickleys.

A small wooden door at the penthouse head of the stairs was hanging half off its hinges. He squeezed through it, hearing the drone of the helicopters, and found himself on the top of the tower, its surrounding parapet crenellated, the masonry weathered and broken and overgrown with a tangle of virginia creeper. Lead sheeting covered the ground, and the gutters to carry off rainwater were blocked with dead leaves and broken stone.

He moved away from the small, wooden pent structure which held the door and guarded the top of the stairs and saw Charlie. He was squatting in a far angle of the parapet wall and had in his hands a tattered old hymn book which he could have carried up from the chapel. He was slowly ripping out the pages, letting them float from him in the morning breeze. Now and again he put one into his mouth to add to the wad he was slowly chewing.

Seeing Rimster, Charlie raised his head and, opening his mouth, stretched it wide, his big lips pulling back over his teeth, exposing the wad of paper. Then, pulling it from his mouth, he began to clap his hands on it, flattening the pulp to a moist pad, and cried *waa waa waa* gently.

Rimster moved slowly to lessen the wide angle between himself and Charlie until he faced him squarely across the top of the tower.

Charlie watched his movements, his dark eyes shining, the sunlight burnishing his brown pelt and, perhaps nervous at the sight of this white-clad, white-hooded, goggled creature, pouted his lips and gave a thin series of whimpers.

Rimster raised the pistol and took aim. For a moment or two he was aware, through the

342

embrasure behind Charlie, of the lake far below, a strengthening breeze ruffling it into rough, polished pewter, a mallard duck taking off, the tall tops of the reeds swaying. This was his last job. A country cottage, a garden . . . maybe do a little fishing. No shooting. He never wanted to touch a gun again.

He fired and, almost before he heard the hiss of the discharge, saw the dart hit Charlie just below his right shoulder. Charlie's reaction did not surprise him. Charlie screamed, jumped to all fours, panicked, and began to run towards him. He stepped quickly aside and then backwards as he fired again.

As he did so, his foot caught the raised edge of a jagged tear in the lead covering of the tower top and he stumbled backwards, out of balance. His right shoulder hit the rotten masonry of the parapet close to an embrasure and it collapsed outwards behind him. As he began to fall, he saw Charlie suddenly collapse in his run and slew sideways like an untidy sack to the ground.

He went down, followed by cascading masonry and torn lengths of virginia creeper, and death took him as, head first, he hit the stone paving of the path at the foot of the tower. He went without time for a prayer or a plea or even a moment of ironical thought that he had not noticed the broken lead when he first came on to the roof as he would have done in the prime of his powers. He went, as he had sent many others in his time, from sunlight and summertime into darkness and eternity.

Envoi

The pre-recorded announcement about Charlie was never made. Nobody retired from political life, though considerable changes in staff and methods were made at Fadledean. And Charlie went back to Fadledean but only until he had passed through his infective stage and eventually became no plague danger. A popular national figure, he was handed over to a wild-life park to spend the rest of his days in honourable and, presumably, happy retirement. But since one swallow does not make a summer, the successful plague-carrying test on Charlie had to be confirmed and reconfirmed to make it safe for men and women to be used as carriers, so another chimpanzee took his place. Everyone was happy, particularly the apes in dark suits who might one day, for political or military reasons decide to use the silent weapon of plague to avoid the open and honest brutality of the sword.

We do hope that you have enjoyed reading this large print book.

Did you know that all of our titles are available for purchase?

We publish a wide range of high quality large print books including:
Romances, Mysteries, Classics
General Fiction
Non Fiction and Westerns

Special interest titles available in large print are:
The Little Oxford Dictionary
Music Book
Song Book
Hymn Book
Service Book

Also available from us courtesy of Oxford University Press:
Young Readers' Dictionary
(large print edition)
Young Readers' Thesaurus
(large print edition)

For further information or a free brochure, please contact us at:
Ulverscroft Large Print Books Ltd.,
The Green, Bradgate Road, Anstey,
Leicester, LE7 7FU, England.
Tel: (00 44) 0116 236 4325
Fax: (00 44) 0116 234 0205

THE CRIMSON CHALICE

Victor Canning

When a party of marauding Saxons destroy her father's villa, young Roman girl Gratia, 'Tia' escapes. She comes upon the body of the heir to the chieftanship of a British tribe in the west. Baradoc, a prisoner of Phoenician traders, was sold as a slave and is also escaping the Saxons. However, after being attacked he was left for dead by his cousin, the next heir. Tia nurses him back to health, and they continue together to the safety of her uncle's villa in Aquae Sulis . . . Their son, Arturo, inherits his father's desire for uniting Britain against the Saxons.

THE CIRCLE OF THE GODS

Victor Canning

Arturo's dream, like that of his father, Baradoc, is to unite Britain against the marauding Saxons. Always a wild and arrogant youth, he grows up and leads a rebellion against Count Ambrosius. He raises a small force of men which attacks Saxon settlements. Then, with Durstan and Lancelo to lead the troops, Arturo's great campaign begins . . .

BIRDS OF A FEATHER

Victor Canning

A fortunate man, Sir Anthony Swale is married to a loyal wife; he lives in a grand house in Somerset and leads a very privileged life. He devotes most of his time to collecting rare art treasures, particularly from behind the Iron Curtain. And he will pay any price for the right piece — including treason. But then his treachery is discovered — and agents working for the Government decide it is time to take discreet action . . .

THE BOY ON PLATFORM ONE

Victor Canning

Cheerful Peter Courtney, a fourteen-year-old, is an unusual boy. Exceptionally gifted, he's able to repeat, fully, any text which is read to him once — even in French. When his widowed father's business fails, he takes Peter around London's social clubs to perform professionally. Because of his skills he finds himself involved with the Secret Service. He is required to use his gift to receive important information regarding traitors to the British and French Governments — but this places Peter and his father in danger. Now they must escape and leave everything behind . . . in hiding from an assassin who is thorough and systematic.

TALES OF MYSTERY AND HORROR: VOL. III

Edgar Allan Poe

These *Tales of Mystery and Horror* include the story of Bedloe, a wealthy young invalid, who has a strange tale to tell his physician, after he experiences a form of time travel, in *A Tale of the Ragged Mountains* . . . And *The Conversation of Eiros and Charmion* is a very strange tale of a comet approaching earth, causing it to contain pure oxygen. The result of this has a devastating effect on people . . .

THE HAPPY PRINCE AND OTHER TALES

Oscar Wilde

The Happy Price and Other Tales is a collection of fables — *The Happy Prince* had been, in life, a joyful personality. However, now, immortalised by a gold and jewel encrusted statue, he's saddened by the poverty of his citizens. Unable to move, he enlists the help of a swallow to help his people . . . In *The Nightinglale and the Rose,* a nightingale overhears a student complaining that his professor's daughter will not dance with him, as he is unable to give her a red rose. But will the nightingale's sacrifice be enough?